THRAXAS
UNDER SIEGE

Baen Books by Martin Scott

THRAXAS
UNDER SIEGE

MARTIN SCOTT

THRAXAS UNDER SIEGE

This a work of fiction. All the characters and events portrayed in this book are fictional, and any resemblance to real people or incidents is purely coincidental.

A Baen Books Original

Baen Publishing Enterprises
P.O. Box 1403
Riverdale, NY 10471
www.baen.com

ISBN 10: 1-4165-2088-0
ISBN 13: 978-1-4165-2088-7

Cover art by Tom Kidd

First U.S. printing, October 2006

Library of Congress Cataloging-in-Publication Data:
Scott, Martin, 1956-
  Thraxas under siege / Martin Scott.
      p. cm.
  "A Baen book"—T.p. verso.
  ISBN-13: 978-1-4165-2088-7
  ISBN-10: 1-4165-2088-0
  1. Thraxas (Fictitious character : Scott)--Fiction. 2. Private
investigators—Fiction. I. Title.

  PR6063.I34T488 2006
  823'.92—dc22
                                    2006021126

Distributed by Simon & Schuster
1230 Avenue of the Americas
New York, NY 10020

Printed in the United States of America

10 9 8 7 6 5 4 3 2 1

THRAXAS
UNDER SIEGE

Chapter One

"Turai is doomed," says old Parax the shoemaker. He never was the most optimistic of men.

"Turai will survive," declares Gurd. "No damned Orc is chasing me out of this city."

He looks to me for support. I shrug. I don't know if we're going to survive or not. With our own army defeated, an Orcish army somewhere outside the walls, and no help on the way, it's hard to be too optimistic. Last month we suffered a catastrophic defeat at the hands of Prince Amrag, Orcish overlord. He took us completely by surprise, trapping and destroying our forces outside the city walls. We hadn't expected an attack in winter. The city authorities ignored the warnings of Lisutaris, head of the Sorcerers Guild, and we paid the price.

Despite their success, the Orcs failed in their attempt to take the city. They'd crossed the wastelands in midwinter, and they'd even managed to bring dragons with them. They were counting on a swift victory. Had they smashed their way into the city they could have wintered in comfort here, allowing fresh troops to join them from the east before mounting their invasion of the Human lands. As it is, they're stuck outside in the snow and that can't be comfortable, even for northern Orcs who are used to the bad weather.

"As soon as spring comes there'll be a relief force on its way," says Gurd.

Gurd is the owner of this tavern, my landlord, and my oldest friend. We've fought beside each other all over the world. These days his hair is grey and he sells beer for a living but his strength and fighting spirit are undiminished. Come the spring he's fully expecting to be marching out of Turai and sending the Orcs back where they belong. It's not such an unreasonable expectation. At this moment armies should be gathering. Simnia and all lands to the west will be arming themselves for war. The Abelasian General Hiffier will be preparing an army from the League of City States. The Elves of the Southern Isles will be preparing their ships and sharpening their spears. In theory, the first day of spring should see a huge force marching towards Turai from the west and another force sailing up from the south.

Unfortunately, we can be sure that at the same time a huge army of Orcs will be moving towards us from the west. Prince Amrag's reinforcements might get here first. And anyway, Prince Amrag might not wait till spring.

"I reckon he'll try and force his way into Turai before then."

Gurd shakes his head.

"He can't. He doesn't have enough Orcs to storm the walls. He doesn't have siege engines and the dragons can't fly so well in winter. Our Sorcerers can hold them off."

It's true. Lisutaris, Mistress of the Sky, still has a formidable array of sorcerous talent under her command. While the Orcs broke our army, they didn't succeed in killing our Sorcerers and they've always been our most potent weapon. Gurd thinks that Prince Amrag miscalculated.

"Good attack, certainly. But not good enough. He didn't get into the city. I don't think he's even close anymore. Why would he spend the winter out there in the snow? He'll head home and try again another time."

I motion for Dandelion to bring me a beer. Winter in Turai is never comfortable and the only reasonable thing for a man to do is sit in front of a roaring fire and drink beer till it's over. Unfortunately, civic duty requires me to spend a long time standing guard at the walls and I'm not enjoying it at all. If it wasn't for my magic warm cloak I'd have passed away already.

I'm an Investigator by trade but I'm not doing any investigating these days. Since the Orcs attacked, I haven't had a case. With the enemy outside the walls, the population is careful of its belongings. There are always shortages in Turai in winter and now it's going to be worse. Dragons burned the storage warehouses and food will soon become scarce. Crime hasn't gone away but with mercenaries, soldiers and Civil Guards everywhere, even the larger gangs that run the underworld have cut back on their activities. It means no one is paying me any money, but it's probably just as well. With my military duty to perform every day, I'd be pushed to find the time to investigate anything.

Gurd's tavern, the Avenging Axe, is very busy. There are plenty of customers trying to forget their troubles. Though Turai lost a lot of men outside the walls, the city is still fuller than I've known it for a long time. Mercenaries are everywhere, along with Turanian citizens from the outlying villages and farms who've made it into the city for shelter. Gurd, Tanrose and Dandelion are all busy serving food and drink, and so is Makri, apart from when she's with Lisutaris, performing her duties as bodyguard.

Makri works here as a barmaid. She used to be a gladiator, in the Orcish slave pits. She's a skilful woman with a sword. She has Orcish blood, as well as Human and Elvish. She's also the half-sister of Prince Amrag, leader of the Orcish forces. I'm the only person in Turai who knows that. I'm not about to pass the information along. The population of Turai hates Orcs. Recently Makri's had more than her usual share of comments and insults in the street, from anyone who feels like noticing her reddish skin, and pointed ears. If it was known that she was actually related to Prince Amrag she'd be in danger of being thrown from the city walls.

Gurd's also been spending time on military duty. Almost everyone has. Every tavern owner, Investigator, shoemaker, warehouseman, wagon driver, docker, and even those who never seem to have any sort of job that you can define, is obliged to report every day, sword in hand, ready to repel the Orcs.

I watch as Dandelion draws a tankard of ale for a mercenary who's still clapping his hands together for warmth and brushing snow from his tunic. She manages the operation reasonably competently, which is something of a surprise. Dandelion, our idiotic barmaid, talks to dolphins and has signs of the zodiac embroidered on her skirt. No one is quite sure how she ended up working in the Avenging Axe. She's not your average sort of barmaid, particularly not in Twelve Seas. This is the bad part of town and anyone working in a tavern has to be tough. Dandelion is not tough. When she first started, her incompetence was staggering, but she's more or less mastered the beer taps now. And while she doesn't have Makri's way of dealing with awkward customers—violence—she seems to get by all right by not exactly realising what's happening around her, and smiling sweetly at even the most hostile mercenary.

Tanrose emerges from the kitchen with a fresh pot of stew. I beat back several rivals in the food queue and take a healthy bowlful off her hands.

"Few more yams if you please, Tanrose."

Tanrose shakes her head.

"Can't give you them, Thraxas. No yams at the market today. There's a shortage."

"Already?"

Tanrose nods. Much of our supply of yams for the winter was burned in the warehouse fires. Immediately I'm depressed. Yams running out, and winter not even halfway through.

"I'll kill those Orcs for that," I mutter darkly, and I mean it. I'm a man with a healthy appetite, and a lot of girth to maintain. Interfere with my food supply and you're going to find yourself in trouble.

Chapter Two

Perturbed by the yam situation, I take a beer upstairs to my office and check my supply of klee. I've only three bottles of the fiery spirit left. Maybe I should go easy. I've been fortifying myself with a few glasses before heading for the ramparts, but if it's going to be a winter of short-ages, perhaps I should cut back. Though how a man is meant to sit in a cold guard post staring out into the snow without a warming glass of klee inside him I really don't know. Living in a city under siege is hell at the best of times. Living in a city under siege without a plentiful sup-ply of alcohol doesn't bear thinking about. A month ago I expected the Orcs to smash their way into Turai. Now, I'm not so sure. Gurd may be right. Perhaps Prince

Amrag has decided they missed their opportunity. We don't even know how many Orcs are still out there. Some are billeted in the Stadium Superbius, outside the city walls to the east, but apart from that, we can't tell. Their forces have withdrawn from sight. Our Sorcerers have scanned the area but the Orcish Sorcerers cast their own spells of hiding and it's hard for anyone to be certain. Lisutaris thinks that there are still Orcish forces guarding every exit from the city, but the main bulk of their troops may have retired southwards towards the forests, where it's not so exposed to the elements. Unfortunately for us, this winter is not as fierce as the last few have been. The Turanian winter can be bitingly cold, but after the first severe snowstorms, this one has turned unusually mild. No aqueducts have frozen up and the alleyways of Twelve Seas, usually clogged with thick drifts of snow, remain clear and passable. It might have been better for us had the weather been worse. The Orcs would have been less likely to remain.

After a glass or two of klee I find myself slightly more optimistic. We'll hold them off till the spring. The armies will arrive from Simnia and the Elves will sail up and we'll survive, just like we did fifteen years ago, last time the Orcs attacked.

The memory makes me frown. Last time we threw them back after a desperate struggle but we wouldn't have if the Elves hadn't arrived at the last moment. I was on the eastern wall when it collapsed and I was a second away from being mowed down by an Orcish squadron when we were rescued. No amount of klee, or passage of time, can make these grim memories fade. I get the uncomfortable feeling that if my life ends right here, then I haven't made that much of a success of it. Failed Sorcerer now scratching a living as an Investigator in the poor part of town, working for impecunious clients on cases so hopeless no one else will take them on. I curse, throw another log on the fire, and wish I'd studied more when I was an apprentice. If I hadn't discovered beer at such a young age, I might have been a real Sorcerer instead of a man who knows a few tricks. I'd be up in the Palace, living in luxury, with enough yams and klee to get me through any shortage.

Possibly the Palace isn't such a great place to be these days. The King is infirm and practically bedridden. The heir to the throne, Prince Frisen Akai, is so far gone on wine and dwa that he's no longer allowed out in public. Young Prince Dees Akan was killed when the Orcs attacked. Consul Kalius is wounded, traumatised, and out of action after the Orcish attack, leaving the administration in the hands of Deputy Consul Cicerius. A good man in his way, but not a warrior. All military planning is in the hands of General Pomius. He at least is an experienced soldier. He might just get us through, particularly as he has a proper respect for Lisutaris, Mistress of the Sky, head of the Sorcerers Guild and one of the most powerful people in the west. With someone like that on our side, there's always a chance of holding off the Orcs, and she's not the only strong Sorcerer in the Guild.

Makri walks into my office.

"Will you never learn to knock?"

She shrugs.

"Why?"

"It's civilised."

"We're under siege."

"No reason to abandon all standards. I thought you were spending the whole day with Lisutaris?"

Makri scowls. She takes off her heavy winter cloak then sits down on the chair nearest the fire.

"Lisutaris had to go to the Palace to meet the King. I couldn't go along."

Her eyes flash.

"Isn't that ridiculous? I can't attend a private meeting with the King because I've got Orcish blood. Who was it that saved Lisutaris from the Orcs?"

Makri is angry, though she knew what she was in for when she took the job. No one hates Orcs more than Makri and she's butchered a lot of them in her time. Nonetheless, she does have one quarter Orcish blood and that's never going to allow her access to the most refined places in the city.

I notice Makri's looking a little skinnier these days. She's still filling out the chainmail bikini well enough to earn a bundle of tips from the mercenaries in the tavern, but between her shifts as a barmaid and working for Lisutaris, I don't think she's been eating properly.

"I hate the way the library shuts in winter," she says. "I need to study."

Makri works here to earn money to pay for her education at the Guild College. I can't believe she's still thinking about education at a time like this.

"The Orcs are about to storm the walls. Can't you ever take a break?"

Makri shrugs.

"I like it. Samanatius isn't taking a break."

Samanatius is a prominent philosopher in Turai. Makri holds him in great respect. I regard him as a fool because he teaches for free. Obviously the man has no knowledge worth selling. To be fair to him, he was on the field of battle when the Orcs attacked, even though he could have been excused military duty because of his age.

Makri runs her hand through her great mane of dark hair. She looks dissatisfied.

"I wanted to dye it blond."

This takes me by surprise. Makri was champion gladiator by the time she was thirteen. She's such a brutal fighter I always think of her with a sword in her hand. Outside the city walls she stood over the unconscious body of Lisutaris and defended it with an astonishing display of savage determination, unflinching in the face of impossible odds. Hearing her come out with anything concerning personal vanity is strange, though since arriving in Turai she has taken on board a few of our feminine fashions, mainly low-class ones like a pierced nose and painted toenails.

"It'll make you look like a whore."

"No it won't. Senator Lodius's daughter has blond hair."

True. Turanian women are generally dark-haired. Blond hair is usually only sported by prostitutes, but the style is also affected by senators' daughters, and sometimes their wives. Why only rich women and prostitutes do this, I don't know.

"No one is going to mistake you for a senator's daughter. But what do you care? You've already managed to outrage the city. What's a little more public opprobrium?"

"I'm not worried about the public," says Makri. "I just don't have time. I have to work and study and be a bodyguard and then the Orcs are going to take the city and I'll be killed which I don't exactly mind but I wish I'd had time to see what I looked like with blond hair."

This is beyond me. My own hair hangs down in a long ponytail like the rest of the humble citizens of Twelve Seas and I never think about it from one day to the next. I ask Makri what news there is from Lisutaris.

"Nothing much. She can't tell how many Orcs are outside the city and General Pomius doesn't want to risk sending men to find out. But the Sorcerers have been busy with the messages. Everyone is making ready to help us in the spring."

Makri doesn't sound convinced. Our neighbours to the west, Simnia, might decide they'd rather hold the line against the Orcs on their own borders, and so might Nioj to our north. Everyone says they'll march to our aid but whether they will or not remains to be seen.

Makri's talk of Lisutaris worsens my mood. For one thing I'm annoyed that I'm reduced to learning news of the war from Makri. I used to be a Senior Investigator at the Palace, abreast of all the city-state's affairs. I was a man with contacts. A man who knew what was happening. Now I'm a man who's dependent on rumour and gossip. It's irritating. What's more irritating is that I have to speak a spell every morning on behalf of Lisutaris. Unbelievable as it may sound, this spell is to help conceal Herminis, a senator's wife whom Makri, Lisutaris and several other criminally minded women broke out of jail just before the Orcs attacked. Herminis had been sentenced to death for the murder of her husband, a senator. The Association of Gentlewomen decided to intervene. As a result of this, Herminis ended up at the Avenging Axe and Lisutaris prevailed on me to help hide her from the authorities. It's not a task I welcome, and had Lisutaris not bribed, cajoled and blackmailed me in the most shocking manner, I'd have refused to have anything to do with it.

"It's not right," I say, quite forcibly.

"What isn't right?"

"Me having to help hide Herminis. If the Abode of Justice finds out I'm involved, they'll be down on me like a bad spell. I blame you."

"Why me?" protests Makri.

"Because you messed up your rescue operation. Not that there should have been any rescue operation in the first place. And then Lisutaris has the nerve to rope me into covering for her. Talk about ingratitude. I picked that woman up and carried her off the battlefield. I saved her life. And did she exhibit the slightest sign of gratitude?"

"Yes. She gave you a new magic warm cloak."

I wave this away.

"A magic warm cloak? Lisutaris can make a magic cloak by snapping her fingers. Not the sort of gift that really says 'thank you for saving my life.' Especially from a woman as rich as Lisutaris. You think it would have harmed her to open up her coffers once in a while? I tell you, these aristocrats are all the same, not a shred of decency among the lot of them."

"Thraxas, is there any chance of you shutting up?"

"Absolutely none. I tell you, next time Lisutaris finds herself on the wrong end of an Orcish phalanx, she can look for someone else to rescue her. The woman's lack of gratitude is a scandal."

"She sent you a gift. It's downstairs."

"What?"

"I brought it down in a wagon. She said to tell you it was for saving her life."

I pause.

"Possibly I spoke harshly. What is it?"

Makri shrugs.

"I lost interest a while ago."

I'm deflated. I wasn't ready to stop complaining yet.

"This doesn't excuse her getting me involved with Herminis."

Makri curses me for a fool, yawns, and departs to her room. I hurry downstairs to take a look at my gift. I can't remember when anyone last sent me a present. Maybe my wife, on my wedding day. That was more years ago than I care to remember. My wife, wherever she is now, probably wouldn't want to remember it either.

The tavern is full of drinkers. There's a very large crate behind the bar. Gurd is curious as to the contents, as are Viriggax and his squadron of northern mercenaries. I ignore them all and drag the box upstairs. If Lisutaris has sent me anything good, I'm not going to share it with a bunch of drunken mercenaries.

I wrench the lid off, drag out some padding, then start emptying the contents on to the table. There's a layer of bottles, and the very first one I take out makes me stop and stare. It's a bottle of klee with three golden moons painted on the side. I know what that means. It's the Abbot's Special Distillation, a brand of klee so rare and fine as to never be seen in Turai outside the Imperial Palace and a few exclusive residences in Thamlin. Compared to the klee I normally drink it's like . . . like . . . well, there's no comparison. The only time in my life I drank this was at a banquet at the Palace, and even then I had to sneak it off the Consul's table. I place the bottle reverently on my table and find there are three more in the box. Four bottles of the Abbot's Special Distillation, made with love and care by the most talented monks in the mountains. Already I can feel my worries fading away.

I burrow further into the box and drag out another bottle, this one being thicker, of brown glass, with fancy calligraphy on the label. As I recognise what it is, my legs go slightly weak. The Grand Abbot's Dark Ale, a brew so precious, so fine in every way, as to be the only beer ever deemed fit for the King. Beer is not normally imbibed by the city's wine-quaffing elite, but an exception is made for the Grand Abbot's Dark Ale. I doubt if the monastery that produces it brews more than fifty barrels a year, and every one of them goes to the Palace. So famous is the Grand Abbot's Dark Ale that a barrel of it was once used as part of a treaty with the Simnians. This beer is the finest beverage in the known world, and I haven't had a drop for more than ten years. Lisutaris, a woman I have always held in the highest regard, has sent me eight bottles. I dab a little moisture from my eyes. Beer like this just doesn't come to a man more than once in a lifetime.

Underneath the beer is a small sack of thazis, but not the dried brown leaves we normally have to put up with in Twelve Seas. This is moist, green, and pungent. Thazis grown by Lisutaris herself. Again, I'm amazed. The sorceress is devoted to thazis. Not only does she have a house in her garden with walls made of glass, specially for growing the plants—an unheard-of extravagance—she has actually developed a spell for making the plants grow faster. There is no finer thazis anywhere, and she's sent me enough to get through the winter, and more.

Underneath the thazis are six bottles of Elvish wine. I'm not a connoisseur of wine but I know, from the standard of the other goods, that this will be from the finest vineyard on the finest grape-growing Elvish isle. At the bottom of the box is an enormous joint of venison, wrapped in an unusual fold of muslin. It doesn't seem to be dried, or salted, as venison usually is in winter. There's a note pinned to it.

From the King's own forest. Will stay fresh till you want to eat it.

My senses pick up the tiniest flicker of sorcery. The joint is magically protected against ageing. I place it with the other goods on my table then sit down to stare in wonder. Four bottles of klee, eight bottles of ale, six bottles of wine, a bag of thazis and a joint of venison. All of a quality never seen in this part of town. It's an outstanding gift. I'm man enough to admit that I was wrong about the Mistress of the Sky. She's a fine woman and a credit to the city. A powerful Sorcerer and sharp as an Elf's ear. I've always said so. Long may she lead the Sorcerers Guild to greater glory.

Before retiring for the night I carefully place locking spells on both my doors. No disreputable inhabitant of Twelve Seas is going to get his hands on my excellent present.

Chapter Three

Next morning I wake feeling more cheerful than I have for weeks. Even the prospect of food shortages can't dim the enthusiasm of a man who's got eight bottles of the Grand Abbot's Dark Ale waiting for his attention. I'm tempted to open one for breakfast but I restrain myself, with an effort. I should wait till I return from guard duty and savour the brew when I'm warm and comfortable. I decide to make do with a little of Lisutaris's thazis instead, and construct a stick of modest size. As I inhale, the world, already not looking so bad, improves considerably.

There are some strange noises outside my inner door, the one that leads down to the bar. Normally I'd be annoyed at such an early interruption to my day but I wander over genially and drag the door open. Out in the corridor I find Palax and Kaby, two young street musicians. There was a time when I'd have been displeased to see them because the young couple are not what you'd call your standard citizens of Turai. They affect the strangest clothes and hairstyles and have facial piercings never seen before in the city, and they live in a caravan which they park behind the tavern. Not the sort of behaviour to endear themselves to the average Turanian, including me. However, I've grown used to them these days, and I've enjoyed some good nights in the Avenging Axe when they've been playing their lute and fiddle.

"We need help," says Palax, anxiously. I notice that Kaby is trembling. I scowl at them.

"Didn't I tell you dwa would kill you?"

Dwa, a powerful drug, has been the bane of the city in recent years.

"She hasn't take dwa. She's sick."

I look more closely at the girl. Her face is red, she's shivering, and sweat is glistening on her forehead. It's obvious what's wrong. I'd have noticed right away had it not been for the unusual potency of Lisutaris's green thazis.

"She's got the winter malady," I say.

"I know," says Palax. "I think she's going to die."

Kaby suddenly sneezes. I step back quickly. The winter malady is not quite as deadly as the summer plague, but it's bad enough. As the city is so crowded I wouldn't be surprised if we were in for an epidemic. Kaby begins to shake, quite violently.

"Palax. Pick up Kaby and take her to the empty guest room at the end of the corridor. Keep her warm with a blanket and give her water and nothing else. Don't leave the room and don't let anyone else in. The malady spreads quickly and if anyone else comes near they'll catch it."

"Is she going to die?" asks Palax, looking quite desperate.

"No. She's young and strong. She'll be better in a few days. Now get her out of here and along to the guest room. I'll get the healer."

Palax does as I say. He has some difficulty carrying Kaby but I don't offer to help. I've had the winter malady before and it's commonly believed this makes a man less liable to get it again, but I don't feel like taking the risk. The disease isn't usually fatal but it's unpredictable. There have been times when it's struck with unusual ferocity. People can die from it. I drink some klee then go downstairs to tell Gurd the bad news in private. Gurd is alarmed.

"How bad is she?"

"Couldn't tell. The malady always looks bad at the start."

"What'll I do?" asks Gurd.

I'm not certain. Any case of the winter malady breaking out in a public building should be reported to the local Prefect's office. Unfortunately the Prefect can then impose a quarantine. If Gurd reports Kaby's illness to Prefect Drinius he's liable to see the Avenging Axe shut for at least a week, and that's a lot of business to lose. He could just keep quiet about it, which is fine if Kaby recovers and no one learns of it. But if the Prefect discovers what's happened, there'll be trouble.

Gurd chews his lip.

"Three years ago that silversmith from Lorn took the malady. He just stayed in his room and he got better. I didn't report it then . . ."

I remember. The incident passed off harmlessly enough. The winter malady often does. Some years very few people catch it, and it doesn't seem virulent enough to kill. Unfortunately there have been years when it's been a lot worse. My younger brother died of the winter malady, a long time ago. A lot of people died of it that year. Gurd decides to look in on Kaby, judge her condition, then visit Chiaraxi the healer in private. Chiaraxi is a friend, and won't close him down if it doesn't seem necessary. I watch him hurry upstairs then walk over to the counter for a beer. Makri is serving.

"What was that about?"

"Nothing," I say. "Have you heard of Moolifi?"

Makri shakes her head.

"She's a singer up at the Golden Unicorn."

Makri sneers. I raise my eyebrows.

"How did a barmaid who grew up in a gladiator slave pit become such a snob?"

"I am not a snob," retorts Makri.

"Oh no? You sneer at anything that wasn't written five hundred years ago by some obscure Elvish bard."

"I sneer at anything which involves the performer taking her clothes off before the end of the first chorus."

"Well it might brighten up some of these musty old Elvish plays. Besides, I hear Moolifi has a terrific voice."

"From who?"

"From Captain Rallee. Who has apparently been stepping out with Moolifi for the past week."

It's an interesting snippet of news, even for Makri, who's not normally one for gossip. Captain Rallee did used to be something of a lady's man, but generally these days he's too busy to pursue them. He's in charge of one of the local Civil Guards posts, and with half his men absent on war duty, he's even more overworked than usual.

"He's as happy as an Elf in a tree. He's been strutting round with her on his arm, making the locals jealous."

I muse for a while on the Captain, and his new lady. I've never seen her perform.

"I haven't been up to the Golden Unicorn for a while."

"Are you feeling the need for some exotic dancers?"

"No. But there's a big game of rak played there every week, lot of rich players. I'd like to sit down at a table with some of them."

"So why don't you?"

"Can't afford it," I admit. A man needs a lot of money before he can play cards with Praetor Capatius and General Acarius."

"You gamble too much," says Makri.

I point out to Makri that she herself has not been averse to the odd wager since arriving in Turai.

"Only because of your bad influence."

"Bad influence? I'd call it rounding out your personality. All you used to do was work and study. These days you're slightly less unbearable."

Tanrose is further along behind the bar, ladling out stew to Viriggax and a few of his mercenaries. When she's filled their bowls she hurries over to me and leans across the bar, lowering her voice so as not to be heard by anyone else.

"Thraxas. I need to consult you."

"You mean an investigation?"

Tanrose nods.

"I'm due for guard duty right now. Can it wait till I get back?"

Tanrose nods, and I tell her to come to my office when my shift at the walls ends. I've no idea what she might want me to investigate, but as she's the finest cook ever seen at the Avenging Axe, I'm more than willing to give her whatever help she requires.

Chapter Four

I have two magic warm cloaks. The first one is a fairly inefficient garment. Keeps out the chill for a while but soon starts to lose its potency. I made it myself but my sorcerous powers just aren't up to the task these days. The cloak which Lisutaris, Mistress of the Sky, made for me is much better. She put a spell on it which only needs a word from me to revitalise it each day. The cloak stays warm for a long time. I've done enough soldiering in freezing weather to appreciate the favour. Not that Lisutaris didn't owe me a favour or two, as I pointed out to Makri, with some justice. As do various others, I reflect, during my long spell on the walls. I gaze out into the frozen waste below with a feeling of dissatisfaction. I've fought for this city. I've lived here, worked here, paid taxes. I've sorted out the problems of the rich and poor. My investigating talents have helped keep Lisutaris in her job and Deputy Consul Cicerius out of disgrace. And where has it got me? Two rooms above a tavern in the poorest part of town with little prospect of improvement.

The wind blows a little colder. I wrap my cloak tighter around me. Down below is the rocky stretch of shoreline that leads to the harbour. Since talking about Captain Rallee and his girlfriend, I keep thinking about the card game in the upstairs room at the Golden Unicorn. General Acarius and Praetor Capatius are both regular visitors to the table. The General has a reputation as the finest gambler in the Turanian army, and he's very wealthy. Half the Turanian fleet is built from wood grown on his family's vast estates. As for Capatius, he's the richest man in Turai. He owns his own bank and his trading empire extends all over the west. If I could just get myself around a rak table with these two I'd soon show them how the game should be played.

I do have a slight connection to the game at the theatre. Ravenius plays there. Ravenius, a senator's son, also comes down to the Avenging Axe to play at our weekly game. The stakes at the Avenging Axe are a lot lower than Ravenius is used to at the Unicorn, but the young man is such a keen gambler he enjoys playing anywhere. Perhaps he could introduce me to General Acarius. I shake my head. It's hopeless. You have to lay down a lot of money before they'll allow you to sit at the table. More than I can raise.

My companion in the lookout post is Ozax, an old soldier now turned master builder. Something catches my eye and I call him over.

"A ship?"

It's an unexpected sight. Ships don't sail these waters in winter; the gales are too severe. Though this winter isn't particularly harsh, there have already been several storms fierce enough to sink any warship or trader foolish enough to venture out. We watch as the vessel limps towards the harbour.

"Trader," mutters Ozax. "Looks like it's barely afloat."

The ship's masts are broken and it's crawling along under one ripped sail. It's low in the water, and though we can't see it clearly at this distance, I'm guessing that all spare hands on board are currently pumping out water for all they're worth, trying to keep the vessel afloat. I can see soldiers hurrying along the harbour walls, ready to deal with any emergency. In time of war, no ship can enter the harbour unbidden. It's protected by both chains and spells, and the harbour master won't admit anyone till he's very sure that it's not an enemy.

As we watch, the stricken ship crawls up to the entrance to the harbour then halts, its bow pressed against the thick chains that block the entrance. Sounds of shouting float over the water. Probably whoever's on board is yelling at the defenders to let them in before they go under, which won't be long. The vessel hovers perilously at the entrance, sinking ever further in the water. Just when it seems it's about to slide beneath the sea, the great chains are pulled back. The Sorcerer on duty at the harbour removes the defensive spells and the ship begins to crawl into the harbour. They've made it to safety.

It's an interesting occurrence. As a curious sort of person, I might be inclined to take a walk over if I hadn't promised to see Tanrose after my shift. I run into Makri as I'm walking back to the Avenging Axe. She's wearing a man's tunic and leggings, and her floppy green pointed hat. Its a foolish item she picked up on the Elvish isle of Avula. Only Elvish children wear them and it looks ridiculous. Along with her new golden nose ring, it makes for a particularly offensive sight. The assorted lowlifes who frequent the Avenging Axe are always going on about how great it is the way Makri bulges out of her tiny chainmail bikini in all the right places, but as far as I can see they're missing the point. For one thing she's far too skinny round the waist, and for another, even if you like the skinny type, a pretty face and figure don't make up for her numerous faults. She paints her toenails gold like a Simnian whore, she has her nose pierced like some refugee from an Orcish brothel, she's got the longest and most unruly hair in the city, and beneath that are a pair of pointed ears. Together with her short temper, her foolish intellectual pursuits and her weird puritanical streak it makes for a very unattractive package. Anyone ending up with Makri as a partner would soon come to regret it.

"What's the hurry, Thraxas?"

"I need a beer."

"Since the Orcs arrived you've hardly been sober."

"Who wants to be sober when the Orcs are outside the walls? Last time they were here I was drunk for three months. And still fought heroically."

There are some people on the streets, but between the cold weather and the war there's not a lot of merriment about. Makri isn't helping. She's unusually gloomy. Even the sight of a new batch of swords being laid out in the armourer's window doesn't bring a smile to her face, and Makri is a great weapons enthusiast.

"You notice how it's not such a bad winter?" she says.

I nod. It's cold, but nothing like last year.

"Wouldn't you say it's warm enough for the Guild College to open?"

Makri has a strange passion for education. It's another of her faults.

"It always shuts in winter. Anyway, you said they'd suspended classes for the duration of the war."

"But they could have stayed open and we'd have been able to take our exams before the spring. Might have got the whole year finished before the Orcs attacked."

"Makri, you must be the only person in the city who's thinking about learning anything right now. Chances are there won't even be a city after the spring."

"That's just the point," says Makri, now agitated. "Supposing the college goes up in flames and all the records are destroyed? I'm number one student, two years at the top. I'm going to finish with distinction this year and who's going to know if they don't give me my certified scroll?"

Poor Makri. If it were anyone else complaining about their education at a time like this I'd ridicule them, but I've realised over the past two years what it all means to her. Makri has moved heaven, earth and the three moons to complete her studies at the Guild College. This college, a place for the sons of the lower classes to further their studies, didn't want to admit her. Makri had to struggle all the way, and she's still struggling, scraping together enough money to pay for her classes, and dealing with a lot of hostility because of her Orcish blood. It's quite an achievement for her to have accomplished as much as she has. Makri's dream is to enter the Imperial University of Turai. It's a hopeless dream, but I've given up mocking her over it.

"Don't worry, we'll hold off the Orcs for a while yet. Hell, we don't even know if Prince Amrag's got any sort of force out there."

Makri shakes her head.

"Even if we win the war it'll still delay the exams. I need my certified scroll to apply to the university."

"Makri, do you have enough money to pay for the university?"

"No."

"Do you have a plan to circumvent the article in the university statutes which forbids the education of women?"

"No."

"Do you have some means of getting round the other part of their constitution, which forbids admitting anyone with Orcish blood?"

Makri purses her lips.

"No," she admits.

"So what's the difference? Even if you nail your scroll to the university doors they still won't let you in."

"I'll think of something," says Makri, stubborn in the face of the uncomfortable truth.

"Think of something? What?"

"I don't know. Just something."

"Threatening them with your axe won't work."

"Then I'll think of something else."

"Maybe," I suggest, "when Prince Amrag takes over the city he might make you a professor."

Makri whirls to face me, a furious look on her face.

"I told you not to mention him!"

"I'm an Investigator. I find it hard not to mention things."

Makri glares at me, but refuses to discuss it further. Since learning that she's half-sister to the new overlord of all the eastern Orcs, I've certainly been curious to learn more. However, apart from the vague information that they had the same father but a different mother, and that Amrag escaped early from the Orcish slave pits, leaving Makri there to fend for herself, I've learned nothing at all. Makri refuses to discuss it and insists that I never mention it to anyone. I'm okay with not mentioning it. It's not the sort of thing she'd want the public to know. But I can't help feeling she ought to tell Lisutaris, Mistress of the Sky. In time of war any information about the enemy leader would surely be helpful, and Lisutaris wouldn't give Makri away.

We walk past some small alleyways. Each one we pass is occupied by someone either selling dwa, or using it. The distinctive smell of the burning substance assails us from all sides. It's impossible to travel more than a few yards along the narrow pavement without being approached by someone trying to make a sale. By the third or fourth time I give up answering and just bat them out the way.

"Turai is going to hell," I mutter, stepping over the prone body of an addict, sprawled out in the street. Many of them are young men who should be doing military duty. "If this gets any worse the city won't be worth defending."

I shake my head.

"I should have left this place long ago."

"So why didn't you?" asks Makri.

"I could never think of any place better to go."

The outskirts of the harbour is a really bad part of town, worse even than the rest of Twelve Seas. Shivering young prostitutes, wrapped in threadbare cloaks, try to attract our attention as we pass. Beggars hold out their hands hopelessly, and a few children, far too raggedly dressed to be out in this weather, stand forlornly outside taverns, waiting for their parents to emerge. Things don't improve when I spot Glixius Dragon Killer coming towards us. He's a large man, broad and vigorous. Even without his rainbow cloak he'd stand out from the poor miserable masses around him.

His eyes narrow as he approaches, and so do mine. Glixius Dragon Killer is an old enemy. He's a powerful Sorcerer, though not one who's ever been a credit to the city. Until recently he was outside the influence of the Sorcerers Guild, though he's been brought back into the fold due to the current crisis. That doesn't alter the fact that he's a criminal. He may have escaped conviction, and he might even be fooling the Sorcerers Guild, but he's not fooling me.

Like any successful Sorcerer, Glixius is wealthy. I wonder what he's doing in the poor part of town. Something illegal no doubt. I'm wearing my spell protection charm but I get ready for action because Glixius is strong, and quite capable of launching a physical assault if he feels like it.

Glixius halts right in front of me.

"Thraxas the cheap Investigator," he says, getting straight to the point. I look him in the eye, but don't bother to reply.

"I've been talking to Ravenius," continues the Sorcerer. "He tells me you play rak every week in your cheap little tavern."

I'm surprised. I can't imagine why this would interest Glixius.

"I usually play with General Acarius and Praetor Capatius at the house of Senator Kevarius. But Kevarius has closed his doors for a few days. His wife is down with the winter malady."

He looks at me mockingly.

"I imagine your stakes are too small to be of much interest."

I'm not certain if he's angling for an invitation to our game or merely taking the opportunity to insult me.

"So why don't you join us?"

"I doubt there'd be enough money on the table to make it worth my while."

"You can stake anything you like. I'll be pleased to take it off you."

Glixius eyes me for a few moments. I think he might be smiling though it's hard to tell. He's a square-jawed, steely-eyed sort of individual, and it would take a lot to brighten up his face.

"I never like to sit at a game without five hundred gurans in front of me."

"Five hundred gurans is fine." I reply. "Bring more if you like. It'll be a pleasure to show you how the game is played."

Glixius sneers, then gives the faintest of nods, and marches off.

Makri is looking puzzled.

"What was that about?"

"He wants to play cards."

"At the Avenging Axe? Why?"

"Because he hates me," I say. "Can't get over the time I punched him in the face. Probably he's been looking for revenge ever since. And now he thinks he can humiliate me at the card table. Poor sap. I'm number one chariot at rak."

Makri is doubtful.

"I still think it's strange the way he just walks up out of nowhere and says he's coming to the Axe to play cards."

"That's because you don't appreciate how much he dislikes me. After all, I did once publicly accuse him of a serious crime when he was completely innocent."

"You've done that to most people in the city," says Makri.

"That's true. But it's probably still on his mind."

We walk on towards Quintessence Street.

"You don't have anything like five hundred gurans, do you?" asks Makri.

I admit I don't. The most I can raise is about forty. Which might be a problem.

"Do you have anything spare?" I ask.

"Of course I don't," says Makri. "Who does?"

Light snow is falling as we reach the Avenging Axe. I'm looking forward to a beer and a seat by the fire.

"Are you meeting Lisutaris soon?"

"Forget it," replies Makri. "I'm not asking her to lend you money."

"You don't need to ask. Just bring up the subject. She'll probably volunteer."

Makri declines, and I'm obliged to drop the subject as Tanrose is waiting for me when we enter the Axe. I'd like to thaw out in front of the great fire downstairs but she doesn't have a lot of time before getting back to her cooking, so I content myself with taking a bottle of beer upstairs to my office, and lighting the fire. The room is cold and I leave my cloak draped around my shoulders as I take a seat at the large, dark wood desk I use to transact my business.

Tanrose sits down opposite me. She's not a thin woman, but she's not as large as might be expected, given the excellence of her cooking. Tanrose is currently one of the Avenging Axe's more cheerful inhabitants. If she's worried about imminent Orcish invasion it doesn't show. Since becoming engaged to Gurd she's been happy.

"It's odd consulting with you professionally, Thraxas."

I shrug.

"It's about my mother."

"How is she?" I ask politely. I've met her once or twice. Before moving to the tavern Tanrose used to live with her up in Pashish.

"Quite well," says Tanrose. "Though her memory's not so good these days."

She hesitates, and taps a finger on the desk.

"Last week she told me her father once buried a cask containing fourteen thousand gurans near the harbour and it's never been recovered."

I raise my eyebrows.

"Fourteen thousand gurans?"

"In gold."

"Where did the money come from?"

"He was captain of a ship which raided a Simnian convoy."

"Your grandfather was a captain in the navy?"

Tanrose nods. I'm surprised. Common sailors have low status in Turai but ship's captains usually come from wealthier backgrounds. If Tanrose's grandfather was a captain, it means the family has come down in the world. Tanrose is aware of it.

"He was put in prison and most of the family's wealth was confiscated. That's how my mother ended up in Pashish."

"Why was he jailed?"

"He was accused in the Senate of profiteering in the war with the Simnians. He was meant to hand over all booty he collected to the King but it was alleged that he'd held on to his."

"Which, according to your mother, he had."

Tanrose nods.

"There was some dispute over how much money he'd brought home, and what was owed to him. Back then I don't think all the captains were actually in the navy. Some of the ships were private, and the navy used them when there was a war."

I nod. It's true. There were various famous seafarers in the last century who fought for Turai but weren't exactly part of the navy. Some of them were little more than pirates before the great war between Simnia and the League of City States. When war came, Turai overlooked their previous crimes and drafted them into the navy. It wouldn't be unheard of for one of these captains to find himself in possession of a lot of booty, and later find himself in dispute with the King over who exactly owned the loot.

"It's an odd story, Tanrose. But maybe not so unbelievable. What happened to your grandfather?"

"He died in prison. Quite soon after the trial, I think."

"Why did your mother never mention this before?"

Tanrose isn't sure. She thinks her mother may have preferred to forget about the disgrace in the family rather than have it all raked up again.

"But now she thinks the city's going to be overrun by the Orcs. So she wants the gold recovered."

"When exactly is this supposed to have happened?"

"After the Battle of Dead Dragon Island. Forty-two years ago."

"And where was the money buried?" I ask.

"Beside the harbour."

"That's not very specific."

"It's all she could tell me."

"There must have been a lot of change round the harbour in forty years. Though I don't remember ever hearing a story about fourteen thousand gurans being unearthed. Maybe it's still there. If it was ever there in the first place."

I eye Tanrose.

"You said your mother's memory was bad. How bad exactly?"

Tanrose shrugs her shoulders.

"Not so bad really for a woman of eighty. Do you think it might be true?"

I extinguish the stub of my thazis stick.

"Perhaps. I'll have to talk to her first."

I agree to visit Tanrose's mother tomorrow. Tanrose hurries off downstairs, to cook. As she leaves, Makri walks into my office.

"What did Tanrose want?"

"A private business affair."

"What was it?"

"Private."

Makri frowns.

"But I want to know what it was."

"Well that's unfortunate. Thraxas the Investigator does not reveal details of private consultations with his clients. Now move out the way, I'm needed downstairs for beer and a roaring fire."

Chapter 5

I'm sitting in front of the fire, musing on Tanrose's tale. There's probably nothing in it other than the confused ramblings of an old woman, but I'm willing to check it out. For one thing, I like Tanrose, and for another I'm greatly in need of money. I need at least 500 gurans to sit down at the card table with Glixius. If I unearth a chest containing 14,000 gurans I'm bound to earn at least that. Possibly more, depending on how grateful Tanrose's mother turns out to be. My thoughts are interrupted by Gurd. Kaby is still sick. Worse, Palax has now come down with the malady. They're both shivering in the guest room. Gurd is still unwilling to notify the authorities.

"They'll close the tavern. First thing I learned about keeping a tavern, don't let the authorities close you down."

Gurd asks me if I'd mind taking a plate of food upstairs for them. I eye him suspiciously.

"Why me?"

"You've had the malady," replies Gurd.

Even though it's generally believed that once you've had the winter malady you won't catch it again, the memory of lying in bed, burning up inside, panting for breath, every bone and muscle in my body racked with pain, makes me unwilling to take any risks. Must have been fifteen years or more since I had it, but I haven't forgotten.

"I had to go a week without beer. It was hell."

Tanrose emerges from the kitchens clutching a pot of stew. She's accompanied by Elsior, the apprentice cook, who's learning the trade.

"I can't believe you went a week without beer, Thraxas," says Tanrose.

"That's how sick I was."

"I was there," says Gurd. "He didn't go a week without beer."

"I did. I remember."

Gurd shakes his head.

"The healer told you to lay off the drink. Two hours later we found you crawling towards the tavern, rambling crazily about how the healers were trying to kill you. It took three men to drag you back to your tent and even then you wouldn't shut up till I brought you a tankard. By that time I was ready to kill you myself, so I figured 'What the hell?' "

Tanrose laughs.

"That's not how I remember the story at all," I protest.

"Enough about the malady," says Gurd, looking round shiftily. "We can't let anyone know."

Gurd is nervous, and not just because his tavern might be quarantined. Since Tanrose agreed to marry him he's been happy and anxious in turns. Tanrose touches his arm. Gurd is embarrassed to be caught in even this mild act of intimacy in front of an old fighting companion like myself. He shoves a bowl of soup towards me. I take it upstairs, unwillingly. Palax and Kaby are a nice enough pair but I don't like them enough to risk a repeat dose of the malady. Besides, I dislike acting as a waiter. Life is demeaning enough. On the other hand, it is a powerful tradition in Turai that you look after anyone who falls sick under your roof. Not taking care of Palax and Kaby would be close to taboo, and bring us bad luck. I'm wary of garnering bad luck with such an important game of cards coming up.

Palax and Kaby are huddled together on the small bed in the guest room. Despite the winter cold, they're both flushed and sweating, and have thrown off their blankets.

"Brought you some soup," I say, setting it down on the floor.

"Thank you," gasps Kaby.

"Don't worry, it'll pass soon. You want anything else, Makri will bring it for you."

I depart as swiftly as I arrived. In the corridor I crash into Makri.

"Hey watch it," she says. "What are you doing?"

"Taking soup to the patients."

"And retreating as fast as possible," notes Makri.

"Damn right I'm retreating as fast as possible. I don't want to come down with the malady again."

"Sickness will come and go. It's part of the natural process of life."

"Says who?"

"Samanatius."

"That old fraud?"

Makri is offended.

"He's the greatest philosopher in the west."

"Then tell him to bring soup for Kaby. And I don't see you volunteering."

Makri looks slightly uncomfortable.

"I don't want to get ill. I've never had the malady. I'm needed for the war effort."

"And I'm needed for an important game of cards."

Makri asks me if I've come up with a plan for raising the money for the game.

"Yes. You ask your employer Lisutaris."

"She won't do it. She's not going to risk five hundred gurans on your dubious card skills."

"My card skills are not dubious."

"Last week you lost money to Gurd, Rallee, Ravenius and Grax. I'd say that was dubious."

"It was a fluke. The cards were against me. It happens to the best players sometimes. I'm number one chariot at rak. Stop smiling."

"Lisutaris will be here soon," says Makri. "You can ask her yourself."

"What's she coming here for?"

Makri isn't sure, though she thinks the Sorcerer might want to check I've been doing the daily incantation for Herminis. If the authorities ever find out that I was involved in her escape they'll be down on me like a bad spell. I wonder if I might be able to use this to apply a little pressure on Lisutaris. Maybe hint that unless she lends me a sum of money I might neglect to do the incantation?

"Don't you dare try and put any pressure on Lisutaris," says Makri, reading my mind. "She's busy keeping up the magical defence of the city against the Orcs. She doesn't need you fooling around with inconsequential matters."

I'm about to point out that winning money at cards is not an inconsequential matter when Lisutaris herself sweeps up the stairs and into the corridor. The Sorcerer is as well dressed as ever, with a thick fur wrap draped elegantly over the rainbow cloak that denotes her rank, and some delicate white shoes that owe more to winter fashion at court than the practicalities of moving around the streets in bad weather. Not that Lisutaris has to walk anywhere. As head of the Sorcerers Guild and an important member of the war council she has a fleet of carriages at her command. Though her hair is carefully styled and her make-up expertly applied by her personal beautician, I'd say she was looking tired. Slightly under the weather even. The strain of doing too many spells, no doubt. Last month on the battlefield she expended a fantastic amount of energy fighting the Orcs. She pulled down two of their greatest beasts, huge war dragons carrying Prince Amrag and Horm the Dead, creatures that were protected by every defensive spell known to the most powerful of Orcish Sorcerers. I was standing next to Lisutaris at the time. I can still hear her voice as she intoned the spell in some dead, dread forgotten language, bending her will to the almost impossible task of overcoming the huge brute strength of the dragons and the powerful sorcery that protected them. I'd say it was one of the greatest feats of sorcery ever performed in the heat of battle. Since then I doubt she's had much time to rest, and it shows.

I thank the Sorcerer for the gift she sent.

"Would you like some . . . ah, Abbot's Ale? Maybe some Elvish wine?"

Lisutaris senses the rather unwilling nature of my offer, and smiles.

"Keep it for yourself, Thraxas, I'd rather see you drink it than some of these people at the Palace. You'd be surprised how many healthy young men have suddenly found themselves keen to work in the administration rather than report for military duty."

Lisutaris frowns.

"I don't remember this happening in the last war. What happened to the people's spirit?"

It beats me. Lisutaris is right. There's a lot less patriotic fervour around these days. I don't exactly know why, unless it's got something to do with the wealth that's flooded into the city in recent years. That and the dwa, I suppose.

Lisutaris comes into my office. Makri follows on, uninvited. I give her a questioning look.

"I'm the bodyguard," says Makri. "And what's this about the Grand Abbot's Dark Ale?"

"A rare and fine brew."

"I want to try it."

"I'm saving it for a special occasion."

I tell Lisutaris that I've been doing the incantation every morning to protect Herminis, though I don't bother to sound enthusiastic about it. Lisutaris assures me it's safe enough.

"No one's looking for Herminis anymore. The city's got enough troubles."

Lisutaris takes a seat, and takes out an elegant little silver case containing thazis.

"I'm in the middle of an investigation," she says. "And you, being an Investigator, might be able to help me."

"Is someone about to pay me for helping?"

The sorceress shakes her head. She's constructing a thazis stick; quite modestly sized by her standards.

"No pay. It's official war work, part of every citizen's duty."

"I tend to starve when I'm doing my duty."

"You could afford to lose some weight," says Lisutaris. "Anyway I'm not here to hire you. Senator Samilius is in charge of the investigation and he's got agents all over Twelve Seas already. I'm just looking for advice."

Lisutaris inhales deeply from her thazis stick.

"Have you heard of the Storm Calmer?"

"No. What is it?"

"A sorcerous item. One of the items I inherited when I became head of the Guild."

"What's it do?"

"It calms storms."

"Right."

Lisutaris explains that the Storm Calmer is a conch shell imbued with powers to quieten the seas.

"It was made by the Grand Sorcerer Elistratis about eight hundred years ago and brought to Turai by her daughter after Elistratis was killed in a sea battle far down to the south. Elistratis's daughter sailed here through the winter storms, using the conch shell to calm the seas. Or so the story goes."

"Sounds like a useful item," I say. "Particularly in this part of the world. How come it's never used? We lose a lot of ships every year to the weather."

"It's too important for that," explains Lisutaris. "The Storm Calmer is part of our national defence, like the green jewel I use for far-seeing. It's kept secret, for use only if a hostile Sorcerer tries to batter down our sea walls by conjuring up a storm."

"Last time you mentioned one of these important items of national security," I say, "it had been lost. Has the Storm Calmer gone missing?"

"No. It's safe. But its brother has gone missing."

"The Storm Calmer has a brother?"

"In a manner of speaking. No one knew about it till recently but apparently there's another shell called the Ocean Storm. A Turanian captain came across it on the uninhabited isle of Evoli last autumn. Or so he claims. It hasn't really been confirmed by anyone else. He sent a message to the Sorcerers Guild, saying he'd bought it from some ancient Elvish hermit."

"On the isle of Evoli?"

"That's right."

"So it's not really uninhabited?"

"It's uninhabited apart from one hermit."

"No one else? A cook, maybe, or a maid?"

Lisutaris looks annoyed.

"What sort of hermit has a maid? Please stop making irrelevant comments."

"I'm an Investigator. I need the full facts."

"We don't have the full facts. Just a story that a sorcerous artefact exists which is powerful enough to whip up a storm that would batter down Turai's sea walls and let the Orcs sail in."

By now the Mistress of the Sky is rolling another thazis stick. She is inordinately fond of the substance.

"The Ocean Storm was on its way to Turai last week. No ships sail in these weathers, but this one did."

"I saw it," I say. "Limped in, just made it."

Lisutaris nods.

"It was brought in by the first mate and the four remaining crew members, all experienced sailors, so I understand."

"And the captain?"

"Captain Arex was nowhere to be seen. He had disappeared."

"Taking the Ocean Storm with him?"

"Exactly. Which is a problem. We don't really know if this item exists or not. None of the surviving crew had ever seen it. According to them they didn't even know their captain had sent a message to the Sorcerers Guild. If it does exist, we can't let it fall into anyone else's hands. Which means that we're now moving heaven, earth and the three moons to find something we're not sure is even in the city. Or even ever existed."

I muse for a moment, and light a thazis stick of my own.

"This all sounds unlikely to me."

"In what way?"

"Every way. A powerful sorcerous item no one's heard of before? You know better than me that these items don't happen along every day of the week."

"True. But we can't take the risk. If an Orcish Sorcerer starts trying to batter down our sea walls with a powerful new weapon, we'll be in trouble."

"It wouldn't be easy to use," I point out.

"True," agrees Lisutaris. "You'd have to be a very powerful Sorcerer indeed to pick up a strange magical talisman and use it right away, particularly for controlling the weather."

She pauses, inhaling from her thazis stick.

"But I could do it. If this Ocean Storm really exists, I could use it. A few others might be able to. The most powerful of the Orcish Sorcerers. Like Horm the Dead. Or Deeziz the Unseen."

I'm slightly surprised to hear the name. Deeziz is reputed to be the most powerful Sorcerer in all the Orcish lands, but he was last sighted somewhere in the mountains of Gzak and no one's heard anything about him for a decade.

"Deeziz? He's not with Amrag's army. No one's seen him since the last war."

"He retreated to a mountaintop to seek wisdom, or so we heard. Some people say he was banished when the Orcs were defeated," says Lisutaris. "Finding out anything about him is next to impossible. He's cloaked himself with so many spells of hiding we can't tell where he is. Even when he did used to appear, no one ever saw his face."

Deeziz always wore a veil. People generally assumed he must be horribly mutilated in some way, and given the brutal nature of Orcish sorcery, it's not unlikely. I ask Lisutaris why she's suddenly mentioned him.

"Has there been news that he's heading this way?"

She shakes her head.

"No news at all. But I thought of him when I heard about the Ocean Storm. He always was a master of the weather. If he suddenly appears outside the city with the Ocean Storm in his hand, we've got a problem. Anyway, it doesn't have to be him. Horm could probably use it. We can't let it fall into their hands."

"Probably it was just some piece of junk the captain was hoping to sell for a profit."

Lisutaris admits this is possible.

"Though I don't know how he'd have hoped to convince me it was real. You don't get to be head of the Sorcerers Guild by buying fake sorcerous items."

"True, it wouldn't have fooled you. But he might've had some idea of selling it to some other hapless member of the government. I've known senators get conned by stupider things than that."

"Can't you use your own sorcery to tell if there's a new sorcerous item in the city?" asks Makri, butting in with a question I was just about to ask myself.

"I haven't come up with anything," replies Lisutaris. "But that's not really conclusive. An unknown sorcerous artefact, inactivated, wouldn't necessarily give out any signals that could be traced. There are a great many objects and people in this city who give off sorcerous vibrations. Picking up some unknown source isn't easy."

"What does the ship's crew say about the captain disappearing?"

"Nothing. They don't know what happened. They were so short-handed that each of the five sailors was at his post, bringing the ship in. And suddenly the captain wasn't there."

"He probably fell overboard drunk," I say. "If he's anything like the other captains around here."

"It might all be nothing," agrees Lisutaris. "But suppose it isn't. Suppose the Ocean Storm is real and someone has stolen it. What would you think?"

"Then I'd think it was serious. It might have fallen into the hands of someone who'd be happy to see the Orcs batter down the harbour walls with a tidal wave and sail their fleet in. Has Samilius found out anything?"

"No."

"No surprise. Samilius is an idiot."

"I know. I've taken charge of the sorcerous part of the investigation and assigned several good Sorcerers to the hunt," says Lisutaris. "I trust you don't think I'm an idiot?"

"I think you're a woman who sent me an excellent gift. What do you want me to do?"

"Help us search," says Lisutaris. "When it comes to asking awkward questions and finding lost goods in strange places, you have some talents."

"I have. Are you sure there's no money involved?"

The Sorcerer looks frustrated.

"Regard it as an extension of the battlefield, Thraxas. This is war."

"Of course. It's my patriotic duty. But there is a matter of supreme importance occupying my attention just now, which really calls for a substantial sum of money. Do you think you could see your way to lending me five hundred gurans?"

Lisutaris is suddenly overtaken by a fit of coughing. I use the opportunity to press my case.

"I'm not asking you to take a risk. It's money loaned at a guaranteed return."

Lisutaris attempts to rise, falters, then falls to the floor. I gaze down at her, perplexed. I didn't think she'd be quite so shocked by a simple request for money.

"Well, you know, maybe three hundred would be enough to get me started—"

"Thraxas, you idiot, can't you see she's sick?" yells Makri.

"Sick?"

Lisutaris's face is turning red and her breath is coming in heavy gasps. Beads of sweat appear on her forehead.

"She's got the winter malady," says Makri.

"She can't have. She's head of the Sorcerers Guild."

I gaze down at her on the floor, cursing my luck. One of the richest women in Turai, right here in the Avenging Axe, and before she can listen to my business proposition she comes down with the malady. I've always felt that the gods had it in for me.

"Get Chiaraxi," says Makri. "I'll put Lisutaris in your bed."

"I don't think that's really the best place for—"

"Get the healer!" yells Makri.

While I'm not at all pleased to have a sufferer from the winter malady dumped on my own bed, there doesn't seem to be a better alternative. It's a serious matter having the head of the Sorcerers Guild fall sick at a time like this.

"If she comes round, ask her about lending me some money."

I depart. Before making my way along Quintessence Street to the home of Chiaraxi, I stop downstairs to appraise Gurd of current events. The brawny old Barbarian looks alarmed.

"Lisutaris? Sick? Here? Can't she go somewhere else?"

"Not in her condition."

Gurd curses under his breath. It's going to be difficult to keep this secret. A quarantine order is looking more and more likely. It's unfortunate timing. The tavern is full of mercenaries and soldiers. Gurd's business has never been so good. Provided the city doesn't get destroyed by the Orcs, he's in line for a healthy profit over the next few months. I leave him to his worries and hurry along to fetch Chiaraxi. Chiaraxi is alarmed as I barge into her office, possibly due to the fact that the last time I arrived here in a hurry was because Makri was about to die from a crossbow bolt, fired into her chest by Sarin the Merciless, one of the worst villains ever to blight Turai.

"Makri? Is she—"

"It's Lisutaris. She's come down with a bad case of the malady."

Chiaraxi frowns, and starts loading herbs into a bag.

"How bad?"

"Very bad, I'd say. Started coughing and then collapsed. I'd have thought such a powerful Sorcerer would have some protection against illness."

Chiaraxi shakes her head.

"Sorcery's no use against the winter malady. You can die just the same."

We hurry back towards the Avenging Axe. Chiaraxi asks me if it's the first case there's been. I admit it isn't.

"Palax and Kaby are sick with it."

"Has Gurd reported it to the Prefect?"

I remain silent. Chiaraxi purses her lips, indicating disapproval. I take the healer up the outside staircase that leads directly into my office, not wanting the customers in the tavern downstairs to suspect what's happening. Unfortunately my office isn't empty. I left without placing a locking spell on the door, and Captain Rallee and his new lady friend Moolifi are sitting together on the couch. Makri is standing uncomfortably by the door into the only other room, where Lisutaris is lying sick.

The Captain is around my age, but better preserved. His blond hair, long and tied at the back, is only just beginning to streak with grey, and his lifetime of pounding the streets has kept him in shape. We used to be friends. We fought together, a long time ago, and we worked together when I was an Investigator at the Palace and he had a far cushier job at Palace Security. Since I got sacked and the Captain got forced out by the endless politicking and favouritism that goes on there, we haven't get on so well. The Captain doesn't like the fact that's he's back on the beat, working a tough patch like Twelve Seas. From his point of view, private Investigators only get in the way.

I've never seen Moolifi before, and know her only by reputation. They say she's got a good voice. She has a lot of fair hair and a good figure, which probably helps things along. She looks quite a lot younger than the Captain. I get the impression he's not displeased to be here with her at his side. Puts him in a good light. A lot of people must have been vying for the singer's attention and the Captain doesn't mind it at all that he's come out the winner.

"Captain? What brings you here?"

The Captain looks at Chiaraxi.

"Who's sick?"

"Me," I reply.

"What's the matter?"

"That's between me and Chiaraxi," I reply.

The Captain looks suspicious. I intimate that I'm in a hurry to get my medical problem attended to so could he please make it quick. It turns out he wants Moolifi to stay at the Avenging Axe for a few days.

"She's had some trouble up at the Golden Unicorn."

"What sort of trouble?"

"Trouble with her manager. She had to leave in a hurry. I'd like you to keep an eye on her for a few days till she gets something sorted out."

Normally I could see reasons for objecting to this. If Moolifi is in trouble in her theatre in Kushni it probably means the Society of Friends is involved, because that criminal organisation runs the Golden Unicorn. I'd rather not offend the Society of Friends. Furthermore, I don't owe the Captain any favours. However, with Lisutaris sick in the next room I'm keen to get the Captain out of here as quickly as possible. I don't want to let the Civil Guards know that Gurd's been hiding a case of the winter malady from the authorities. So I tell him it's fine with me.

"If Gurd has a spare room for her I'll check she's safe. Now if you'd let me get on with my examination?"

As soon as they're gone I take Chiaraxi through to the bedroom. Lisutaris looks bad. Paying no further attention to either Makri or me, Chiaraxi takes out her herbs and potions and gets to work.

I tell Makri that we've got a problem.

"Captain Rallee wants to put Moolifi in the guest room. We can't let him find Palax and Kaby in there."

"So what are we going to do?"

"Carry them into your room."

Makri's face twitches.

"I don't want them in there."

"There's nowhere else."

"Couldn't they come here?"

"I've already got one sick person. You want me to look after everyone?"

Chiaraxi abruptly halts our argument by rising swiftly and issuing orders.

"Lisutaris is very ill. I want her isolated. She can't be moved and no one else is to come in here. If you have to move Palax and Kaby take them to Makri's room."

"I don't want them there," protests Makri again.

"I don't want Lisutaris in my room," I add.

"I don't care what you want," says Chiaraxi. "Do as I tell you."

Makri looks nonplussed. She turns to me.

"Can she order us around like this?"

"Stop wasting time and do as I say," says Chiaraxi.

It's difficult to argue with a healer when she's engaged in ministering to the sick. Makri and I reluctantly comply with her instructions. We swiftly haul Palax and Kaby into Makri's room.

"This can't be right," complains Makri. "I've only got one small room. How come I have to take two sick people? How can I study when they're here? What if I get the malady?"

We only just get the moving of sickly bodies completed before Moolifi and Gurd arrive upstairs. Gurd looks at me questioningly. I give a slight nod to indicate that it's safe to let her into the guest room. Moolifi thanks Gurd. Her voice is rather cool and gracious, less rough than I'd have expected a Kushni entertainer's to be. She says she's tired, and would like to lie down for a while.

"This is bad," says Gurd, after the singer departs.

"You're right it's bad. The head of the Sorcerers Guild is about to die in my bed and God knows what the *Renowned and Truthful Chronicle* will say about that."

We return to my office. Chiaraxi appears from the bedroom, briskly efficient.

"You must inform the authorities," she says.

"I can't," says Gurd. "They'll shut me down."

"They'll do a lot worse if they find you're trying to conceal an outbreak of the malady," points out the healer.

"I won't report it," says Gurd, stubbornly.

"Then I will," replies Chiaraxi.

"We can't keep it secret anyway," points out Makri. "People are going to notice if the head of the Sorcerers Guild isn't around."

True, of course. Lisutaris is among the most important people in the city. She can't just disappear. It's our duty to let the authorities know what's happened. It seems as if Gurd has no alternative but to report it all to the local prefect.

There's a very light tap on the inside door. Everyone looks towards it, suspiciously. I open it carefully. I'm confronted by a small, pale woman with dark hair who I'd take to be a worker in the local market if I didn't recognise her as Hanama, number three in the Assassins Guild. I stare at her balefully.

"What do you want?"

"Makri."

Hanama is softly spoken. Listening to her talk, you'd never believe she'd killed so many people. I detest her, as I do all Assassins. A foul and murderous breed without whom the city would be far better off. I'm about to slam the door in her face when Makri hurries over.

"What is it?" she asks.

Hanama puts her mouth to Makri's ear and whispers.

"Stop having murderous Assassins' conversations at my door," I say, harshly.

Hanama suddenly clutches at her throat and falls forward. A rather puzzling occurrence. She's not the sort of woman to take an insult so badly.

"She's got the malady," cries Makri.

"She can't have," I yell. "Not her. Not in my office."

I turn towards Gurd.

"This is getting out of hand. We have to get these sick people out of the tavern."

Chiaraxi bends over the Assassin.

"Carry her to the couch," she says.

"I refuse to let a sick Assassin lie on my couch."

Chiaraxi and Makri ignore me. Hanama is laid on my couch. Sweat pours from her forehead and her breath comes in heavy gasps. I glare at Hanama.

"Couldn't you get sick somewhere else? You're not staying here. I refuse to allow it."

"No one in Turai can refuse aid to a sick guest," says Chiaraxi.

"She's not a guest. She just barged her way in here."

It's hopeless. Chiaraxi is already busy with her herbs.

"Bring a blanket," she instructs.

"I refuse to let you cover Hanama with my blanket," I protest, but it's useless. Makri is already fetching it.

"How can Hanama be my guest? I don't even like her. Ask anyone."

No one is listening to me. I take out a bottle of klee and drink a good shot, shuddering as it burns my throat. Now I've got a sick Sorcerer in my bedroom and a sick Assassin in my office. I shake my head, and wonder how it can possibly have happened. It's not like these people don't have homes of their own where they could be ill.

Chapter Six

Deputy Consul Cicerius hurries down to Twelve Seas as soon as he receives my message. I haven't yet informed Prefect Drinius. I'm on bad terms with our local prefect and will leave it to Cicerius to do what's necessary. When Cicerius arrives I'm hesitant about actually letting him in my office. The way things are going I'm half expecting him to plummet to the floor the moment he enters.

"I have had the malady," he says, and sweeps past me. His assistant, Hansius, doesn't look quite so comfortable in the presence of disease. Cicerius is surprised to see Hanama lying on the couch. I'm not certain if he recognises her. Asleep, she looks more child-like than ever. Not at all like a woman who once killed an Elf lord and an Orc lord both in the same day, and a senator as well, as Hanama is reputed to have done.

"There is more than one victim? Where is Lisutaris?"

"In the next room."

I'm not thrilled at the prospect of the Deputy Consul of Turai entering my only private room, not least because it's even more untidy than my office. I get the strange feeling that I'm back in the army and my personal kit is about to be inspected by an officer. I start to bridle. One comment about the state of my rooms and I'll sling them out. Chiaraxi accompanies them into the bedroom. Gurd has gone back downstairs, leaving me alone for the moment with Makri, apart from Hanama, who's sleeping under the influence of some medicinal draught. Even so, I draw Makri to the far side of the room and talk to her in a low voice, careful lest Hanama should overhear. You can't trust an Assassin, even a sick one.

"What did Hanama want? Is it something I should know about?"

Makri shrugs.

"I don't know. She collapsed before she could tell me."

"Didn't she even give you a hint?"

Makri shakes her head.

"You saw how quickly she went down."

It's a mystery. Damn Hanama. Couldn't she have stayed on her feet for another thirty seconds?

"It must be something really serious," says Makri.

"I suppose so. Unless she just felt like talking to you."

"What's that supposed to mean?" declares Makri, sharply.

"Last month she brought you flowers."

"Will you just drop that?" says Makri. "There's no need to keep going on and on about it. Don't you have something else to think about?"

Hansius reappears and asks me to join the Deputy Consul. I notice his eyes flicker towards Makri. Hansius has been in my office before but I don't think he's ever encountered Makri in her chainmail bikini. Plenty of people regard it as a remarkable sight. Not just her breasts; Makri is the only woman I've ever seen with tightly defined stomach muscles. Even the dancers in the theatres up-town tend to have softer bellies. Of course, all decent women keep their stomachs well covered up.

Knowing that if Hansius keeps staring, Makri will say something rude, I take his arm and guide him back into my private room where Deputy Consul Cicerius is standing beside Lisutaris, looking thoughtful. The sorceress is conscious, but very weak.

Cicerius thanks me for notifying him.

"This is bad. I do not want news of Lisutaris's illness to be made known. It would be disastrous for the city's morale. Furthermore, and most importantly, the Orcs must not learn of it."

What the Deputy Consul says is true. Lisutaris is so important to the defence of the city that news of her incapacity might be all the Orcs needed before staging an attack.

Cicerius is a thin, grey-haired man, trusted by the population though not loved. He's too vain and too austere to generate much affection. But he's a better man than our highest official, Consul Kalius. Kalius was injured on the battlefield, and not gloriously. He's now recuperating but is too traumatised to take the reins of power, which leaves Cicerius in charge. The strain is showing. His face is thinner and his toga, normally as clean, white and well pressed as it could be, shows signs of having been put on in a hurry.

"The healer is concerned by Lisutaris's condition but not overly so. The Mistress of the Sky is a strong woman and should recover."

I glance at Lisutaris. Her eyes are open, but I'm not sure if she can hear us or not.

"So are you going to send a wagon to ship her back home?"

"No. She must stay here while she recovers," continues Cicerius. "Your healer advocates complete rest."

I start complaining loudly. Cicerius glares at me.

"Do you not trust this healer Chiaraxi?"

I'm forced to admit I do.

"She keeps people going in Twelve Seas and that's not easy."

Cicerius nods.

"I have the feeling she is to be trusted. I could send down healers from the Palace, but . . ."

He ponders for a while.

"But I would rather as few people learn of this as possible. Already this month our intelligence services have rooted out an Orcish spy in the Palace and another one in the senate. There are probably more. I'd far rather leave Lisutaris to recover here, away from all prying eyes. Makri is already employed as bodyguard to protect her. I'll send down a few other agents, discreetly, to ensure her safety. All being well, our sorceress should recover fully in a few days with no one even knowing she was ill."

"Won't people miss her at the Palace? Or on the war council?"

Cicerius shakes his head.

"I can assign her duties which would keep her away from the war council for a few days. And we can use her double for some public appearances, to allay any suspicions."

"Her double?"

Cicerius informs me that the Consul's office has people ready to play the parts of various important citizens in Turai, for precisely this sort of emergency.

"There is an employee at the Palace—a keeper of imperial records—who has already served in this capacity on occasion."

I'm impressed. I didn't realise our government was so organised.

"What about quarantine?"

Cicerius shakes his head.

"Prefect Drinius is not to be informed and the Avenging Axe is not to be quarantined. Do nothing which might attract attention to this tavern, until Lisutaris has fully recovered."

"And Hanama?"

"She must stay here. We cannot risk her leaving. She might let it be known that Lisutaris is ill."

"But it's not safe having her here. What if she assassinates Lisutaris?"

"That hardly seems likely," says Cicerius. "Assassins do not kill at random. They work to contract."

"I don't like this at all. Why should I look after a sick Assassin?"

"You are aware, of course," says Cicerius, "of the Turanian tradition which requires all citizens to give hospitality to a sick guest?"

"Of course. I just don't think it should apply to Assassins."

"It applies to everyone," says Cicerius, who's always keen on Turanian traditions, no matter how stupid they are. "Simply care for them, go about your business, and Lisutaris's illness should pass unnoticed."

I give up the argument. At least if the tavern isn't quarantined the card game can go ahead. I get the insane notion to ask Cicerius for 500 gurans but dismiss it immediately. He's not known for his generosity. Besides, he'd probably find it impossible to imagine that anyone could think of playing cards at a time like this.

Inspiration suddenly strikes.

"How is the hunt for the Ocean Storm?"

Cicerius looks at me suspiciously.

"You know of that?"

"Of course. Lisutaris came down to consult me. She knows I'm number one chariot at finding missing items."

"Any help you can give will be appreciated," says Cicerius, brusquely. "But there are already many people looking. Praetor Samilius is organising the search."

"Then you can expect not to find it. Best hire me. I've come through for you before. Shouldn't take more than— let me see—five hundred gurans should do it."

The Deputy Consul looks shocked.

"Are you trying to extort money for finding an item on which national security may depend?"

"Extort? You call asking for a decent wage extortion?"

"As I recall, your normal daily rate is thirty gurans," says Cicerius. "It saddens me to see any citizen of Turai trying to make money from the crisis."

"And me. But it so happens I need five hundred gurans in a hurry. That's not a great sum. You could lose it in the treasury accounts easily enough. So how about offering a reward of five hundred gurans for the swift locating of the Ocean Storm?"

Cicerius gives me a withering look. He clearly regards me among the ranks of the profiteers who buy up supplies in times of hardship and sell them for vastly inflated prices to the suffering population.

"If you locate the item I may authorise a small reward. But do not expect me to do you any favours in future."

"I never noticed you doing me any favours in the past."

Hansius reminds the Deputy Consul that they have an urgent appointment at the Palace. Cicerius nods.

"Thraxas. It is your responsibility to look after Lisutaris. While she is under this roof, I suggest you moderate your habits. For once in you life, try putting the interests of the city before your own."

Cicerius departs. It was typical of him to insult me at the same time as requesting I work hard for him. Cicerius can be a great speaker—in the law courts he's a fabulous orator—but he doesn't spend a lot of time working on his personal charm.

Chiaraxi provides instructions for the care of Lisutaris and Hanama. They're simple enough. Plenty of water, and the herbal concoction every few hours.

"Make sure they're kept warm. That should be easy enough for you."

I look at her blankly.

"Sorcery," says Chiaraxi. "You can light your fire with a spell."

"Right," I say.

It's a long time since my fire-lighting spell worked. These days I just don't have the power. After Chiaraxi leaves I check on Lisutaris and Hanama. Neither look like they're about to die in the next few moments so I do what I've been wanting to for some time, and hurry downstairs to the bar.

"Happy Guildsman, and make it quick."

Gurd hands me over the extra-large-sized tankard. From the expression on his face he could do with a few Happy Guildsmen himself.

"It's terrible," he hisses.

"Not so bad," I tell him, quietly. "No quarantine."

Gurd is still troubled.

"What if Lisutaris dies?"

"They can hardly blame you."

"Can't they? I never reported it when Kaby went sick. I should have."

I tell Gurd to relax.

"The Deputy Consul has entrusted the whole affair into my hands."

"What do you know about healing the sick?"

"Not much," I admit. "But all that seems to be required is regular doses of Chiaraxi's herbal concoction. Just pour it into the patients and wait for them to get better. Easy enough. I always knew these healers were making too much out of the whole thing. Probably helps them to bump up their fees."

I point out to Gurd that once Lisutaris has been successfully brought back to health the Avenging Axe could even benefit.

"Might get a reputation among Sorcerers as a good place to go, and Sorcerers are big drinkers. When I went to the last Sorcerers Assemblage they were taking it in like their lives depended on it."

Sorcerers rarely seem to practice moderation. Whether it's alcohol, dwa or, as in Lisutaris's case, thazis, they always need to go to excess.

Makri arrives with a tray full of empty tankards.

"Where are you going to sleep?" she asks.

"In the guest room, I suppose."

"You can't. Moolifi's in the guest room."

I forgot about that. I don't know where I'm going to sleep. Makri announces that she's sleeping next to Lisutaris, on the floor.

"Says who?"

"Me. It's my job. I'm her bodyguard."

Suddenly everything seems worse. Makri sleeping on my bedroom floor. Time was when no one entered my office apart from the occasional hopeless client. Now there's hardly room for a man to sit and drink beer.

I turn to Gurd.

"Looks like you'll have to put me up in your room. Be like sharing a tent in the war."

Gurd looks embarrassed.

"That would be, ah—"

Gurd abruptly feels the need to polish the far end of the bar, and moves away rapidly, working his cloth furiously. I'm baffled.

"What's the matter with him?"

Makri gives me a pitying look.

"You can't share his room. Tanrose shares his room. Didn't you know that?"

"Of course I didn't know that. When did this happen?"

"Right after he asked her to marry him," Makri informs me.

Now I'm stuck for inspiration.

"Maybe I can sleep behind the bar," I muse.

"Just sleep on the floor in your office."

"Sleep in the same room as an Assassin? No chance."

"You might form a bond," says Makri. "It's time you got yourself some female companionship. Hey, even Gurd's not alone these days."

Tanrose appears from the kitchen, carrying a tray of pastries.

"Tanrose, don't you think it's time Thraxas got himself a woman?" calls Makri.

"Definitely," says Tanrose. "I've been telling him for years he should settle down."

"Of course, Hanama's on the small side, so you'll have to be careful . . ."

No wishing to listen to any more mockery, I take a bowl of stew—with no yams—and depart to the far corner of the room, where I sit in front of the fire, listening to mercenaries talk about fighting. I wonder about the Ocean Storm, and I wonder about Tanrose's mother's tale of buried gold. Which is most likely to earn me some money in a short space of time? It's a difficult choice. I decide to investigate each one tomorrow, and see where it takes me.

Chapter Seven

Next day I'm out on the streets early enough to catch the first beer delivery. I recognise the large, red-haired man who's rolling barrels down to the cellar.

"What are you doing on a wagon, Partulax?"

Partulax gave up working the wagons a few years ago when he became an official in the Transport Guild. These days he spends most of his time sitting in an office giving out jobs and contracts.

"Driver shortage," he replies. "Most of the Guild's been called up for the war. Your delivery man's up at the Gardens."

Turai has a regiment of troops stationed close to the Pleasure Gardens defending the East Gate. There's been some suggestion of mounting an attack on the Stadium, but I think General Pomius is against it. We don't know how many Orcs are there and he'd rather not open any of the city gates till a relief force arrives.

"No shortages in the beer department?"

"Not yet," replies Partulax.

Just as well. If beer runs out it will be a crushing, demoralising blow for the city. I'd find it hard to carry on. Again it's a mild day, and Gurd is sweating as he helps fill the cellar.

"Off to the walls?"

I shake my head.

"My day off military duty."

"Then what are you doing up at this time?"

"Working on a case."

No one has been able to shed any light on the mysterious disappearance of the captain of the ship that was supposed to be bringing the Ocean Storm to Turai, so I'm off to interview the first mate. He's holed up at the Mermaid Tavern. An interesting choice, given that the Mermaid is the local headquarters for the Brotherhood. Not the sort of place an innocent man generally chooses for his residence, though it doesn't necessarily mean the sailor is part of the criminal gang. He might just need to be near to a supply of dwa. Or maybe he's sick of being investigated, and wants to be somewhere where the law doesn't go. Between the Civil Guards, Palace Security and the local prefect, he's already suffered a lot of investigation.

The lane that leads to the Mermaid is full of dwa dealers, small-timers at the mouth of the alley and a few more important figures close to the tavern. Trade is brisk, as always. Once more, I'm struck by the number of men who should be on military duty but aren't. Very lucrative for the Brotherhood, but maybe they won't think it was such a smart way to make a profit when the Orcs storm the walls and put them all to the sword.

As I'm about to enter the tavern, Glixius Dragon Killer strides out the front door. His great black boots, handcrafted by the master leather workers of Juval and probably costing more than I earn in three months, are scuffed and muddied from the alleyway. If I had such a fancy pair of boots I wouldn't wear them to the Mermaid. I'm surprised to find him here. As far as I know, Glixius doesn't use dwa. When I try to walk round him he gets in the way.

"I'm looking forward to our game," he says.

"Me too. Now move over, I'm busy."

"You're not calling it off then?" says Glixius, loud enough so the people hovering round the doorway can hear. "For lack of money?"

"I'll be there."

"I'll see you soon," he says, and strides off, his long rainbow cloak trailing behind him. It's an unusual sight, a Sorcerer in this alleyway, but I wouldn't say it attracts that much attention from the dwa dealers or their customers. They're all too busy with their own business.

Inside the tavern the first person I meet is Casax, local head of the Brotherhood.

"Well, well," says Casax. "Two Sorcerers in two minutes."

That's a joke, sort of. My failure at sorcery is well known. It doesn't help my mood.

Casax has a shaven head, dark features, and a gold earring in each ear. He's intelligent, and ruthless when he has to be. He's a powerful man, large, though not as large as Karlox, his enforcer, who stands beside him dwarfing everyone, even me, and I take a lot of dwarfing.

"You never told me you had a special game lined up," says Casax.

"What special game?"

"With Glixius and General Acarius. How did you manage to get the General to come to the Avenging Axe?"

"I didn't know he was," I admit. "But Glixius just invited himself."

"Well I hear he's invited Acarius. They usually play with Praetor Capatius. If the Praetor comes down it'll be the richest game ever seen in Twelve Seas."

He looks at me like I'm a man who doesn't have a lot of money.

"I can cope," I say.

Casax shrugs.

"You better make sure you've got a good stake to start with. Otherwise they'll just force you off the table."

Casax comes most weeks to play in the rak game at the Avenging Axe. Big money won't be a problem for him. Since he took over the Brotherhood in Twelve Seas they've tightened their stranglehold on crime and increased their profits.

"How's the Captain?"

"Rallee? He's fine. Why?"

"You might tell him to watch his back. You know that woman he's running around with's in trouble with the Society of Friends? She owes them money. Probably took up with Rallee for some protection," says Casax. "I quite like the Captain. Always admire an honest man."

"As long as he doesn't interfere with your business."

"It's a long time since the Civil Guards could interfere with my business."

Casax frowns at a sailor at the bar who's making a lot of noise. The sailor shuts up.

"Anyway they won't come after her in Twelve Seas," says Casax. "So you don't have to worry."

I move a little closer to Casax.

"The Society worry me as much as the Brotherhood. Which is to say not at all."

"You hear that, Karlox?" says Casax. "We don't worry him. Better take care not to upset such a tough guy."

Karlox grins. I've had some run-ins with him in the past. He's dumb as an Orc but good at violence.

"What did Glixius want?" I ask, not really expecting a reply.

"To talk to a sailor about a missing item."

Casax points to a figure at a table, just discernible through the perpetual smoky gloom inside the Mermaid. I wonder if Glixius Dragon Killer has been looking for the Ocean Storm on behalf of the Sorcerers Guild. Lisutaris said she'd sent out some people. But Glixius isn't trustworthy. More likely he's working some angle of his own.

Casax loses interest in me. He doesn't care about me questioning the first mate. Maybe he figures it would be wise to cooperate, with the Sorcerers, the Civil Guards and Prefect Drinius all buzzing around. Or maybe he just feels like being polite because he's looking forward to the card game. He's not a bad player, Casax. Sharp as an elf's ear, or near enough, and difficult to read.

I sit down next to the sailor. His eyes are dull and they don't light up when I appear.

"I don't know anything about the Ocean Storm," he says, before I can even frame a question.

"How d'you know I was going to ask you about it?"

"Everybody else has. The Prefect. The Civil Guards. The Sorcerers."

His voice sounds weary. Perhaps the result of his arduous sea voyage. More likely he's midway between doses of dwa.

"What happened to Captain Arex?"

"He disappeared. We just made it into harbour, and when we got there, no Captain Arex."

"He just disappeared?"

"That's what I said."

"I saw the ship come in. The weather was calm. He couldn't have been washed overboard. Where'd he go?"

The first mate shakes his head. He doesn't know.

"You feel anything strange? Sorcery maybe?"

He shakes his head again. Of course, there are plenty of spells that can't be sensed by your average citizen.

"Tell me about the Ocean Storm."

"I don't know anything about it."

A waitress passes. I order a beer and sit in silence till it arrives. My companion doesn't volunteer any more information. He doesn't seem worried. He doesn't even seem interested. I sip my beer.

"When these people asked you questions—the Guards, the Prefect, the Sorcerers—did any of them offer you some financial reward for your trouble?"

This gets his attention. He looks straight at me.

"Now that you mention it, they didn't."

I take out my purse.

"None of them really know how to investigate," I tell him. "They're amateurs. Just get in my way, really."

I take out two gurans and lay them on the table. It's more than I'd normally pay for information in a place like this.

"Why did you go to the isle of Evoli?"

The first mate slides the coins off the table and into the pocket inside his tunic.

"To take on water. Not unusual."

"But something unusual happened?"

"The captain disappeared inland with a few sailors and he came back with something in a bag. Didn't say what it was and he didn't tell me where he'd been. Later the sailors told me he went to see some old monk. An Elf. I didn't know there was anyone on Evoli, it's just a rock in the sea really. A few trees and a stream."

"Was it on your normal trade route?"

"No. We made a diversion."

"Strange time to make a diversion, with the stormy season due."

"It was. We were lucky to make it back to Turai."

"So what happened to the captain?"

The first mate shakes his head.

"I don't know. I was busy working a pump when we came into port. We were shipping so much water we damned near went under."

I stare at him.

"I didn't pay you to tell me the same story you told the Prefect. I've been at sea. I don't imagine a ship's captain ever disappeared without someone on board knowing where he went. And I don't believe he was spirited away by a spell either. Where'd he go?"

The first mate looks at me pointedly. I slide another guran across the table.

"He has a woman in Silver Lane."

"Then give me the address and I'll be on my way."

He gives me the address. I finish my beer and depart, satisfied. Having cleared up any foolish notions of mysterious disappearances, I've more of an idea what's been going on. The captain might have been in negotiations with the Sorcerers Guild but he's obviously got an idea of how he might earn himself more than they were willing to pay. I'm guessing he's had a better offer from elsewhere, and has dropped out of sight while he tries to do a deal. Theft and greed. I'm back on familiar ground.

Silver Lane isn't far away. It's one of the many small streets in Twelve Seas with tall tenements crowding in on each side, dwellings which are never comfortable and often dangerous. The landlords bribe the city officials to look the other way while they build them up too high. Every year there's some disaster when one of them collapses and there's an outcry in the city for a while, but it never changes. I'd expect a sea captain to live in a slightly better area, but if he's on the run it's not a bad place to go, though the Guards or the Sorcerers would have found him soon enough if they weren't so dramatically bad at investigating.

The stairway is narrow, dark and dirty. I walk up three flights and knock on the door. There's no reply. Maybe they're out. Maybe they're not keen on visitors. I speak a minor word of power and the door swings inwards, easily enough. I'm pleased. I always am when any of my small knowledge of sorcery pays off. The hallway is neat, with a small table and a clean rug. The captain's lady keeps a nice slum. I can smell freshly baked bread. I glance in the first room, which is empty. I look in the second, which is not so empty. There's a few sticks of furniture and two dead bodies. One male, around my age, face somewhat gnarled, probable effects of a life at sea, stabbed in the back. One female, younger, rather plump, wearing the sort of dress a poor woman buys to greet her lover. Also stabbed, and also dead.

It's a depressing sight. The neatness of the room makes it worse. The woman lives in the poorest part of town but makes an effort to keep things tidy. Her lover arrives back with a plan for making some money, presumably to take them somewhere better. Soon afterwards they're both dead. Not such a great plan, all in all.

I take a look around. I'm not expecting to find anything and I don't. If the captain had the Ocean Storm on him, it's long gone. In the tiny kitchen there's a loaf on the table, newly baked. The captain's woman was skilful in the kitchen. He should have stuck with his homely comforts instead of trying move up in the world. I tear off a hunk of bread, cram it in my mouth, and close the door on my way out.

After I leave I feel downcast. I've spent too long sorting out problems in this city. With the Orcs outside the walls, I wonder why I bother. A beggar holds out his hand as I pass by. He's dressed in rags, and suffering in the cold. When winter is harsh, the beggars die. Maybe this year they'll make it through to spring. I should question him. He might have seen someone coming out from the tenement. But I hurry past, suddenly uncomfortable from the feeling that I'm going to end up like him, destitute and on the streets. The way my life has been going for the past few years, I wouldn't say it was impossible. My mood worsens when I pass a tavern at the foot of Moon and Stars Boulevard which has a quarantine sign outside it, a large black cross painted on the white door. The winter malady is starting to spread.

I'm not too far away from the tenement where Tanrose's mother lives. I could go and question her. I hesitate. Having just encountered two corpses I'm not really in the right state of mind to launch into a fresh investigation. But time is short, and I need money. I sigh, and head over to visit her.

Chapter Eight

Tanrose's mother is quite a frail, grey-haired woman. She's made it to eighty, which is old in these parts, but I wouldn't say she was going to be with us for too many more years. She has one servant, paid for by Tanrose, who leads me into their only large room where Tanrose's mother is sitting in a large chair with a brown blanket over her legs. Though the family isn't wealthy, the tenement they live in isn't as bad as many of the others in the poorer areas. It's small but comfortable, and well decorated, with some small tapestries on the walls, clean, uncracked glass in the windows, and polished floorboards covered by thick rugs. I catch a glimpse of the family shrine off the hallway and it's bright and clean, and smells of incense.

After the servant has brought me a glass of wine I wait for Tanrose's mother to get down to business. It takes a little while, and as she tells me the story there's an edge of bitterness in her voice. She hasn't forgiven the authorities for putting her father in prison.

"The privateers had an agreement with the King that they could keep whatever booty they took before they joined up with the navy. My father, Captain Maxius, attacked a Simnian treasure ship the day before he was due to meet with the squadron he'd been assigned to. Everything he took that day was his by right."

As she tells it, the authorities didn't see it that way. Captain Maxius took part in the Battle of Dead Dragon Island honourably enough, but when he arrived back in port he found himself summoned to the Palace, where he was accused of withholding treasure from the King.

"Other captains were jealous because he was so successful. The trial wasn't fair. He was put in prison when he refused to hand over the money."

Tanrose's mother coughs, and looks frail and upset. Some tears form in her eyes.

"He died soon after. He wasn't well after the voyage and he couldn't recover in prison. They killed him. Afterwards they were always questioning my mother but she never told them anything."

She sighs, and looks off into the distance for a while.

"That was all a long time ago. Now the Orcs are going to take over the city. Good, I say."

"Good?"

"Why should I care? The city ruined my family. My father was wealthy. Look at us now."

She pauses again. She seems to be tiring. She revives long enough to look up at me sharply.

"But the Orcs can't get my father's money. Find it for me. There's fourteen thousand gurans. If you find it you can have one thousand."

"Where exactly did he bury it?"

"Near the harbour. Under the whale."

"What?"

"Under the whale."

I scratch my chin.

"I don't know of any whale at the harbour."

"That's what he told my mother. Under the whale. And that's what she told me."

"I really don't think there's a whale in Turai harbour."

"Not in the harbour. Beside it."

"Even so—"

I break off. Tanrose's mother's eyelids are starting to droop. Any second now she's going to nod off.

The servant comes in and looks questioningly at me.

"I'm leaving," I say, and bid farewell. I leave the tenement very thoughtfully. She didn't seem crazy and her memory seemed to be intact. Her story wasn't that unlikely, given the history of Turai's naval past, and the greed of the Palace. Any captain arriving back with a fortune might well find someone there trying to relieve him of it. Besides, I've been offered a reward of 1,000 gurans for finding the loot, which makes me even more inclined to believe the story.

The only problem is I'd swear there isn't a whale beside the harbour. I'm still musing on it as I arrive back at the Avenging Axe. I'm not pleased to find Makri in my office and my mood isn't improved by the way she's kneeling over Hanama, their faces almost touching.

"What the hell are you doing?" I demand. "No, don't answer that. Just do it somewhere else."

I grab a bottle of klee and take a slug. All these sick women in my private quarters, it's starting to unnerve me. Makri springs lithely to her feet. Everything she does is lithe, agile and nimble. I never noticed before how annoying it can be.

"Hanama was trying to tell me something," says Makri.

I sit down at my desk. There's a brief silence.

"Stop pretending you're not interested."

"Nothing an Assassin says is of any interest to me."

"Isn't it time you lightened up on this hating Assassins all the time, Thraxas? It's getting tedious."

"Tedious? This woman kills for money. It's a vile trade that should have been outlawed long ago."

"You were a soldier. You killed for money."

"That's different."

"How?"

"It just is. And don't try and confuse the issue with some smart argument you learned from Samanatius the so-called philosopher."

Makri looks frustrated.

"Do you want to hear what Hanama had to say or not?"

"No."

"Fine," says Makri.

She sits down on the couch. I try to ignore her. After a few minutes I glance up. She's studying her nails. I tap my fingers on the desk, and take out today's edition of the *Chronicle*. It's full of news about the winter malady. There's been a major outbreak in the north of the city and it's expected to spread. Makri's still studying her nails.

"What the hell did Hanama have to say!" I roar.

Makri looks up.

"Pardon?"

"What was it?"

"I can't remember."

I've really had enough of this. I rise to my feet.

"Makri, I've got an office full of sick Assassins and Sorcerers and it's starting to get on my nerves. I'm not in the mood for you to hang around acting like an imbecile. What did Hanama say?"

Makri rises to her feet too.

"She said if that fat Investigator comes back tell him he's a drunken oaf."

I put my hand to my sword and draw it a few inches from its scabbard.

"Tell me what she said."

Makri's eyes blaze. She wrenches a long knife out of her boot and steps towards me.

"What if I don't?"

Makri brandishes her knife. I draw my sword. There's a knock on the inside door and Tanrose comes into the office. She looks aghast at my drawn sword and Makri's knife.

"What's going on?"

I sheathe my sword, with dignity.

"A private disagreement."

"You should both be ashamed of yourselves," says Tanrose. "What sort of way is this to behave?"

Makri puts her knife back in her boot and looks sulky.

"He started it," she mutters.

Tanrose frowns.

"I was going to ask you to look after the bar while I went to the fishmonger's. But I think I'll ask Dandelion instead. Try not to kill each other while I'm gone."

Tanrose departs. I sit back down at my desk. I light a thazis stick and throw one to Makri. She catches it and places it between her lips. There's a few moments' silence.

"That was strange," says Makri.

"What?"

"The argument. Even by our standards it didn't seem like time for drawing weapons."

I shrug.

"Everyone in Turai is crazy right now, with the Orcs outside the walls. Always happens. A city under siege is never a good place to be. Now that the malady's arrived, I expect a lot more citizens to start exhibiting their craziness."

I draw on the thazis; the mild narcotic calms me down.

"So what did Hanama have to say?"

"She says there's going to be an attempt on Lisutaris's life."

"Who from?"

"She passed out again before she could say any more."

I turn to look at the small Assassin, who's murmuring to herself, lost in the troubled sleep that comes with the malady.

"That's great. Couldn't she have stayed awake another ten seconds?"

"At least we got the warning," says Makri.

"It's not a lot of use. The way things are just now, half the city could be planning a bit of treachery to save their skins from the Orcs."

"What did Tanrose's mother want?" asks Makri.

I'm immediately suspicious.

"How did you know about that?"

"I heard someone mention it," says Makri, vaguely.

"It's a private investigation. A little trouble with her neighbours. Nothing important."

I'm not about to let Makri know that I'm hot on the trail of 14,000 gurans. Once word got out, there's no knowing what might happen. In a city as avaricious as Turai, half the citizens would be down at the harbour in no time, digging for gold.

Before Makri can attempt to prise any more information out of me we're interrupted by a knock on the door. It's a young man from the Messengers Guild. He hands over a sealed scroll. I sign for it, and close the door. The message is from Deputy Consul Cicerius.

Situation now grave. Lisutaris in great danger. Do nothing whatsoever that might draw attention to this tavern. Am sending Tirini Snake Smiter to provide sorcerous protection.

"I told you Lisutaris was in danger," says Makri.

I'm not that impressed by Cicerius sending Tirini Snake Smiter to help. She's not the sort of Sorcerer you'd turn to in a crisis. I'd be happier if he sent a regiment of troops to ring the tavern. Unfortunately this might alert the Orcs to Lisutaris's illness, which might precipitate an immediate attack.

"Are you going to cancel the card game?" asks Makri.

I'm puzzled.

"Why would I do that?"

"It'll draw attention to the tavern."

"No it won't."

"Of course it will. People are bound to talk about it, especially if General Acarius brings Praetor Capatius."

I get the slight feeling that things are spinning out of control, with sick people everywhere and the city's richest gamblers heading in my direction, but I force the thought away.

"In times of crisis, a man has to carry on as normal. I can't go around cancelling card games. It would be unpatriotic."

Makri scoffs at this.

"You're meant to be not drawing attention to the Avenging Axe. Staging the biggest card game in Twelve Seas' history might technically be seen as drawing attention."

"Cancelling it would only raise suspicions."

"Have you raised the money yet?"

"Not quite. But I can feel things moving my way."

Chapter Nine

I spend the evening sitting in front of the fire downstairs in the tavern, sipping beer and working my way through an enormous venison pie. Salted venison rather than fresh, as it's winter, but Tanrose has a way of bringing it back to life. My mood improves. True, the rooms upstairs are full of sick people, and the pie isn't quite the same without a few yams to mash up in the gravy, but looking on the bright side, I'm feeling on firmer ground with regard to the missing Ocean Storm. Now I've cleared up the matter of the so-called mysterious disappearance of the ship's captain, at least I know where I stand. I've no idea who might have killed him after he slipped away quietly into his lover's arms, but when it comes to a murder in Twelve Seas, I can generally sort it out. Criminals round here are careless. They make mistakes. I find them out. Sometimes it takes a smart piece of thinking. Sometimes just the willingness to plod on till I find the solution. I generally get there in the end.

Gurd's tavern is full, but despite the raucous drinking contest going on between a group of northern mercenaries and a company of crossbowmen from the Turanian village of Geslax, most people's attention is drawn to Moolifi. The Avenging Axe has never before played host to such a famous entertainer. Captain Rallee pretends not to notice but I can tell he's as pleased as a pixie. He loves it that he can sit at a table with Moolifi and let people see the way she looks into his eyes. He's replaced his tired old black uniform with a smart new one, polished up his boots and trimmed his moustache. Drinkers pause as they lift their flagons to their lips and glance over at the couple, jealous that the Captain has made such a catch. Singers and dancers are very low down in Turai's social strata, but even so, a golden-haired beauty like Moolifi would normally be spending her time with a wealthy member of the Honourable Merchants Association, or maybe even a senator. Now Rallee's hooked up with her, even though he's only a poorly paid captain in the Civil Guard. It says something for his qualities as a man, or so he likes to think.

Some drinkers call over to the Captain, asking if his lady would like to give us a song. The Captain waves their requests away for a while, and starts to look annoyed when a few young mercenaries are too persistent in their attentions. Rallee starts to get angry but Moolifi ends any bad feelings by smiling at the mercenaries and calling over that she'll be pleased to sing. She rises to her feet, a confident woman who's used to entertaining an audience. As the tavern goes quiet, Makri sits down heavily at my table, looking a little fatigued after her long evening shift.

"The men in Turai are fools," she says.

"We're in the middle of a war. Nothing wrong with a little entertainment."

Makri sneers. She lights a thazis stick, and keeps her back towards Moolifi, determined not to show any interest in her performance. She's the only one to do so. Voices are hushed and the drinking contest comes to a halt as Moolifi starts to sing. The hush doesn't last for long. As Moolifi launches into "Love Me Through the Winter," there are roars of appreciation. "Love Me Through the Winter" is her most popular song, and delivery boys and wagon drivers have been whistling it for months. It has a strong tune and by the time she's reached the first chorus tankards are starting to beat out time. As the song comes to an end the audience erupts with applause. Tankards, fists and sword pommels are banged on tables in thunderous approval.

"That was awful," says Makri. "What sort of idiot would enjoy that sort of thing? Thraxas, stop banging your tankard on the table."

"How could you not like it? She's a great performer."

I bang my tankard some more. Makri shakes her head in disgust and rises to her feet. She snatches my tankard off me and puts it on her tray.

"Bring me another beer!" I roar.

"Some time tomorrow," mutters Makri, and departs into the throng of drinkers with her tray, snatching tankards right and left.

Moolifi sings a few more songs for the customers. It's a memorable night. Worries about the war are banished, and people still grieving for the friends and relatives they lost in the battle forget them for a while. Makri might not approve of cheap entertainment but it certainly goes down well at the Avenging Axe. As for Captain Rallee, I've never seen him looking so cheerful. He's in such a benevolent mood he forgets to be annoyed about the fact that we're both working on the same case.

"Thraxas. I hear you've been looking for the Ocean Storm."

I nod.

"Any success?"

I shake my head. I sent a message to the Guards telling them about the two bodies in Silver Lane, so Captain Rallee now knows about the murders. I sent the message anonymously so he doesn't know it was me who found them. Or possibly he does; Captain Rallee isn't a fool.

"It's a big thing for the city," says the Captain. "If you do somehow stumble across it, get it to the Sorcerers as soon as possible. You know there was a report of an Orcish fleet not far along the coast?"

I'd heard about it. I'm not sure if I believe it.

"I don't think they'll be out in this weather. There's no good anchorage along the coast. If they got caught in a storm they'd be done for."

"Maybe they don't plan to be out there for long."

The Captain's point being, of course, that if the Orcs get hold of the Ocean Storm they can use the magical talisman to batter down our defences around the harbour and sail right in. It's a good option for Prince Amrag. He doesn't have siege engines and it's hard to see how he can storm the walls in winter. The eastern and western gates of the city are heavily guarded by men and sorcery, and the North Gate, where the river flows into the city, is extremely well protected. Battering his way into the harbour might be his best plan.

Captain Rallee has a lot of men engaged in the hunt. So far they've had no more success than the Sorcerers Guild or Praetor Samilius. The Captain glances round to where Moolifi is engaged in a conversation with Dandelion and Tanrose. Then he looks at me. I figure I'm expected to say something.

"She's a fine woman. Must be making your life brighter."

"She is."

The Captain suddenly looks downcast.

"Of course she's just hooked up with me for the duration of the war. You know how everyone goes crazy when the enemy is at the gates."

He looks at me again, but if he's expecting me to reassure him that Moolifi will love him forever, he's come to the wrong man.

"When were we first in action together?" asks the Captain.

I shrug.

"About twenty years ago."

"We made it through a lot of fighting."

Captain Rallee stares into his drink.

"I'm not expecting to make it through this."

"Why not?"

"I just don't think anyone will come and help us. Turai's luck has run out."

I'm surprised to hear the Captain so pessimistic. He's always been a man who is confident of finding his way through, even in difficult circumstances.

"At least you've got Moolifi to cheer up your final days."

"True. But she picked a poor time to arrive in this city."

"Lucky for you though."

The Captain nods.

"Strange the way she hooked up with me," he says.

"That's the second time you've said that."

"So?"

"So what's your problem? You think Moolifi might be after you for your money?"

This make the Captain laugh. We both know that a captain in the Civil Guards doesn't earn enough to attract fortune-hunters.

Makri arrives, still scowling.

"Enjoy the singing?" asks the Captain.

"No," snaps Makri, grabbing his empty tankard and departing without another word. Rallee looks startled.

"What the hell?"

"She has harsh critical standards," I explain. "Doesn't really like anything if it's not Elvish. And old."

He shakes his head

"Makri the intellectual. I don't envy the man who ends up with her."

He looks straight at me. The Captain seems to be doing that a lot.

"I always figured you had a thing for her."

"Then you figured wrong. I'm going to my grave clutching a beer tankard."

"That still leaves one hand free."

"Then I'll pick up another beer."

"Maybe you ought to think about it more. None of us are liable to be here come the spring."

"Goddamn it, Rallee, since when did you become as miserable as a Niojan whore? Your pretty singer doesn't seem to be making you that cheerful."

"The pretty singer makes me wish I might live a bit longer."

I spend a very unsatisfactory night sleeping on my office floor in front of the fire. Lisutaris is still in my private room, with Makri on the floor by her side. Hanama is lying on the couch. I'm used to a bit of privacy and I'm finding this assortment of Turai's least desirable women hard to take. I'd considered sleeping in the store room downstairs, or even the corridor, but brief investigation reminds me that these places are all as cold as the ice queen's grave, and I'm not prepared to freeze to death just to get away from them all. I wrap myself in my cloak and lie in front of the fire, cursing the winter malady and everyone who's suffering from it.

At least I have the card game to look forward to. The evening after tomorrow I'll be sitting at a table with Glixius, Praetor Capatius and General Acarius. I'll show them a thing or two. I remember I haven't got enough money to play and feel downcast for a moment. I'd better do something about it. I resolve to head out early tomorrow and find the buried gold. Maybe I'll come across the Ocean Storm while I'm at it. I could do with some spectacular success. It has to happen to everyone sometime.

Next morning I wrap my magic warm cloak around me and head out early to visit Kerk, an informer of mine. In Quintessence Street the stall-holders are already at work, shivering behind their meagre displays of goods. I'm grateful for my warm cloak. It gives me a slight feeling of superiority to the procession of cold figures hurrying about their business in Twelve Seas. None of them have a magic item keeping them warm.

Kerk is at home; he's living in one squalid room at the top of a ramshackle tenement at the far end of St. Rominius's Lane. It's the sort of place where the very poorest people end up; one step up from sleeping in an alleyway. The landlords divide and subdivide the floors into smaller and smaller rooms, till they're barely sufficient for humans to live in. Nothing is good in a place like this: no sanitation, ventilation, hygiene, privacy, nothing.

Kerk opens the door and looks disappointed when he sees me. He has a slightly Elvish look to him, something about his eyes. If he does have a touch of Elvish blood it was no doubt deposited by some visiting Elf into a whore in Twelve Seas. Even visiting Elves need a little entertainment. I think he might have been a smart guy when he was younger. Occasionally he still is, but he's too far gone with dwa to ever get out of it. He scrapes up what little money he can, uses it to buy the drug, and then looks for more money to buy more dwa. The same thing, over and over, destroying himself a little more each time. I doubt he's eaten a proper meal in years. It doesn't seem like much of an existence. Maybe the Orcs will be doing him a favour if they destroy the city. Even if they don't, he'll be dead soon enough.

I tell him I'm looking for the beggar I saw outside the tenement in Silver Lane.

"The place where that sea captain was murdered?"

"The same."

Kerk holds out one hand. This early in the morning he's fairly lucid, but already trembling, in need of dwa. I hand over a very small coin.

"More," he says.

"More when you tell me something."

"I know where you can find him. Give me more."

I hand over another small coin. Kerk used to be a reliable informer. These days he's not so reliable and I'm not paying him too much in advance only to find he knows nothing. Kerk scowls at the two small coins in his hand.

"His name's Nerinax. He usually begs in front of St. Volinius's church in the morning. Good spot, usually gets something from the pontifex."

I give Kerk a larger coin. He stops scowling. I leave, picking my way carefully down the dark, litter-strewn stairway into the street below. It's not far to the church. A chill rain starts to fall and I walk swiftly over the frozen streets. I'm hoping I don't run into the priest, Derlex. He's had it in for me ever since I got into an argument with his superior, Bishop Gzekius. While I admit that I've never been the most godly of men, I still say it was going too far to use me as the main example in his famous sermon against the four great vices—gluttony, gambling, drunkenness and violence. Children still point at me in the street.

Nerinax the beggar is sitting right in front of the church. The last time I was inside the building I encountered some Orcs. Makri killed them. She was so keen to kill them I was left trailing in her wake.

Nerinax has a bowl in front of him containing a few small coins. There's a crutch propped up on the wall beside him, and one of his legs ends just below the knee. When I approach him he looks up hopefully. I take another small coin from my purse.

"Do you have a spot for begging up in Silver Lane?"

He stares at me, no longer hopeful. Now I'm not a person who's about to give him money. I'm a person who wants to ask questions, never a popular thing in Twelve Seas.

"Silver Lane," I repeat. "Do you beg there?"

"What about it?"

"Who did you see coming out of the building?"

"No one."

I drop the coin into his bowl and take out another one. So far I've bribed the sailor in the Mermaid, Kerk, and now Nerinax. It's the easiest way to get information. At least I haven't had to think too much.

"Are you from the Guards?"

"No. I'm an Investigator. And Captain Arex was murdered inside the building you were outside of. As I'm sure you know. So tell me about the people you saw coming out."

"I saw you."

"Who else?"

"Civil Guards. After you."

"What about before me?"

Nerinax looks round uncomfortably. He'd like me to drop another coin in his bowl but he doesn't want anyone to see him giving information to an Investigator. Giving information can be an unhealthy pastime in Twelve Seas. There's no one around. I drop the coin into his bowl.

"A few people were in and out of the building. A Sorcerer."

"A Sorcerer? A big man? Long cloak and fancy black boots?"

The beggar nods. So Glixius Dragon Killer was there. That's interesting.

"Who else?"

"A thin man in a cloak."

"What did he look like?"

Nerinax shrugs.

"He had his hood up. He was thin. He was looking down like he didn't want to be recognised."

"Was this before the Sorcerer?"

He nods. I question him some more but he can't give me a better description. A thin man in a cloak. Medium height, wearing a grey tunic, same as most people in Twelve Seas. It's not much of a description.

"Anyone else?"

He glances round nervously again. Fearing he's about to clam up, I take out another coin.

"Borinbax," he says, quite nervously.

I've heard of Borinbax. He works for the Brotherhood, which is enough reason for Nerinax not to want anyone to know he saw him. Borinbax is a thief by trade. Not famous for his exploits, but busy enough. Mainly works around the harbour warehouses but has been known to rob wagons coming into the city. He could be the sort of man to steal the Ocean Storm, though I never heard that he was a killer. If he does have it, it might be in the hands of the Brotherhood by now, which will make it very awkward to retrieve.

I hand over another coin. By now the rain has started to fall more heavily. The beggar shivers, and looks uncomfortable. The front door of the church opens. I glance up. It's Derlex, the pontifex. He glares at me. I depart swiftly.

Borinbax rents some rooms above a sailmaker's shop close to the docks. By the time I get there the sky is dark grey and the rain is coming down heavily. The water in the harbour is choppy. Out beyond the harbour walls the sea is cutting up quite roughly. If there are any Orcish ships out there they might be in for an uncomfortable time. Perhaps Prince Amrag and his whole army will drown. That would save us a lot of trouble.

Before calling on Borinbax, I look around for a whale, or something which might resemble one. I don't see anything. I wasn't expecting to. I've lived close to the harbour most of my life and I've never heard of anything called the whale. But Tanrose's mother definitely recalled that her father said the gold was buried under the whale. After some fruitless tramping of the streets I start to wonder if perhaps she's losing her mind. Always a possibility, after a long life in Twelve Seas.

There are various taverns dotted around the docks. I wonder if any of them might once have been called the Whale. It's a possibility. I'll check it out later. I abandon the hunt and turn my mind back to Borinbax.

There's a door beside the sailmaker's shop and a staircase leading up to Borinbax's rooms. The door isn't locked and I climb the stairs carefully. Whoever's taken the Ocean Storm hasn't hesitated to kill, and I keep my hand on my sword pommel as I make the ascent. I've got a sleep spell ready to knock out anyone who gets in my way. It's a small piece of sorcery but it's often helped me out of a jam.

Borinbax's front door is painted white. Most front doors in Turai are. It's the lucky colour for front doors. It's freshly painted, probably a sign that he isn't doing too badly for himself. The door swings open easily. Odd. No self-respecting thief leaves his front door open. I draw my sword and advance carefully into the hallway. It's dark, with no torch lit, so I take out my illuminated staff and speak the word to make it work. The hall lights up with a golden glow. My illuminated staff is a fine piece of craftsmanship. I won it from an Elf lord playing niarit. He was a fool to play me. I'm number one chariot at niarit.

The hallway is neat and clean. Fresh plaster on the walls and a small religious icon with a picture of St. Quatinius, picked out in gold. There's a rug on the floor, another good item, Abelasian wool, better quality than you'd find in most places in Twelve Seas. Borinbax must be doing well for himself. Or was doing well for himself, I should say, because he's lying face down in the hallway, dead, and no longer enjoying his furnishings.

I creep further along the hall, examining each of his rooms. They're all neat and they're all empty. I go back to the body and turn it over carefully. There's an ugly wound in his chest. I stare at it for a few moments. Doesn't quite look like a stab wound. I try sensing the air for sorcery. I can't pick up anything. I take a further look around but I'm not expecting to find anything, and I don't. The Ocean Storm has eluded me again.

Chapter Ten

In the street below I call into the first tavern, buy a beer and down it in one gulp, then set off towards the Avenging Axe. Three people have now died because of the Ocean Storm. Every time I get close someone beats me to it. I wonder who else might be on the trail. I wonder about the oddly shaped wound in Borinbax's chest.

There's a cold mist rolling in off the sea which doesn't improve my mood. Nor does the thought that my office is currently infested with sick people. How long is Lisutaris going to loll around in my bed? It seems like time she was getting better. As for Hanama, the woman is meant to be a deadly Assassin. You might think she'd be healthy enough to just shake off an attack of the malady rather than collapse in my office and refuse to budge. I decide to ask Gurd if he can do something about clearing a store room. Maybe I could just throw Hanama in the cellar till she recovers, and to hell with what Chiaraxi says. I've had enough of that healer ordering me around.

I'm no closer to raising the required funds for the card game. No Ocean Storm and no sign of the buried gold. Unless I get some sudden inspiration as to what Captain Maxius meant by "under the whale," the treasure is going to remain undisturbed. The thought of not having enough money to play cards fills me with gloom. Might there be anyone else in the Avenging Axe who could lend me something? Dandelion for instance. She gets paid every week and what does she have to spend money on? As far as anyone knows, the only thing she ever does is go down to the coast and talk to the dolphins. She might have a few gurans laid by somewhere.

I trudge into the Avenging Axe with a mighty scowl on my face. Ignoring various friendly greetings from some of the regular customers, I march up to the bar and tell Dandelion to pour me a Happy Guildsman and be quick about it. Remembering that I'm about to ask her for money, I say thank you when she lays it on the counter. Makri emerges from the back room with a case of klee, replenishing the stocks behind the bar.

"You look as miserable as a Niojan whore," she says.

"No doubt. I have a lot to put up with. Dandelion, can you lend me any money?"

Dandelion looks surprised.

"Are you having problems?"

I've been considering spinning some lie, but I don't have the energy.

"I need it to play cards."

"All right," says Dandelion.

Makri interrupts, inevitably.

"You're crazy Dandelion."

"Makri, shut up. How much can you lend me?"

Dandelion thinks for a minute.

"Fifty gurans."

"Excellent. I appreciate it."

"That's the last you'll see of it," says Makri, quite mockingly.

"But Thraxas is an excellent card player," says Dandelion. "Doesn't he always win?"

"I do. And I appreciate the loan. You can count on a good return on your money, Dandelion. A pity more people in this tavern don't share your faith in a man."

I ask Makri whether Lisutaris is showing any sign of recovering.

"Not much. She's got it bad."

Palax and Kaby are a little better, but still unable to leave Makri's room, which doesn't please her at all. Makri is also worried about falling ill herself. Chiaraxi is still calling in regularly to minister to her patients, which is something. According to her, the malady is spreading and it looks like the city might be in for a full-scale epidemic. Bad news, with the Orcs outside the walls. We're short of fighting men as it is.

"I heard people in the market talking about the Orcs breaching the sea wall," says Makri.

"What? Who said that?"

"Just some people at the stalls. They'd heard the Orcs have got a new weapon and they're going to smash their way into the harbour."

I suppose the rumour was bound to leak out. With the Civil Guards, the Sorcerers Guild, and the prefects' office all looking for the Ocean Storm, word was bound to spread.

Makri notices I'm looking thoughtful.

"Do you think you can find it?"

"I don't know. Whoever else is looking for it keeps getting there ahead of me. And he isn't shy of killing either."

Makri wonders why whoever else is looking for the Ocean Storm killed the captain and Borinbax. I admit I don't know.

"Maybe just to protect his identity. It's odd that no one seems to know who exactly is involved. The Sorcerers and the Guards are all looking; you'd think they might have come up with something."

I wonder about the odd wound in Borinbax's chest. It didn't look like it came from a sword or a dagger.

"It looked like your chest."

"What?" says Makri.

"Your chest after we pulled that crossbow bolt out of you."

Makri looks interested.

"A crossbow bolt?"

A killer called Sarin the Merciless once fired a crossbow bolt into Makri's chest, nearly killing her. She's been keen for revenge ever since.

"I wonder if Sarin's involved. She's smart and she likes her crossbow. She might have removed the bolt afterwards to avoid giving herself away. And she wouldn't mind killing anyone who got in her way."

"If she shows up again I'll kill her," says Makri, brightening up at the prospect.

I finish my beer, and consider another. I need some sustenance, particularly as I've been obliged to sleep on the floor. I can still feel my back aching. It strikes me that as Tanrose has apparently moved in with Gurd, her room downstairs is now free.

"Of course," I say, slapping my palm on the bar. "I should have thought of it before. I can move into Tanrose's room till the sick people get the hell out of mine."

"You can't," says Dandelion.

"Why not? Tanrose won't mind."

"It's not empty."

"I thought Tanrose was—"

I stop, not wishing to complete the sentence in front of Dandelion.

"Sleeping with Gurd," says Makri, who has no delicacy about her at all.

"She is. But Chiaraxi is in Tanrose's room."

"What do you mean?"

"She got sick."

I gape at Dandelion, as does Makri.

"Dandelion, don't babble. She can't get sick, she's the healer."

"Well she did," replies Dandelion, placidly. "This afternoon. Just fell over when she was making potions. So we had to put her in Tanrose's room. I'm going to make up potions for everyone later, she gave me the recipe. We'll all have to work extra hard to look after people now the healer is sick."

I'm practically speechless and Makri isn't looking too pleased either.

"Well, this seems bad," she says. "Rather shakes my confidence in Chiaraxi."

"Mine too. The least you could expect from a healer is not to get ill."

"Damn them all! Can't they get sick somewhere else?" says Makri.

"You were the one who encouraged them all to hang around."

"I did not," retorts Makri. "Apart from Lisutaris. And maybe Hanama. I don't like this at all, Thraxas. Everyone's getting sick. Is it some sort of spell?"

Makri seems quite disconcerted by the whole thing. It's unusual for her to show signs of nervousness in any circumstances. I guess she really doesn't like the idea of becoming ill.

"Relax. If you catch it you'll get better."

"I'm not taking potions to anyone," she says.

"We all have to pull together," says Dandelion.

"Damn them all," says Makri again.

All thoughts of the winter malady are banished next moment when Captain Rallee, accompanied by four excited-looking Civil Guards, rushes into the tavern. He bangs his fist on the table for silence then shouts out to everyone in the room.

"There's a report of Orcs in Twelve Seas! Down by the church. Everyone with a sword follow me!"

There's a mass scramble for weapons. Viriggax and his mercenaries leap to their feet, hastily grab their swords and make for the door. Gurd appears from behind the bar, axe in hand, and runs after them. Meanwhile I'm moving as fast as I can in the same direction. If the Orcs have somehow arrived in Twelve Seas undetected the city might be about to fall a lot sooner than anyone expected. Makri disappears up the stairs to fetch her weapons and is so quick that's she's coming down the steps from my office to the street outside by the time I get there. We hurry along after the mercenaries and the Captain, towards the church. Unfortunately, by this time the wind has dropped and the mist that came in earlier has now enveloped Twelve Seas in thick white gloom. The Captain and his men have already disappeared from view, and those who are trying to keep up with him find themselves crashing into passers-by attempting to make their way home through the gloom. The city's lamplighters have already lit the torches that stand on most street corners, but their light barely cuts through the mist, making it almost impossible to see where I'm going.

Thick winter fogs are not that uncommon in Turai but I'm not certain whether this is completely natural. If the

Orcs are indeed attacking, then sending in a sorcerous blanket of freezing mist as cover wouldn't be a bad idea. Controlling the weather by means of magic is extremely difficult, but everything we've learned about the Orcish Sorcerers in the past few years seems to indicate that they're growing stronger.

By the time I'm close to the church I've lost sight of everyone, including Makri. Somewhere ahead of me I can hear Viriggax bellowing at his mercenary company, ordering them to form up and advance behind him. I can't hear the clash of weapons but there's a lot of shouting coming from all directions, and several people crash into me from behind, rushing to the scene as word spreads that the Orcs are in the city. Suddenly the great bell at the harbour starts booming out a warning.

"Orcish ships!" screams someone, though from where we are, we can't see the sea. But the cry is taken up and soon the whole area around the church is a mass of people rushing blindly about in the mist, brandishing weapons and screaming that the Orcs are coming. I can't see more than a sword's length in front of me, and the way things are going I'm expecting to be run through by an overexcited mercenary before I come to grips with the enemy. I actually bump into Captain Rallee between the church and the harbour. He's lost all his men and he's sweating with the exertion of running around Twelve Seas.

"Have you seen anything?" he barks at me. I shake my head and he hurries off, blowing a whistle to rally his men, which isn't going to work in this confusion. Bells, whistles, shouts and screams rend the air from every direction. Having failed to locate any Orcs around the church, I'm making my way down towards the harbour, ready to repel invaders. It's slow progress. I give up running and pick my way carefully along. I know every inch of these streets but the torches haven't carried away any of the mist and visibility is almost zero. Inevitably, I find myself trampling over beggars and comatose dwa addicts, lying in front of alleyways, impervious to the excitement. I'm continually jostled by soldiers, Civil Guards, mercenaries, not to mention Twelve Seas civilians carrying whatever weapons they can find. I march round a corner with a sword in my hand and nearly decapitate a funeral party, two men in black cloaks and hoods, and a veiled woman, all treading slowly homewards, heads solemnly bowed. I cast a swift suspicious glance at their concealed faces—you wouldn't expect Orcs to invade the city disguised as a funeral party, but who knows what they might be up to these days—but they're Human, not Orcs. I can always sense the presence of Orcs. A useful talent that's stayed with me from my days as a Sorcerer's apprentice. As it happens, I do see one of their faces, when I tread on someone's toes and he lifts his hood to give me an angry scowl.

"Watch where you're going," he barks.

"Possible Orcish invasion," I mutter back, by way of explanation, and plunge back into the mist.

When I'm almost at the harbour I bump right into Makri. She's carrying her black Orcish sword in one hand and a medium-sized axe in the other. Her Elvish sword is slung over her back.

"Have you seen the Orcs?" she cries.

"No. Have you?"

She shakes her head.

"No sign of them. Though I've bumped into most other people in Twelve Seas."

"Me too."

We stand in silence for a moment, as the chaos continues all around.

"We must have covered a fair bit of ground between us," says Makri. "You think we'd have come across an Orc by now."

She looks disappointed.

"You think it might be a false alarm?"

I nod.

"It's starting to look that way."

The great bell at the harbour has stopped ringing, though there's still a lot of confused shouting in the distance. Makri shivers. She ran out of the Avenging Axe wearing only her chainmail bikini, and now that the excitement is wearing off she's noticing that it's not an appropriate garment for walking around in a freezing fog.

"I need a beer. I'm going back to the Axe."

Makri hesitates. She likes to fight and she likes to kill Orcs. She's disappointed not to get the chance.

"Maybe they're hiding somewhere."

By now other people are starting to leave the area, looming in twos and threes out of the mist, muttering to each other about being called from the warmth of their homes to fight enemies that weren't there.

"I doubt it. Orcs aren't that good at hiding. We'd have found them by now. It's a false alarm."

We walk on up the street, through the mist. I pause, then walk on, then pause again.

"What's wrong?" says Makri.

"Nothing," I reply, but as we carry on along the road I lean over to whisper in her ear.

"I think someone's following us."

Makri raises her eyebrows, but carries on walking, careful not to let whoever might be behind us know that we've noticed. I whisper to her again.

"We better sort this out before we reach the tavern. Don't want to lead anyone to Lisutaris."

Makri nods. The mist is now thicker than ever. I can't see more than a few feet in front of my face, but every so often I'm certain I can hear a soft footfall behind us. As we pass the next alleyway Makri disappears into it completely silently, while I carry on.

I keep talking, as if she's still beside me.

"You're right, Makri. I was heroic on the battlefield last month. I expect the city will erect a statue in my honour. This city's been looking for a good man to lead it for a long time now. I wouldn't be surprised if they drafted me into the senate. Just fit me into a toga and I'd sort things out."

If our pursuer hasn't noticed that Makri went into the alleyway, he should now be between us. I turn round and retrace my steps.

"Makri," says a voice, quite clearly through the fog. I can't see anything. I walk quicker. I hear Makri's voice replying.

"Marizaz."

At the sound of the Orcish name I start to run, fearing that Makri has encountered an invasion force, but when I arrive on the scene I find her face to face with a lone Orc. Not tall, by Orcish standards, but very broad. He's carrying a sword in each hand and wearing a cloak and hood which might have got him through the foggy streets undetected. The Orc glances at me as I arrive.

"Who is this?"

"A friend of mine," says Makri.

"You have Human friends now?"

"Yes."

The Orc looks at me contemptuously. It's obvious I haven't made a great impression on him. I take out my sword. Perhaps that will help.

"We heard tales you'd joined the Humans," says the Orc. "But I didn't believe it till now."

They're talking in common Orcish, which I can also speak.

"Are you old friends?" I ask Makri, who's sheathed her axe and now holds a sword in each hand.

"This is Marizaz," replies Makri. "Number two gladiator in the Orcish arena."

"Now number one."

"Only because I left."

"I'd have killed you soon enough," says Marizaz.

"What are you doing here?" asks Makri.

"I'm here to kill your Sorcerer chief."

"That's not likely to happen," I say.

"I'd have killed her already had she not fled her household."

At the news that this Orcish Assassin has already visited Lisutaris's villa, I start to worry. I'm presuming he didn't just walk into Turai and wander round Thamlin without some help.

"How did you get into the city?" I demand.

"As easily as Amrag will, very soon," he replies, which isn't a lot of help really.

From the way Marizaz and Makri are staring at each other, I'd say they'd never been friends in the arena.

"You should have remained a gladiator," says Makri. "Assassination doesn't suit you."

"It suits me well enough. Killing you will be a fine bonus."

"Maybe you've forgotten the way I fight?"

Marizaz sneers.

"They gave you easy opponents because you were a woman."

Makri's expression is grim. I've rarely seen her so offended, and I've insulted her plenty of times. She turns her head towards me.

"Thraxas. Don't interfere."

Back when Makri was training a young Elf to fight on Avula, she once explained to me two different modes of combat she'd learned in the gladiator pits. One, the Way of the Gaxeen, seemed to involve being as insanely aggressive as possible and hacking your opponent to death no matter what the cost. The other, the Way of Sarazu, was more contemplative. Something to do with being at one with the water and the sky. I never quite understood it. It seemed like an overcomplicated way of thinking about fighting, though as the end result was killing your opponent, and Makri is always very good at that, I'm not going to criticise her for it. As she confronts Marizaz, I'd say there is more Sarazu going on than Gaxeen. She doesn't charge in aggressively; in fact they don't engage at all at first, but circle round each other warily looking for an opening. Finally Makri halts, and stands quite motionless, her eyes fixed on her opponent, her swords raised, not moving a muscle. Marizaz does the same. Makri withdraws her twin swords, holding one above her head with the point facing her opponent, and the other in front of her body, slanted sideways. It's an unusual posture, not one I've ever seen before. Marizaz does something similar, and stands in front of her as solidly as an oak tree.

For the first time in a long time, I feel a flicker of worry about Makri's skills. I was never a gladiator, but I've fought all over the world, and in my younger days I won the sword-fighting championship in far-off Samsarina. You get to recognise a good opponent by the way he carries himself. I'd say that Marizaz is a very good opponent. He has to be, to have survived the Orcish gladiator pits. He's got a lot of weight advantage, and studying his posture, I don't see any flaws in his defence. He's a little taller than Makri and he has a longer reach. I leave my hand on my sword pommel, ready to help out if necessary.

They stare at each other for a long time. Far too long for my liking. I'm not used to contemplating an opponent. I've never seen Makri take such a long time to get down to business. Usually when confronted by an enemy she just charges in and kills him.

Finally Marizaz moves, and he attacks so quickly it's hard to tell exactly what happens. He leaps forward in one smooth but explosive movement, his twin swords flashing towards Makri faster than the eye can follow. Makri, nimble as she is, doesn't move her feet. Her own swords descend, there's a clash of steel on steel, and a sudden sharp cry. Marizaz falls to the ground, still clutching his swords, blood pumping from a fatal wound in his neck. Makri watches him carefully, her swords now back in their defensive guard. As far as I could see she deflected both of his blades with her black Orcish sword then slashed his neck with her silver Elvish blade, although to be honest it all happened so quickly it's hard to be sure.

Marizaz dies quickly, expiring in seconds from his fatal wound. Makri regards his body quite calmly, finally lowering her guard.

"Congratulations," I say.

Makri nods.

"He was a good fighter. He should have stayed at home."

I drag the body into a an alleyway and pull some tattered fragments of sailcloth over it.

"I'll send a message to the Guards when we reach the Axe."

We start to walk away.

"I hate Orcs," says Makri.

She shivers.

"Give me your cloak," she says.

"My cloak? I need it."

"I'm only wearing this bikini."

"You should have put more clothes on before you came out. You don't catch me chasing Orcs in a bikini."

"Thank the gods for that. I'm freezing, give me your cloak."

Makri curses me in Orcish.

"Will you stop cursing in Orcish? Goddamn, between that and the pointy ears and the Orcish sword you're lucky people don't mistake you for the enemy."

Makri curses me further, using some quite obscene pidgin-Orcish words probably never heard before outside the gladiator pits. I shake my head, and take off my cloak, though I'm none too pleased about it. The freezing mist quickly penetrates my tunic.

Makri tells me to stop scowling.

"I can't believe how unhelpful you are sometimes. I've just killed the deadliest Orc swordsman this side of Gzak and you're complaining about lending me your cloak. Anyone would think you wanted me to catch the malady."

"If you do, you're on your own. I'm not feeding you any of that foul potion."

Makri halts, and looks at me quite sternly.

"You mean you wouldn't look after me?"

"Not a chance. I've had it with sick people."

"I saved your life."

"When?"

"Hundreds of times."

"Okay you've helped me out occasionally."

"So?" demands Makri.

I sigh.

"Fine. If you get sick, I'll feed you potion."

"You'd better."

We advance a few paces. Makri halts again.

"Will you mop my brow?"

"Not a chance."

"What do you mean, not a chance? You'd do it for Lisutaris."

"She's the head of the Sorcerers Guild."

"So that's the way it is," says Makri, raising her voice. "You'll spend endless time mopping someone's brow if they're important, but when it comes to me, a woman without whose help you'd have been dead and buried long ago, you're just going to leave me to die in the gutter?"

I make an exasperated gesture.

"How did gutters enter into this? Who said anything about you dying in a gutter?"

"Well, obviously I'd be just as well off lying in a gutter as being looked after by you. You probably wouldn't feed me any potion at all, you'd just get drunk and forget about it. Don't worry about Makri, she's an Orc with pointy ears, she can just get the malady and die for all anybody cares."

"Will you shut up? Did I ever let you die?"

"You can't wait to let me die. You're probably looking forward to it."

I stop, and look at Makri suspiciously. Is she becoming feverish?

"Are you feeling all right?"

"I'm fine," declares Makri.

"Then what's this about?"

Makri looks awkward.

"Nothing," she mumbles.

"Are you scared of getting sick?"

"I'm not scared of anything," says Makri, fiercely.

"Yes, I know you're not scared of anything. But apart from that, are you scared of getting sick?"

"A little," admits Makri. "I've never been sick. I hate the way these people are all sweating and tossing and turning. I don't want it to happen to me."

I try and speak reassuringly, not something I'm very good at.

"You probably won't get sick. You've lasted this long. And if you do, I'll feed you potion."

Makri looks placated.

"Well you'd better, or there'll be trouble."

"If I have to stand out here like a frozen pixie any longer there's going to be more trouble."

We make our way home.

"It's been a strange winter so far," muses Makri. "The Orcs defeat Turai in battle, we all get stuck inside the city and catch this disease, and now we're just waiting for the Orcs to force their way in. Plus Orcish Assassins are now in the city. How did that happen?"

I admit I don't know.

"Our Sorcerers should have detected any Orcish incursions."

"We shouldn't wait around to be picked off," says Makri. "We should do something."

"What?"

"Round up everyone that's healthy and attack."

"The city's too weak."

Makri doesn't like hanging round waiting for the Orcs. She'd rather gather up everyone in Turai who can carry a sword and go out and confront them. I point out that we don't even know where they are, but Makri thinks she'd find them if she had to. And she doesn't care how many of them there are. I don't scoff at her idea. I've been in campaigns which have been won by the smaller force taking swift decisive action. But General Pomius, head of the Turanian army, is quite a cautious man. Far too cautious to march out and confront an enemy of unknown size.

"Amrag doesn't have that big a force," says Makri. "He beat us because he took us by surprise. We ought to try doing the same to him."

"We don't know what's going on out there. He might have a larger army by now."

"More reason to attack him quickly," says Makri. "I'd get in a chariot and head right for him. Cut off Amrag's head and his army would melt away."

"We'll make it through all right till reinforcements arrive in the spring."

Makri doubts that they will. The gossip round the markets is that the western forces will hold the line on the Simnian border, leaving Turai to its fate. It might be true.

"Fine," says Makri. "We just wait here till the Orcs overwhelm us. I never get my diploma from college. I never get to go to the university. I never see what my hair looks like yellow and I never hear from my Elf again."

"Are you still going on about that Elf?"

"No."

Makri scowls. She had a brief romance with an Elf when we visited the southern islands. It's a continual disappointment to her that he hasn't been in touch since.

"You're lucky," she says.

"Lucky? How?"

"You don't have any ambitions left."

It's true enough. Though I did always feel I might one day go through the card at the Turai memorial chariot races and pick every winner.

Turai's morale isn't helped by the fruitless hunt in Twelve Seas. Next day the story is all over the city that Orcs were inside the walls and somehow escaped. In fact, Makri and I were the only people who did meet an Orc, and he was a lone Assassin, not an invasion force. I inform Lisutaris, but she's still so sick I'm not certain that she takes it in properly. I sent a message to Cicerius outlining what happened, and another message to Captain Rallee. The Captain picked up the body before anyone found it, preventing the city's population from panicking even more.

The citizenry are in a bad enough state of mind already, struggling under siege and illness. It isn't helped by news of the Ocean Storm leaking out. Soon the whole of Turai is aware that there's a sorcerous weapon capable of battering down our sea walls and letting the Orcish fleet sail in, and no one knows where it is. The *Renowned and Truthful Chronicle* runs an article on the affair;

questions are asked in the senate. Deputy Consul Cicerius is forced to assure the senators that he has matters in hand. He sends more troops to the south of the city, along with Sorcerers to strengthen our protection. This carries some risk as it means leaving the other parts of the city less well guarded than they should be, though we still have enough Sorcerers in Turai to maintain our defensive spells. In reply to some harsh questioning from Senator Lodius, Cicerius assures him that Lisutaris, Mistress of the Sky, has our defences well in hand. As Lisutaris is currently lying ill in the Avenging Axe, this is not strictly true.

Lisutaris seems to be making a very slow recovery. She's taken the malady badly. I'm quite certain I got over it a lot quicker than our head of the Sorcerers Guild. Of course, I've always been strong. "Thraxas the Ox," they used to call me in my younger days. I was famous for my feats of strength. Ask anyone, they'll remember.

Chapter Eleven

Hanama, third in command in the Assassins Guild, slumbers on my couch. I look at her with distaste, and for the fiftieth time contemplate picking her up and slinging her out. Whoever made it taboo to abuse a sick house guest never had to put up with this sort of thing. I'm still not entirely convinced it isn't all some plot on her part. If she were to suddenly leap up and assassinate someone, I wouldn't be all that surprised.

I settle down at my desk and open a book about Turai's naval history which I borrowed without asking from Makri's room. She has a lot more books and scrolls in her room these days. They're expensive items, mostly out of her budget, but she's managed to fool Samanatius and his cronies into thinking she's a worthwhile student and they've been lending her more.

I peer at the book, frowning at the smallness of the writing and the dullness of the text. The historian manages to make some epic battles sound like very dull affairs indeed, and he has an annoying habit of quoting sources from all over the place, as if anyone really cares. I'm wading through the chapter on the Battle of Dead Dragon Island, hoping to pick up something which might help me locate Tanrose's mother's buried gold. I'm now fairly certain there's nothing in the vicinity of the harbour which could be referred to as a whale, but who knows, maybe these sailors used "whale" as a name for something else.

There's an oil lamp on the desk and I've got my illuminated staff cranked up to full power, but it's still not easy reading the endless pages of tedious facts. I realise why I never read a history book before. They're dreadfully dull. Soon I hate everyone involved, and I'm hoping they're all dead by the end of the chapter.

There's a knock at the door. Before I can answer it Makri strolls in. I glare at her.

"What?" she says. "I knocked."

"You're supposed to wait till I answer it."

"You're never satisfied, are you? Maybe I should send a message saying I'm coming."

Makri glances at the book on my desk and looks surprised.

"You're reading?"

"Yes."

"Why?"

"Just broadening my knowledge."

Makri looks suspicious.

"You don't have any knowledge to broaden. What is it?"

She lifts the cover to see the title.

"That's my book. Did you take it from my room?"

"Of course I took it from your room. Why, do you need it?"

Makri admits she doesn't at this moment, but she's displeased that I've taken it. I get the impression she doesn't trust me with it.

"It's only a book. What can happen?"

"Plenty of things. You might spill beer on it. Who can forget the incident at the library?"

I nudge my tankard away from the book.

"Preposterous. And why are you complaining anyway? You should be pleased I'm gathering a little knowledge."

Makri looks dubious.

"You're up to something. Tell me what it is."

"I'm not up to anything. Can't a man read a book without people making a fuss? What do you want anyway?"

"It's potion time," says Makri, and right on cue, Dandelion walks into the room with a steaming bowl of herbal medicine.

"How's Chiaraxi?" I ask, hoping she might have made a miraculous recovery.

"Not too bad," says Dandelion. "She doesn't seem as serious as everyone else. She wanted to get up and give everyone potion. But I told her I could do it."

It strikes me that the healer may regret this when Dandelion kills all her patients, but I don't mention it. Dandelion lent me money. I have to be polite to her, for a few days at least.

Dandelion doesn't wear shoes. The sight of her wandering round my room in bare feet makes me uncomfortable. Naked female feet are not exactly taboo in Turai but they're a rare sight. As for the circlet of flowers around her brow, it's frankly offensive. She holds Hanama's head and pours her medicine into her. Hanama is only partially conscious and some of the liquid dribbles down her chin. It's not an attractive sight. Makri places her hand on Manama's forehead.

"Still very feverish," she says.

"Any chance of her dying soon?" I ask, not entirely giving up hope.

Dandelion and Makri go through to the bedroom to minister to Lisutaris. I splash some water on my face and glance at the small cupboard behind my desk where my present from Lisutaris is hidden. I could do with a drink of the Grand Abbot's Ale right now but I'm not about to risk taking it out when Makri and Dandelion are around. I'm not planning on sharing it with anyone.

Dandelion and Makri reappear. Dandelion stands and looks at me.

"Don't let me detain you," I say, by way of a hint.

"Dandelion has something to tell you," says Makri. There's a slight glint in Makri's eye which immediately makes me suspicious. Makri always finds it amusing when Dandelion's strange ramblings start to infuriate me.

"I'm busy."

"It's very important," says Dandelion. "It's about the dragon line."

"The what?"

"The dragon line."

I frown.

"There's no such thing."

"There is. One of them runs right from the dolphins' cave through the Avenging Axe and up to the Palace."

I shake my head. Dragon lines are supposed to be mystical lines of power which cover the earth. Cheap charlatans, the sort who sometimes appear in the city before the Sorcerers Guild chases them out, tend to talk about them a lot. They promise gullible people cures for their problems if they walk along dragon lines, or dance on them, or whatever it is phoney mystics are recommending that day. It's all nonsense. They don't exist. Only people like Dandelion, who talk to dolphins and dabble in astrology, believe in them. Proper Sorcerers know they aren't real.

"They are real," says Dandelion, and looks surprised that I can possibly doubt it. "Why do you think the dolphins love that cave?"

"Maybe it's comfortable as caves go."

"It's on a dragon line," insists Dandelion. "Its energy draws them there. For healing. And spiritual advancement."

I tap my fingers on my desk. Now we've reached the spiritual advancement of dolphins, I'm about as far into the strange and fanciful realms inhabited by Dandelion as I care to go.

"Well that's very interesting, Dandelion, but I'm—"

"I really feel it's important, with the Ocean Storm still not found."

I halt. Dandelion lives so much in her own world I'm surprised she's even heard of the Ocean Storm.

"What are you talking about?"

"Don't you see?" says Dandelion. "If the Orcs find the Ocean Storm they'll use it on the dragon line. It's bound to make it more powerful."

"What?"

"They'll use it to send a huge storm right from the dolphins' cave over the city walls and up to the Avenging Axe."

Dandelion looks worried.

"I'm very concerned about the dolphins."

I notice my mouth is hanging open. I close it.

"You can see it's a serious problem," says Makri, deadpan.

I crash my fist on to the desk. The aged black wood trembles under the blow.

"I've never heard such nonsense in all my life! A dragon line coming up from the dolphins' cave to the

Avenging Axe? Are you completely crazy? No, don't answer that. For one thing, dragon lines don't exist, and for another, if they did exist don't you think we should be worrying about the people in the city rather than a few dolphins?"

"People can look after themselves," says Dandelion. "We have to help the dolphins."

I'm about to pick up Dandelion and bodily eject her from the office when I remember I'm meant to be polite to her. A physical assault may lead to a withdrawal of vital funding. I control myself, with difficulty.

"Dandelion. I really don't think the dolphins are in danger. If an Orcish fleet arrives they're probably smart enough to swim away. Besides, the Orcs aren't going to get hold of the Ocean Storm. I'm looking for it and so are a lot of other people. We'll find it before the Orcs."

"Really?" says Dandelion.

"Yes."

"All right," she says, gathering up her jars of herbal potion. "I'll go and reassure the dolphins." She departs, apparently satisfied that I'm doing my bit to help.

Makri takes a thazis stick from my desk and lights it. I scowl at her.

"Did you encourage her to do that?"

"Certainly not."

"You always think it's funny when Dandelion starts rambling about dolphins."

"Only when she's rambling in your direction. If it's me, I just walk away."

Makri looks thoughtful.

"Do dragon lines really not exist?"

"No. They're for fakers and fortune-tellers."

"I never had much involvement with Orcish Sorcerers when I was in the slave pits. But I seem to remember talk of dragon lines."

I light a thazis stick. I remember the high-quality thazis from Lisutaris I've got hidden away. Makri would enjoy that. She'd enjoy it too much. I don't bring it out.

"They don't exist."

Makri shrugs.

"Whatever you say."

It's time for me to abandon my studies and hit the streets. I take my best magic cloak and mutter the words to make it warm. It heats up immediately and I start loading thazis sticks and a small flask of klee into the pockets, enough to get me through a day's investigating. I'm humming a tune, without really noticing it, till Makri interrupts.

"Love me through the winter."

"What?"

"That tune you're humming. It's the one Moolifi was singing. 'Love Me Through the Winter'."

"It's a catchy tune."

Makri hasn't softened her opinions on Moolifi's performance.

"She's a terrible singer. No wonder she has to take her clothes off as well. And the tune's only catchy because it's stolen from an old Elvish ballad."

"What?"

"The Song of the Doomed Elvish Sea Lord."

"I've never heard of it."

"It's quite obscure," admits Makri. "It comes from an Elvish play by Ariath-Ar-Mith. He was never that well known, even among the Elves. I doubt his plays have been performed for four hundred years, maybe more."

"Makri, doesn't it worry you that you're starting to know more about ancient Elvish culture than the Elves themselves?"

"I like to know things. But don't you think it's strange Moolifi was singing something based on that tune? It's very obscure."

"It's probably a coincidence. How many tunes are there? They all sound the same after a while."

"Not really," says Makri. "There are fourteen main groups of—"

I recognise the signs, and hold up my hand.

"Spare me the lecture on every form of music ever known in the west. I have some investigating to do."

Makri would like to come out and investigate with me. Ever since I mentioned the possibility of Sarin the Merciless being involved, she's been eager to confront her. Unfortunately for Makri, she has to work all day.

"If I meet her I'll kill her for you."

Hanama rolls over on the couch and groans. Makri looks concerned. I stub out my thazis stick and head downstairs. I have investigating to do and I'm planning on filling up with stew before hitting the streets. Gurd is at the bar, alongside Dandelion. They're looking pensive.

"What's wrong?"

"Tanrose got the malady."

I stare at them, horrified.

"It can't be true."

Gurd nods miserably. I sink on to a stool, stricken with grief.

"Is there no end to it?" I mutter, and motion for drink. "We're cursed."

"I don't think she's so bad—" says Dandelion.

I wave her quiet.

"Tanrose. Ill. Who's going to cook?"

"Elsior can take over," says Dandelion.

"Elsior? She can't cook a proper stew. What have we done to deserve this?"

I start mentally shaking my fist at the gods. They've played a few nasty tricks on me in the past, but striking down the best cook in Twelve Seas goes beyond all reason.

"I just don't think I can carry on."

Dandelion puts her hand on my shoulder.

"You have to be strong, Thraxas. We can get through it."

"No. It's the end."

I look up at Gurd.

"This is your fault. You should have reported the malady as soon as Kaby got sick. Then the tavern wouldn't be full of sick people and Tanrose might have escaped. How could you be so irresponsible?"

"We're talking about the woman I'm engaged to," says Gurd, raising his voice. "It was your idea not to report the malady!"

"What?"

"You didn't want to report it so your card game didn't get cancelled!"

"Ridiculous! You were too worried about your profits. A bit less thinking about money and a bit more consideration for the welfare of others and this wouldn't have happened!"

"Tanrose is sick, and all you can think about is your stomach!" roars Gurd.

"If Tanrose dies you'll be sorry you forced her to work in dangerous circumstances!"

"I did not force her to work!"

Gurd is furious. So am I. He leans over the bar and I rise from my stool, ready to do battle.

"Stop this!" yells Dandelion. "You should be ashamed of yourselves."

I glare at Dandelion, then at Gurd.

"I have investigating to do," I say, stiffly. "Try not to kill off anyone else while I'm gone."

With that I leave. The thought of struggling through even a few days in Twelve Seas without Tanrose's cooking to keep me going is almost enough to make me give up altogether. You'd have to go a long way in this city for a better meal, and you'd need to pay a lot more money.

Perhaps I can win enough at cards to dine out for a while? Maybe even go up to that eatery near Thamlin I used to frequent, back when I was Senior Investigator at the Palace? Their food was worth travelling for. I shake my head. I'll be back on guard duty soon, trapped on a cold wall, staring out into space. Little opportunity for travelling the city in search of a decent meal. I might as well face it, I'm not going to get a proper bowl of stew till Tanrose recovers.

Maybe that won't be too long. She's a hearty sort of woman. People like Tanrose and me, we're good strong Turanian stock. We don't lie around complaining of slight illnesses. We just rest briefly then get on with things, unlike these degenerate Sorcerers and Assassins currently plaguing the Avenging Axe.

I curse them all, and drag my attention back to investigating. The idea that Borinbax's oddly shaped wound might have been caused by a crossbow bolt, subsequently removed, isn't much to go on, but I have a feeling for these things and my feeling is that Sarin is connected to this affair. She's quite capable of killing anyone who gets in her way and she wouldn't have any scruples about selling a vital sorcerous item to the Orcs. I know from experience that she's a resourceful opponent. She once killed Tas of the Eastern Lightning, a very powerful Sorcerer who had the misfortune to form an alliance with her.

I have two days off from my duty on the walls, which allows me to devote my full concentration to investigating. The day is again mild and I let my cloak slip open as I stride through Twelve Seas. I pass several companies of soldiers marching down towards the harbour. Cicerius is making good on his promise to reinforce the defences around the sea walls. A few ragged children cheer as they pass. I also notice Harmon Half Elf, an eminent Turanian Sorcerer, talking with a shopkeeper outside the candle shop. It's unusual to see Harmon in Twelve Seas. At a guess, I'd say he's looking for the Ocean Storm. Now that news has leaked out, there's no need for anyone to do their investigating in secret. Harmon won't be the only one currently scouring the city. I'll be surprised if any of them find it. Investigating is a specialist art. Besides, Harmon is not what you'd call smart. He once called me an imbecile, thereby proving he's a man of poor judgement. When it comes to investigating, everyone knows I'm as sharp as an Elf's ear.

I get the sudden feeling that maybe it's all a waste of time. Perhaps the Ocean Storm doesn't even exist. Maybe Captain Arex was just a conman, hoping to wrest a few gurans from the Sorcerers Guild. Still, there's nothing to do but keep on looking.

I walk towards the southern end of Moon and Stars Boulevard, looking for a landus. I'm out of luck. They can be hard to find south of the river, and I end up walking all the way up to Pashish. I'm planning to visit Astrath Triple Moon. Astrath's an old friend of mine. Since being sacked from his position as Sorcerer at the Stadium Superbius, Astrath has eked out a fairly poor existence. Now the Orcs are causing trouble again, he's been brought back into the fold of the Sorcerers Guild. Turai needs all its Sorcerers at a time like this, honest or not. If Astrath has a good war he'll be right back in business and he's been going all out to show his worth. When the Orcs attacked he arrived early on the battlefield, and since then he's been so busy that I've hardly seen him.

I strike lucky. Astrath is home and he invites me to join him for dinner. His table is better provisioned than it has been for some time.

"How's life in the investigating business?"

"Better than rowing a slave galley, or just about. How about you?"

"I'm close to being a full member of the Sorcerers Guild again."

Astrath has a thick grey beard. When he's in a good mood it makes him look benevolent, jovial even.

"It's good to be back," he says.

I nod. It was tough for Astrath, being cast into disgrace. I load up with a good-sized portion of venison and half a bottle of wine before I mention the reason for my visit.

"I'm looking for the Ocean Storm."

The Sorcerer isn't surprised.

"Everyone is."

"Can you fill me in on some more of the background?"

"Astrath rings for more wine. I notice he's engaged a few more servants, a sure sign that things are looking up. He must be one of the few people in the city whose life has been improved by the war.

"There's not a great deal to tell. No one knows much about it. Even if we find it I doubt there's many people in Turai who could use it. Lisutaris, I expect. Maybe Coranius the Grinder."

"What about the Orcs? Could their Sorcerers use it?"

Astrath considers for a moment.

"I don't think most of them could. Not at short notice anyway. An item like that takes time to get used to. A few of their most powerful adepts, perhaps. Horm the Dead, maybe, or Deeziz the Unseen. Though Deeziz doesn't seem to be with Amrag."

"You really think it might be powerful enough to cause a storm to batter down the city walls?"

"Possibly. Our own Storm Calmer is an extremely powerful sorcerous tool. It can bring a hurricane to a standstill. If there's some sort of equivalent item for starting a storm, it could be strong enough to break through the sea wall. Remember, the Orcs have a lot of sorcery already. Even if the Ocean Storm only cancels out the effects of the Storm Calmer, it might allow them enough time to force their way through with their own spells."

Astrath pours more wine. It's some time since I've seen him so convivial.

"Firing spells on the battlefield. Made me feel alive again."

"My phalanx was wiped out," I remind him.

Astrath acknowledges this.

"A lot of people died, I know. But Thraxas, I've been expecting the Orcs to overrun Turai for the past thirty years. I've never thought we could hold them off for ever. I'm just glad to be back in the thick of it for the last battle."

"You sound like you're looking forward to it."

Astrath shrugs.

"I don't mind. It's not such a bad way to die."

"You're right, it's not. But I sometimes get the feeling I could have died for someplace better than Turai."

I ask Astrath if he's heard any war news through the Sorcerers Guild that hasn't been released to the public. He tells me that the Guild thinks they might have detected a large force of Orcs some way to the northeast of the city.

"Coming from Soraz, possibly."

"You mean Rezaz the Butcher?"

Astrath nods.

Rezaz the Butcher, Lord of Soraz, was one of the leaders of the Orcish army who almost captured Turai seventeen years ago. He wasn't with Prince Amrag when he attacked and no one knows for sure if he's pledged his allegiance to Amrag. There has recently been some sort of cooperation between Turai and Lord Rezaz, on economic matters which were beneficial to both sides, but that's not to say the Butcher wouldn't welcome another chance to march into Turai.

"We don't know for sure. The whole area is blanketed with Orcish spells of concealment. It might be Rezaz or it might be Amrag's army."

"I'd guess Amrag's army's gone south," I say. "There have been sightings of his fleet along the coast."

"It's possible," agrees Astrath. "Though we're fairly sure Queen Direeva in the Southern Hills hasn't joined up with him, which makes his going south less likely. But really, it's impossible to say what's going on."

I drink another goblet of wine, and take a small bolt out from my bag.

"A crossbow bolt?"

"It's the one that Sarin the Merciless once fired into Makri."

Astrath grins.

"How is Makri? Still tantalising the clientele?"

"If you call walking round almost naked with a permanent frown on your face tantalising, then yes."

I produce a small scrap of cloth, stained dark with blood.

"This is part of the tunic of a man I think was killed by Sarin. She wrenched a bolt out of his chest, which means she's touched this cloth. Can you use these two items to locate her?"

Astrath picks up the bolt and the cloth, one in each hand, as if weighing them. He studies them for a few moments.

"Maybe. I think they've both got some of her aura on them. Is it urgent?"

I tell him it is.

"Do you want to come back in an hour, say?"

"It's more urgent than that."

Astrath shrugs. I've done him some favours in the past and he knows I wouldn't press him if I didn't have to. He instructs a servant to provide me with anything I want, and takes the crossbow bolt and the scrap of cloth through to his private workspace at the back of his house. He scoops up a half-full bottle of wine before leaving the room. I finish off the venison on my plate, take the rest from the silver salver in the middle of the table, and ring for the servant.

"Any more venison?"

The servant politely tells me that no, there isn't. I look at her suspiciously.

"You did hear Astrath saying to bring me whatever I wanted?"

"I'm sorry, sir, that's the last of our supply."

A likely story. The servants are no doubt being economical with their master's household goods, possibly figuring that if they have to get through a winter on short rations, they're not about to share the supplies with a rather large Investigator.

"Anything in the way of spicy yams?"

"I'm afraid we finished the last of them yesterday."

I look her in the eye but she stares straight back at me, unflinching. Eventually I have to make do with a few pastries and a small bottle of wine. According to the servant—rather a harsh-faced woman, now I think about it—Astrath is not currently holding any beer in his cellar.

The servant leaves me to my wine. I pick up a magical text from a shelf and flick through it. It's a standard work, nothing too advanced, which doesn't mean there aren't plenty of spells in it I've never heard of. They had this book in class when I was an apprentice, yet I'd swear I've never seen most of the spells before. It shows how little attention I paid.

Astrath hurries back into the room. I'm considering asking him straight out, man to man, if he really doesn't have any beer in his cellar, but he appears to be agitated and waves me quiet.

"Did you say these were from Sarin?"

"That's right."

"And she's a killer?"

"She is."

"Then you'd better get back to the Avenging Axe immediately," says Astrath.

"Why?"

"Because she's heading that way right now."

"Are you sure?"

"Quite sure."

I rise, finish my goblet of wine, and throw my cloak around my shoulders in double-quick time.

"Can you find me a landus around here?"

"Take my carriage," says Astrath.

I'm surprised.

"You have a carriage?"

"Issued to all Sorcerers in wartime," explains Astrath.

I'm impressed. He really is going up in the world.

Minutes later I'm at the reins, thundering through the narrow streets of Pashish towards Twelve Seas. I turn into Moon and Stars Boulevard and head south, scattering pedestrians as I go.

"Out of the way, dogs!" I scream, as a tutor with three children fails to cross the road quickly enough. I thunder on. At this moment the head of the Turanian Sorcerers Guild is lying sick in my bed, and one of the most deadly killers ever seen in Turai is heading towards the Avenging Axe.

Chapter Twelve

I make it to the Avenging Axe in record time, pulling up outside the front door and leaping from the wagon like a hungry dragon going after a plump sheep. The first person I run into is Makri, carrying a tray of tankards.

"Sarin's here," I mutter, and head for the stairs.

Makri isn't far behind me as I burst into my office, though she's taken a diversion to pick up her axe. My sword is in my hand, ready for action. The outside door is open, and Sarin the Merciless is standing by the couch, looking down at the still-sleeping Hanama.

"Does your locking spell ever keep anyone out?" demands Makri, and raises her axe. I get myself in between them.

"Makri. Wait till I know why she came here before you kill her."

Sarin regards us with her cold eyes.

"No one is about to kill me."

Sarin's a tall woman, with her dark hair cropped short, which is very unusual in Turai. Unlike almost every other woman in the city, from the market workers to the senators' wives, she wears no make-up of any kind, and her man's tunic is plain and undecorated. For some reason she has a liking for earrings, and there must be at least eight silver rings pierced through each of her ears. She wears a short, curved sword at her hip, and she's pointing a small crossbow at my heart.

"Don't you know it's illegal to carry a crossbow in the city?"

"And yet I never seem to get arrested," says Sarin.

She gazes first at me, then at Makri. There's a peculiar deadness to Sarin's eyes which is slightly unsettling.

"I've been looking for something that belongs to me," she says. "It wasn't there. But I believe you were."

She holds out her hand.

"Give me the Ocean Storm."

I'm staggered by the audacity of this woman, having the nerve to march into my office and demand I hand over a stolen item like she has some rights over it.

"Why would I give it to you?"

"Because I'm pointing a crossbow at you."

"So you are. Maybe you'd like me to roast your insides with a spell?"

"You can't," says Sarin, flatly. "You don't have the power. And I don't like long conversations. Give me the Ocean Storm."

"I'd like to, Sarin, but I just don't believe it belongs to you."

"I made an agreement with Captain Arex."

"Too bad for you someone else got there first."

"Too bad indeed. Hand it over or I'll kill you."

Makri suddenly makes a move. She hurls her axe, moving so quickly that the spinning blade knocks the crossbow from Sarin's hands before she can pull the trigger. Sarin curses and pulls her sword from its sheath. Then she coughs, puts her hand to her head, and sinks gently forward on her knees, sweat pouring from her brow. The sword drops to the floor.

"Oh come on," says Makri, and looks frustrated. Sarin continues to sink, ending up on the floor, her breath coming in short gasps.

I turn to look at Makri.

"What is this? Is there a sign up somewhere saying go to Thraxas's office if you get the malady?"

"I'm going to kill her anyway," declares Makri.

"Okay with me. I'm damned if I want another patient taking up space."

There's the sound of footsteps on the stairs and Hansius walks in through the open door. When he sees Sarin he looks alarmed.

"Didn't the Deputy Consul instruct you to maintain strict privacy? Why is the door open like this? And why is there another malady victim sprawled here for all to see? Get her out of sight this instant."

I stare at Hansius. Just because Cicerius can come down here and order me about doesn't mean his assistant can.

"What do you want?"

"Is that—"

"Sarin the Merciless."

Hansius frowns. Sarin once blackmailed the government out of ten thousand gurans, and they haven't forgotten.

"Why did you let her in?"

"I didn't let her in. She countermanded my locking spell."

"Thraxas's locking spell is useless," says Makri. "Anyone can get past it."

"Why did Sarin come here?" demands Hansius.

"Who knows? People just seem to like to visit these days."

Hansius eyes us with some distaste.

"Didn't the Deputy Consul inform you that we suspect a plot has been hatched to kill Lisutaris and betray the city?"

I look at Makri.

"I can't remember. Did he tell us?"

Makri shrugs.

"There's so many plots. It's hard to remember them all."

"You must be aware of security at all times!" insists Hansius.

I bend down to grab hold of Sarin.

"What are you doing?" asks Hansius

"Throwing her out."

"But I want to kill her," protests Makri.

"She'll die on the street anyway," I point out.

Hansius practically throws himself in front of the door.

"Have you no idea what it means to maintain security? This woman has heard us talk of Lisutaris. No one who knows that Lisutaris is ill in this tavern can be allowed to leave. We might as well just send a message to the Orcs inviting them to attack."

"Fine," says Makri, stepping forward. "I'll kill her now."

The inside door bursts open.

"What are you doing?" cries a very loud voice.

It's Dandelion, clutching potions.

"I'm about to stab Sarin the Merciless," explains Makri.

Dandelion hurries forward, a horrified look on her face.

"You're about to stab a sick woman? Shame on you, Makri."

Makri looks confused.

"But she deserves it."

"Put that sword away," demands Dandelion.

"Absolutely not," retorts Makri.

Dandelion confronts her.

"You can't kill a sick person."

"Yes I can. I'm going to do it now."

"You are not," states Dandelion, quite emphatically. "No one kills any person that I'm ministering to."

"Since when are you ministering to her?"

"Since I took over from Chiaraxi."

"Well this is just ridiculous," says Makri. "You're not a proper healer. You can't order us around."

"I'm the healer," says Dandelion firmly. "I look after everyone that's sick."

I've never seen Dandelion so determined before. She even casts a defiant glance towards Hansius, in case he might be about to argue with her.

"I'm going to kill her," insists Makri.

"You can't kill a sick guest," says Dandelion.

"A person who breaks in to commit crimes doesn't count as a guest!" retorts Makri.

"Well . . ." says Hansius. "That's a moot point. We do have a strong tradition of hospitality."

Makri curses in Orcish. That's also taboo in Turai, and Hansius is annoyed.

"But if Sarin hadn't suddenly fallen sick I'd have killed her by now anyway," says Makri.

"Not necessarily," says Hansius.

"What?"

"She might have survived the combat. She might even have defeated you."

Makri looks aghast at the thought. I weigh in on her side.

"Ridiculous. Makri's a far better fighter. She'd already got rid of the crossbow with her axe."

Hansius glances at the floor.

"But Sarin has a sword. You companion had thrown her axe, and seems not to have brought another weapon."

"I'd still have beaten her," says Makri. "And why do you care about her anyway?"

"I don't care about her at all," says Hansius. "I'm just pointing out the foolishness and unpredictability of women fighting. Women should not be fighting. It's not their place."

Makri reaches down to pick up her axe, whether to show Hansius her place or whether to kill Sarin, I'm not certain. Either one would be fine with me but Dandelion interrupts us again.

"Stop this. It doesn't matter who would have won the fight. Sarin's sick with the malady and now we're going to look after her."

"No we're not," says Makri.

"You can't kill a sick person!" says Dandelion. "It's wrong. And it's bad luck. Isn't that right?"

Dandelion looks towards Hansius for support. There's no denying that the taboo against killing a sick person is very strong.

"I agree. Sarin should be cared for until she recovers, and then taken into custody for her crimes."

"Good," says Dandelion, ignoring the look of loathing currently being directed towards her by Makri. "Now help me get her to a chair."

Dandelion drags Sarin to a chair. No one helps her.

"I'm really not happy about this," says Makri. "How come it's all right for her to go around shooting crossbows at people and then it's not okay for me to stab her? It goes against natural justice. All these taboos are stupid. Don't blame me if the city gets overrun."

Sarin has now lost consciousness and is sweating profusely.

"It's a serious case," mutters Dandelion. "She's going to need a lot of looking after."

I turn to Hansius.

"Why did you come here anyway?"

"The Deputy Consul has instructed Tirini Snake Smiter to add her powers to Lisutaris's protection. I escorted her down. She should be here any moment."

On cue, Tirini Snake Smiter walks into my office. She is Turai's most glamorous Sorcerer, known far and wide as the woman who spent an arduous six months perfecting a new spell for preserving her nail varnish in perfect condition, no matter how trying the circumstances. And, it has to be said, her nails are never less than perfect. She arrives looking as elegant, glamorous, and about as out of place among the clutter as a person can possibly be. She's draped in a golden fur cloak that's so thick I'm surprised she can move. Her hair, the colour of gleaming corn, cascades around her shoulders in a way that makes me suspect it might be permanently controlled by a spell. The woman is obsessed with her appearance. Tirini has been wooed by princes, generals and senators, envied by their wives and daughters, denounced by bishops, and occupied more space in Turai's scandal sheets than any other person in history.

Despite all this, I know that Lisutaris regards her as a powerful Sorcerer, sharp as an Elf's ear when it comes to working her magics. I'm not at all convinced about this. Tirini is too young to have featured in the last war, so there's no way of knowing how she'll react in battle. I wouldn't wager a great deal of money on her prowess. It's all very well being clever with sorcery to make your hair look better. It's a lot different when there's a dragon diving out of the sky towards you, with an Orcish Sorcerer on its back firing spells, and a squadron of Orcish archers trying to outflank you at the same time.

I greet her, rather wearily.

"Cicerius asked me to check on dear Lisutaris's health," she says

She looks rather dubiously around the room.

"He didn't tell me there were other sick people."

"There are sick people everywhere."

"Who are they?"

"Murderous killer, murderous Assassin," I say, nodding towards the prostrate bodies of Hanama and Sarin.

"Really? How thrilling for you. Where is Lisutaris?"

"In the bedroom."

"Take me to her."

"You sure? So far everyone who's gone in there has fallen sick."

"I've had the malady," says Tirini. "And frightfully boring it was, as I recall."

Tirini walks into my bedroom, followed by Hansius.

Dandelion is meanwhile giving the medicinal potion to Hanama and Sarin. Hanama is still badly sick. Her brow is covered in perspiration. She winces as she moves her mouth towards the cup. The muscle pains brought on by the malady can be very severe, and she's still suffering.

"You'll be better soon," says Dandelion, encouragingly.

"I know," whispers Hanama, and manages to look determined for a few seconds. Her eyes close and she drifts back to sleep. I wonder what would happen if the situation was reversed. Somehow I can't see Hanama feeding medicine to anyone. Caring for people isn't in her nature. There again, nor is it in mine.

Tirini emerges from my bedroom.

"I would hardly say that this is a suitable place for dear Lisutaris to lie ill," she says.

"Neither would I. If you want to move her somewhere go right ahead."

"Cicerius has issued instructions that she should not be moved."

Tirini frowns.

"I have little confidence in Cicerius. Were it not for the efforts of the Sorcerers Guild, the city would have fallen to those dreadful Orcs by now."

The sorceress glances at her hands with distaste.

"I'm covered in dust. Does your maid never clean in there?"

"I don't have a maid."

Tirini looks at me like I'm mentally deficient. The possibility of not having a maid has probably never entered her mind. Her look of distaste intensifies as she glances at the small sink in the corner of my office.

"Where might a woman wash her hands?"

I direct her to Tanrose's room downstairs, probably her best chance of finding something clean and pleasant. It also contains a sick healer, but everywhere you go, someone is sick. It's not just the Avenging Axe. The malady has now made inroads into much of the population. Already there are shortages among the guards at the walls as men fail to report for duty.

Tirini departs, leaving the room with the slow, delicate gait of a woman who's wearing heels which might be suitable for tripping round a ballroom at the Palace but are far too high for the rough terrain you meet in Twelve Seas. In the last twenty years or so, upper-class Turanian women's heels have been becoming higher and higher, a fashion which has led to adverse comment from the Church, and other guardians of the nation's morals. For once I agree with them. Bishop Gzekius might have been talking nonsense when he condemned gambling as the quick way to hell, but he was spot on with his sermon pointing out the iniquities of frivolous footwear. Tirini's shoes, stitched from some yellow fabric with pink flowers embroidered over the toes, with the heel and sole decorated with beaten gold, are surely a sign of a society in decay. I doubt that a sailmaker would earn enough in a year to pay for them.

Makri regards Tirini balefully as she exits.

"I don't think she's the best person to protect Lisutaris. Anyway, *I'm* protecting her."

Before Hansius leaves he questions us about our encounter with the Orcish Assassin. I can't tell him much more than I did in my message to the Deputy Consul, though I do my best to let Hansius know every detail I can remember. Turai's security has been breached by Orcs before, but now, in time of war, with our defensive sorcery at maximum power, it's far more serious. Old Hasius the Brilliant, Chief Sorcerer at the Abode of Justice, has been down at the harbour, checking on the scene of the fight, trying to pick up clues as to how the Orc Marizaz might have entered the city.

With a final admonition to maintain our own security and look after Lisutaris, Hansius departs. Makri turns towards Sarin the Merciless.

"I'm still going to kill her when she gets better."

"At least you have something to look forward to."

I step towards the bedroom.

"Where are you going?" demands Makri.

"Just checking on Lisutaris."

"Keep out of that room."

"What the hell do you mean, keep out? It's my bedroom."

"You're planning on asking her for money."

"Preposterous. I have a duty to look after her too, you know."

I slip into the bedroom, pursued by Makri.

"I refuse to let you borrow money from a sick woman."

"I'm not going to borrow money. What's it got to do with you anyway?"

"I'm her bodyguard."

"So what? You're meant to protect her from Orcish Assassins, not Investigators in need. Besides, I have some important questions regarding the Ocean Storm."

I stare at Makri.

"Questions that need to be asked in private."

"Not a chance," says Makri. "The minute I'm out that door you'll be scrounging money."

"I order you to get out of my bedroom."

"You can't order a Sorcerer's bodyguard around," states Makri, firmly. "I'm staying."

Lisutaris groans.

"You see?" I say to Makri. "You're upsetting her. She needs peace and quiet."

"She's not going to get peace and quiet with you trying to get your hands on her money."

"What's a few hundred gurans to Lisutaris? She's rolling in money. Goddamn, it's not like she'd be taking a risk."

"You just said you weren't here to borrow money."

"I'm not. But if I was, I'd be doing Lisutaris a favour. She enjoys gambling."

"She's got a city to defend!" yells Makri. "We're meant to be getting her healthy so she can fight the Orcs! Have you forgotten that?"

"Life doesn't stop just because the Orcs are besieging the city!" I roar back. "All citizens have a duty to keep things going. It's good for morale."

"Playing cards doesn't count as keeping things going," protests Makri.

We're interrupted by some movement on the bed. Lisutaris struggles to raise her head.

"I'll give you the money if you'll just leave me in peace," she whispers.

"No, don't—" says Makri.

"I accept," I say, butting in quickly. "Very sporting of you, Lisutaris, and I won't forget you when I'm counting my winnings."

Makri looks furious. I hurry to Lisutaris's bedside. The sorceress lifts her head a few inches.

"How much do you need?"

"Don't give it to him," says Makri.

Lisutaris manages a thin smile.

"Makri. Thraxas has been looking after me. Which is so against his nature, I think he deserves something for his trouble."

She motions for me to hand her a fancy embroidered bag, which I do, hastily. Lisutaris fumbles inside the bag. It takes some effort on her part and I start to worry that she might pass out before she finds her purse. If she does, I'll probably have to engage Makri in combat before I can take possession.

Lisutaris finds her purse, and opens it with an effort.

"How much is there?"

I look inside. There are seven coins. Seven silver fifty guran pieces. Not a common sight in Twelve Seas.

"Three hundred and fifty gurans."

"Is that enough?"

"Just about."

Lisutaris hands them to me. I'm deeply moved. Surely this is one of the finest citizens Turai has ever produced. I cram the coins into the pocket of my tunic.

"Do you want anything?" I ask.

"Some peace," whispers Lisutaris.

"Absolutely, peace is what you need."

I rise swiftly and turn to Makri.

"You heard her. Absolute peace. From now on, make sure no one disturbs Lisutaris."

I leave the room quickly, delighted after a successful operation. I now have 440 gurans and require only sixty more. Surely I can raise that in the next few hours. I'm just strapping on my sword when I am struck by an annoying piece of inspiration about the Ocean Storm. Right now I'm not looking for inspiration. I'm more concerned with raising the cash for tomorrow night's gambling extravaganza. I hesitate. I could ignore it, or deal with it later. I head for the door, but turn back with a sigh. It's no use. No matter how I try, I never seem to be able to ignore an investigation.

I stride back into my bedroom. Makri is sitting beside Lisutaris's bed, not actually mopping her brow but looking like she might do it any moment. She glares angrily at me as I reappear.

"Need more money already?"

I ignore her.

"Lisutaris. I just had some sudden inspiration."

Lisutaris turns her face towards me. She's still looking very unhealthy. The head of the Sorcerers Guild has really taken the malady badly. I've known far less healthy people than her recover from it quicker.

"What inspiration?"

"Yesterday we met an Orcish Assassin. No one knows how he could have got into the city without being detected. Have you had any thoughts on that?"

The Sorcerer shakes her head.

"We're working on it," she whispers.

"Before we met him I passed some mourners, close to the harbour. A couple of men and a woman. Or I thought it was a woman. She was wearing a veil. But now I'm wondering if it might have been Deeziz the Unseen."

Lisutaris stares at me. She stares at me for so long I wonder if she might not be completely with us. Finally she manages the smallest of smiles.

"Deeziz the Unseen? I thought I was the one who was sick. You must be hallucinating."

"I wasn't hallucinating. I didn't see anything strange. Just a standard Human mourner, in a veil. Deeziz is known for wearing a veil. So I'm wondering if it might have been him."

"But mourners often wear veils," says Makri, which is true.

"Did you sense sorcery?" asks Lisutaris.

"No, nothing."

"Did you sense Orcs?" asks Makri.

I admit I didn't.

"It's just a feeling."

Lisutaris tries to raise herself on one elbow, but can't quite make it, and sinks down again.

"Deeziz the Unseen is on top of a mountain hundreds of miles away. We'd have detected him if he'd come anywhere near Turai. Cicerius's intelligence service would have heard something about it."

"Maybe not," I say. "It's not unheard of for an Orcish Sorcerer to infiltrate the city. Makri ran into one only a few months ago when she rescued Herminis"—I break off to cast a dirty look at Makri, signifying my continuing disapproval—"and we both came across one at the races a year or so ago."

"True," replies Lisutaris. "But every Sorcerer in the city has been on the highest alert since Amrag attacked. I think we'd have detected an intruder. And General Pomius doesn't even think Deeziz has joined Prince Amrag."

Lisutaris motions to Makri for water, and Makri raises a beaker to her lips.

"You don't have any reason for thinking it was Deeziz the Unseen, do you? Apart from your intuition?"

"No. I don't. But I've made it a long way on my intuition. Now I think about it, isn't it strange the way you've taken the malady so badly? You should have been starting to recover by now. What if it's Deeziz attacking you with a spell? Sorcery can prolong an illness."

Lisutaris has already thought of this.

"I checked. I'm not being affected by any spell."

"You think you're not. What if you're wrong?"

"I'm not."

"I think you might be."

A hint of colour appears in Lisutaris's cheeks. Lisutaris, Mistress of the Sky, does not appreciate anything which might be construed as criticism of her power.

"I'm the head of the Sorcerers Guild."

"And I'm an Investigator who's got you out of a few jams in the past. What if I'm right? What if the most powerful Orcish Sorcerer is wandering around in Turai? Who knows what new spells he might have brought with him?"

"You don't know what you're talking about. No one can catch me unaware."

Lisutaris is angry.

"I just gave you three hundred and fifty gurans to leave me in peace and now you're bothering me with this foolishness. Makri, get rid of him so I can sleep."

"No," says Makri.

"What?" Lisutaris looks surprised. "But you're my bodyguard."

"What if Thraxas is right?" says Makri.

Lisutaris finds the strength to haul herself up into a sitting position.

"I always thought you were the smart one."

"I am the smart one," says Makri. "But Thraxas often succeeds in his investigating. I don't think you should ignore him. Maybe Deeziz is here. Maybe he's attacking you and you don't know it."

"How many times do I have to repeat, I can't be attacked without me knowing it," insists Lisutaris. "I've had enough of this. What was Cicerius thinking, leaving me in this place? I need to be at home where I can recover without being surrounded by idiots."

Lisutaris makes an attempt to haul herself out of bed. Makri puts a hand on her shoulder and firmly pushes her back. Lisutaris's eyes widen in amazement.

"You can't leave," says Makri, firmly. "You have to rest and get better. Meanwhile Thraxas can investigate more."

"Would you like me to blast you with a spell?"

"Well that wouldn't be a very smart thing to do to your own bodyguard," says Makri, logically.

Lisutaris sinks back into the bed.

"I need thazis," she says.

"You can't have it," says Makri. "The healer says it's bad for you."

"To hell with the healer," says Lisutaris. She waves her hand, summoning her bag. It rises from the floor but Makri intercepts it and throws it in a drawer.

"No thazis till you're better," she says, sternly.

Fearing that Lisutaris might actually carry out her threat to start blasting people with spells, I decide it's time to go. As I leave the room Lisutaris is still complaining about not being allowed any thazis, and Makri is ignoring her.

I need food. I head downstairs to see what's on offer. Elsior the apprentice cook is standing behind the bar as I approach, with an apron round her waist, loading some pastries into a jar. I ask if there's anything more substantial on offer. There are plenty of hungry dock workers who visit the tavern at lunchtime so the cooking generally starts early.

"I'm a bit rushed," says Elsior, apologetically. "But the first batch of stew will be ready soon."

She puts her hand to her forehead.

"It's hot in here today."

"Hot? I hadn't noticed."

"Must be the heat in the kitchen getting to me," says Elsior.

I have a strong suspicion about what's going to happen next. Elsior blinks a few times, and brushes perspiration from her forehead. Then she leans forward, clutches the bar for support, and sinks slowly to the floor. I look down at her.

"So is the stew almost ready? Could I just take a bowl from the kitchen?"

Elsior doesn't reply. Makri appears from upstairs.

"Another casualty?"

"I'm afraid so. And the stew isn't ready yet."

"Tough break," says Makri.

We look down at Elsior's prone body.

"I'm starting to get quite fed up with all this," says Makri.

"Me too."

"Do you think these people are really trying to get better? Palax and Kaby have been sick for ages. Shouldn't they be healthy by now?"

I shrug.

"Difficult to say. Sometimes the malady's like that. At least no one's died yet."

"So where are we going to put her?"

Hanama and Sarin are sick in my office and Lisutaris is in my bedroom. Palax and Kaby are in Makri's room and Chiaraxi is lying ill in Tanrose's room. Moolifi is in the only spare guest room.

"Have to be Dandelion's room, I'd say."

Dandelion sleeps in a small room at the back of the tavern, when she's not down at the shore, talking to the dolphins. We pick Elsior up and start to carry her through the kitchen towards the back. As we do so we meet Dandelion bustling towards us.

"Oh dear," says Dandelion. Another one?"

"We were going to put her in your room."

Dandelion accepts it with good grace.

"You best tell Gurd," I say. "He's going to have a lot of hungry dockers and mercenaries here in a few hours and nothing to feed them."

Dandelion wrinkles her brow.

"I'm not a very good cook."

She turns to Makri.

"Can you cook?"

Makri looks quite offended, and shakes her head.

"Well, I'm off to investigate," I say, and depart briskly. I'm not so bad at mixing up a stew on a campfire, but I'm not planning on pitching in and helping. The thought of me cooking for dockers and mercenaries is quite ridiculous, but the way things are going, I wouldn't put it past someone to suggest it.

Chapter Thirteen

I return to my office to pick up my sword and load up with a spell or two. I cram some thazis sticks and a flask of klee into a pocket. When I turn round I find Sarin the Merciless staring at me. I glare at her.

"Aren't you better yet?"

She doesn't reply. She's huddled up in one of my blankets, as is Hanama. Hanama at least contrives to look innocent. Sarin just looks like a killer.

"I'm off to find the Ocean Storm. No doubt you intended to find it and sell it to the Orcs. Well, you can forget it."

"I'd have it already if I hadn't got sick," she whispers.

"No you wouldn't."

"I've outwitted you in the past."

"So you claim. And here you are, sick on my couch. Try outwitting that."

"You're not making sense," sneers Sarin.

"Not making sense? Try this. I work every day and I fight for my city. You're a parasite who feeds off honest people. Does that make sense?"

Sarin mops her brow. She's bathed in perspiration, suffering badly from the disease.

"There's no difference between us," she says. "We're both empty. I fill it up with crime. You fill it up with food and beer."

I blink. It's an odd thing to say.

"You're rambling, Sarin. The malady does that. When you get healthy you'll remember which one of us is the honest upright citizen. And you're not going to be healthy for long once Makri's done with you."

Sarin sneers.

"If she had any sense she'd have done with me already. But at least her life isn't empty like yours."

"Oh no?"

"No."

"She works as a barmaid and wastes her time listening to Samanatius the phoney philosopher."

"You don't like Samanatius?" says Sarin.

"I don't."

"That shows what a fool you are."

Not willing to engage in further conversation with a woman who is clearly delirious, I leave through the outside door, place the locking spell on it, and hurry down the steps into Quintessence Street. As soon as I hit the cold thoroughfare it strikes me that I don't really know what I'm looking for. Whales, maybe, but I've already checked Twelve Seas quite thoroughly, and I'd swear there wasn't one lurking in the shadows. As for the Ocean Storm, who knows where that might be? As far as

I can gather, it was gone from Borinbax's house before Sarin killed him. If it hadn't been she'd have it by now, and wouldn't be troubling me.

A squadron of troops marches by, on their way to bolster the harbour defences. Each man has a long spear and a shield over his shoulder. By this time the city is awash with rumours that the Orcs are going to batter down the sea wall, and the area is continually being reinforced. As well as additional soldiers, Cicerius has assigned more Sorcerers to the sea defences. Even Kemlath Orc Slayer is down there, in charge of one section of wall. Kemlath was banished for his crimes, crimes which I detected, but he's been recalled for the duration of the war. I'm not objecting. The city needs the services of everyone who can wield a spell.

I find myself in the narrow street where Makri and I met Marizaz, Orcish Assassin. What a strange affair that was. One that I really should have looked into further. I would have had my mind not been preoccupied with raising money, and looking after the sick. I can hardly be blamed for some neglect when it comes to investigating. The way the Avenging Axe is bulging with ailing people just now is enough to put anyone off. Once more I find myself wondering if there might be some sorcery behind it. Lisutaris can insist all she wants that no magic is involved, but I still say it's unnatural the way no one can set foot in my office without catching the malady. It goes against all reason.

I glance down at the spot where Makri killed Marizaz. A tiny splash of colour catches my eye, bright against the dull frozen mud. I reach down to pick it up. It's a small scrap of cloth, a few threads of pink. Unusual. There's not that much pink fabric to be found in Twelve Seas. It's an expensive colour. The dye has to be imported from the far west. Upper-class women might flaunt their wealth by wearing pink garments, but no one does in Twelve Seas. I wonder how it got here. As far as I remember, Marizaz wasn't wearing pink. I put the threads in my pocket and look around some more, without finding anything. Then I return to the Avenging Axe. I've made no progress and I'm stuck for inspiration.

Captain Rallee is sitting at a table with Moolifi. I decline his invitation to join them. The Captain is more gregarious these days but I'm not in the mood for admiring the fineness of his lady friend. I'm starting to resent the way he's sitting around here being pleased with himself while I'm out investigating in the cold streets. I make a brief enquiry about the likelihood of food and learn that Gurd has sent out for an emergency cook. Meanwhile he and Dandelion are attempting to manufacture some sort of stew. Knowing Gurd's lack of culinary expertise, I don't hold out much hope, unless the emergency cook turns out to be a woman of extraordinary skill, which isn't that likely.

By now in a thoroughly bad mood, I traipse upstairs to my room to have another look at Makri's book. Unfortunately it's not there. I glance suspiciously at Hanama but she's sleeping and she isn't holding a book. I'm concerned. If someone's stolen Makri's book she'll go crazy, and probably accuse me of not looking after it properly. I hunt round my room, without success. Finally I put my nose through the bedroom door, in case Lisutaris might have it. I'm surprised to find Makri sitting on the floor, reading the book in question. She looks up as I enter, and shifts uncomfortably.

"Thraxas. Finished investigating?"

"Just came back to do some research."

I stare at the book.

"Some research from that book, as it happens."

I hold out my hand.

"You can't have it," says Makri.

"What do you mean, I can't have it? I need it."

"So do I."

"What for?"

"College."

"College is closed."

"I have to prepare a seminar. For next year. On naval history."

I stare at Makri.

"Makri, you are a terrible liar. You don't have a seminar to prepare, whatever that means. If you did you wouldn't have lent me the book."

I take a step towards her.

"Hand it over."

Makri leaps to her feet.

"Back off," she says. "I need this book."

"You're researching whales, aren't you!" I cry.

"Whales? You're talking rubbish. Why would I be researching whales?"

"Because you're trying to get your hands on Tanrose's gold! How did you learn about it?"

"I don't know what you're talking about," says Makri, not very convincingly. She really is a bad liar. Faced with a master of the art like me, she's wasting her time. Nonetheless, she doesn't look like she's going to give up the book without a fight. I take a step backwards, and draw myself up to my full height.

"I might have expected this from you. I'm out there doing an honest day's work and the moment I get home I find you stabbing me in the back."

"No one is stabbing you in the back. And what do you mean, you might have expected it of me?" demands Makri.

"The Orcish blood. Never trust a person with pointed ears."

Makri narrows her eyes. When she does that they have an odd, slanted appearance. Another sure sign of her non-Human untrustworthiness.

"I'm getting fed up of your Orcish insults," she says.

"Feel free to leave the city any time," I respond, and I mean it. We stare at each other angrily for a few seconds.

"How did you learn about the whale story?" I demand.

"Everyone knows about it," snaps Makri. "Glixius Dragon Killer was in here asking about whales while you were out."

"Glixius? How did he learn about it?"

"Servant gossip. Tanrose's mother's servant is the sister of one of Glixius's cooks."

Servants are notorious for gossiping. I should have guessed it wouldn't remain a secret. I'd better find this gold, and soon. If I don't, there's no telling how many people might start trying to muscle in. I curse Glixius. This man really is the bane of my life. Not only is he searching for the Ocean Storm, he's apparently looking for the hidden gold. It's not like the man is poor. He doesn't need a share of 14,000 gurans the way I do. The thought makes me even angrier. I feel slightly better when I remember that I'll soon have the chance to take some of his money from him at the card table. Unfortunately I'm immediately reminded that I don't have enough money to sit down with yet, and I get angry again.

I leave the room. To hell with them all. I've got about thirty-six hours before Turai's richest gamblers roll up to the Avenging Axe, and nothing is going to prevent me from finding the cash I need to play with them. There's a knock on the inner door. I open it to find Tirini Snake Smiter outside. I glare at her. Tirini hasn't actually stabbed me in the back but she's an associate of Lisutaris's and Makri is Lisutaris's bodyguard, so I'm annoyed at her by association.

"What do you want?" I ask.

Tirini looks surprised.

"To protect Lisutaris, of course. That's what I'm here for, remember?"

I let her in, muttering under my breath all the while.

Tirini eyes me with mild distaste.

"Don't blame me. This tavern is the last place I'd choose to spend my time. But some of us have to make sacrifices for the good of the city. Did you give up guarding the walls?"

"I have a few days off."

"Really," says Tirini, raising her eyebrows. "How reassuring. One trusts the Orcs are also enjoying a holiday."

Tirini sweeps past me and on into the bedroom to check on Lisutaris. I notice she's wearing another fancy pair of shoes with pink and gold embroidery. Was she wearing them before? I can't remember. The pink looks rather similar to the threads I have in my pocket. The ones I picked up from where we left Marizaz.

There's probably nothing in it. Lots of rich Turanian women have embroidery on their shoes. It's a popular way of showing off your wealth. But maybe I'll examine them later to see if there are any threads missing. I don't completely trust Tirini. She never appeared on the battlefield. For all anyone knows she could be an Orcish spy. Lisutaris trusts her. But Lisutaris also employs Makri as a bodyguard, so it's not like you can trust her judgement in everything.

There's a knock on the outside door.

"Go to hell!" I shout.

The door flies open. Harmon Half Elf strolls into the room. He has long fair hair, and an elegant green cloak with the rainbow motif of the Sorcerers Guild embroidered around the hem.

"Where is the meeting?" he asks, politely enough for a man who just countermanded my locking spell and barged into my office.

"What meeting?"

"The Sorcerers' meeting."

"What Sorcerers' meeting?"

Before I can reply, Coranius the Grinder strides in though the door. Coranius is one of Turai's most powerful Sorcerers, and a man of notoriously short temper.

"Where is the meeting?" he asks, curtly.

I'm starting to feel annoyed.

"There isn't any meeting."

Coranius stares at me.

"Stop talking rubbish."

A carriage draws up outside. Anumaris Thunderbolt, one of our younger Sorcerers, hurries into the office.

"Am I late for the meeting?" she asks. "Hello, Thraxas."

I nod at her politely. I fought at Anumaris's side only a month or two ago, when the Orcs attacked us outside the walls. It was her first time in battle and she did well, so I greet her rather more politely, but tell her once more there isn't a meeting.

My bedroom door opens. Tirini leans out.

"In here, everyone," she says.

"What's going on? Did you organise a meeting in my room without telling me?"

No one listens. Before Harmon, Coranius and Anumaris have disappeared through the door, Lanius Suncatcher, Chief Sorcerer from Palace Security, is hurrying in, followed by Melus the Fair, resident Sorcerer at the Stadium Superbius.

"Is there any chance of a glass of wine?" asks Melus.

I'm speechless. If a bunch of Sorcerers think they can just turn up and start demanding wine from me they're sadly mistaken. I'm about to give them all a piece of my mind when old Hasius the Brilliant himself hobbles into the room complete with three attendants. Old Hasius is reputed to be 112 years old, and he's starting to look it. He very rarely leaves his chambers at the Abode of Justice yet here he is, walking into a tavern in Twelve Seas like it's the most natural thing in the world.

Various other Sorcerers crowd in, some powerful, some less so, and some I don't even know. I fight my way to the door of my bedroom and peer over their shoulders. My bedroom is a mass of rainbow cloaks of every description. Sorcerers are perched everywhere, on the floor, on the bed, all acting like they belong here. Meanwhile Makri is sitting calmly beside Lisutaris. It's enough to test anyone's patience.

"Would someone tell me what's going on?" I yell, loud enough to stop their babbling. They all turn to look at me.

"Sorcerers' meeting," says Coranius, sternly.

"Yes, I know it's a Sorcerers' meeting. But why in my bedroom?"

"Because Lisutaris is here."

"And she can't be moved."

"Sorry Thraxas," says Lisutaris, who's still looking weak, but has managed to sit up in bed. She has her cloak draped round her shoulders, and looks rather regal.

"Isn't it meant to be a secret that she's here?" I ask.

"It remains a secret," says Coranius.

"Not much of a secret if every Sorcerer in Turai suddenly appears."

"We're Sorcerers," says Coranius. "We can cover our tracks."

I'm about to raise several more objections when Glixius Dragon Killer suddenly appears.

"Sorry to be late," he booms, brushing past me. "Has the meeting started yet?"

I give up in disgust. My own private space invaded by my enemies, and there's nothing to be done about it. Much as I'd like to sling every one of them out into the street, I can't. The weakest Sorcerer here still has more power than me. Unable to think of even a good line to leave on, I turn on my heel and depart. I'm seething, not least because Makri seems to be welcome at the meeting whereas I'm obviously not. I head straight downstairs to the bar. I need beer, and plenty of it. And I need it quickly. Gurd is standing behind the bar, a welcoming sight.

"Beer. Quickly. My rooms are full of Sorcerers."

Gurd pours me a beer. He hands it over with a sympathetic look.

"It's an outrage," I say. "A man can't even call his room his own anymore. First it was invaded by sick people and now it's Sorcerers. I detest them all."

"Perhaps the Sorcerers will get sick," says Gurd.

"I hope so. I tell you, Gurd, this city makes me sick. Apart from you, I hate every inhabitant."

Gurd grins, but his smile fades quite suddenly and he starts to look vague. He puts his hand to his forehead, then stares at his palm, which is damp with sweat.

"Is it hot in here?" he asks.

Before I can reply, Gurd is sinking gently to the floor.

"And you're sick as well," I say, and shake my head sadly. "Now I don't like anyone."

"Look after the tavern," gasps Gurd.

Dandelion appears on the scene. She gives a small cry when she sees Gurd lying on the floor.

"Oh my goodness, Gurd is sick. Help me get him to his room. Thraxas? What are you doing?"

"Pouring myself a beer."

"We have to help Gurd."

"I will. I just need a beer first."

At this rate there will soon be no one left. Gurd was my last ally. Now he's gone it's just me against the hostile world, and at this moment the hostile world seems to be winning.

Makri suddenly appears at my side.

"Shouldn't you be with your Sorcerer buddies?"

"They threw me out," says Makri. "I'm completely offended."

"Well, Sorcerers are always secretive."

"But I'm Lisutaris's bodyguard."

Poor Makri. She's under the misapprehension that this gives her some sort of status. It doesn't really. She's acknowledged to be a good woman with a sword, but fighting abilities alone don't win status in this city.

"Help us get Gurd into his room."

"I hate all these sick people everywhere," says Makri.

Chapter Fourteen

It's a chaotic evening at the Avenging Axe. Dandelion and Makri are both serving behind the bar, which means there's no waitress service, which in turn leads to a long queue of thirsty drinkers all competing for service. Mercenaries and dockers become impatient. They're not used to waiting so long for their tankards of ale, and they're not shy about complaining. The food is being prepared by some temporary cook whose name I don't even know. She seems to be taking a long time about it, which leads to more impatience. There are more than a few angry words and sharp exchanges as Makri and Dandelion struggle to cope. It's a bad situation, and a less experienced drinker than myself might be inclined to panic. Fortunately I've had a great deal of practice and I've got a lot of weight on my side. I lever some mercenaries out of the way, force back a sailmaker, and slide up to the bar without too much trouble.

"Happy Guildsman, Makri," I say, holding out my extra-large tankard for a refill.

Makri looks at me balefully.

"Have you considered helping out?"

"Helping out? Why?"

"Because we need help," she says, logically enough. Logical or not, I brush it aside.

"I'm not employed here. I'm a paying customer."

Even Dandelion is slightly harassed as Barbarian mercenaries compete for her attention.

"It really would be nice if you were to help, Thraxas," she says.

"Afraid I can't do that."

Makri hands a tankard of ale over to a customer, then pauses.

"Then you're not being served," she says.

I gape at her.

"What do you mean?"

"If you won't help, I'm banning you from the tavern."

Only the crush of bodies prevents me from reeling backwards in shock. I'm not used to being banned from taverns. Or rather, I am used to being banned from taverns, but not the one I reside in.

"Don't be ridiculous. You can't ban me. I live here."

"I don't care," says Makri. "You're not getting any drinks. Either help out or step aside. There are people waiting."

"You dog!" I roar, and reach for my sword. "This time you've gone too far!"

I start heaving my way through the press of bodies to the hatch in the bar, intent on getting behind it and skewering Makri at the first opportunity. Makri grabs the axe she keeps for emergencies and waits for me to arrive.

"No one refuses beer to Thraxas!" I yell, still struggling through the crowd. I find my way blocked by a Barbarian mercenary who stands about seven feet tall and almost as wide. It takes me a while to work my way round him and it doesn't calm my temper. Meanwhile I'm yelling insults at Makri and she's yelling insults back at me. By the time I make it behind the bar, fifty or so assorted mercenaries, dockers and other Twelve Seas lowlifes are looking on with some amusement. I ignore them.

"Pour me a beer or I'll run you through like a dog."

Makri raises her axe.

"Get out from behind the bar or I'll chop your head off, you cusux."

Even in the company of mercenaries and dock workers, not the most refined of people, Makri's use of an Orcish insult causes a few raised eyebrows. I take a step forward. Dandelion suddenly leaps in front of me.

"Stop this at once," she says. "With everyone sick we all have to work together."

I eye her with loathing.

"Dandelion, have I ever told you how much I despise you?"

"Don't pick on her, you fat oaf," shouts Makri. "Dandelion, get out the way so I can chop his head off."

Dandelion turns to face Makri.

"You have to stop it as well. We shouldn't be fighting among ourselves."

"Goddamn you, you ignorant zutha bitch," roars Makri, giving vent to another of her favourite foul Orcish insults. "Get out the way or I'll chop you in half."

Dandelion takes a step backwards, intimidated. She turns to me, and then back to Makri. And then, quite abruptly, she bursts into tears.

"I was only trying to help," she wails, then runs off into the back room, leaving me and Makri staring at each other with weapons raised, feeling a little foolish.

"Well there was no need to make the girl cry," says one of the loudest voices in Turai. It's Viriggax, who's standing at the bar with a look of disapproval in his eye.

"Poor little soul," says Parax the shoemaker, agreeing with him. "Always tries to do her best."

"I never like to see a young woman bullied," growls Viriggax. "Goes against the grain."

"Oh come on," I protest. "We weren't bullying her. Everyone knows Dandelion is an idiot."

Another mercenary at the bar, a man with a scar running from his ear to his chin, clucks in disapproval.

"Always thought she was a helpful young wench. Don't see any reason for threatening her with swords and axes."

There are mutters of agreement from all over the tavern.

"I wasn't really going to attack her," protests Makri.

"You insulted her in Orcish," says the mercenary, and looks at her suspiciously.

"Are we ever going to get a drink?" demands another large mercenary, and bangs his fist on the bar. Realising that the mob is against us, and remembering that Gurd's last words were to look after his tavern, I sigh, and sheathe my sword. If these people don't get drinks soon there will probably be a riot. I pick up an empty tankard, and place it under the beer tap. I can't believe it. Thraxas, once Senior Investigator at the Imperial Palace, now reduced to serving beer.

"I'll get you for this," I mutter to Makri.

She puts her axe away and picks up an empty tankard.

"You started it," she mutters back.

Chapter Fifteen

In the early hours of the morning I'm slumped on the floor, my back against the bar, exhausted.

"That was one of the worst nights of my life."

"I told you it's not so easy serving beer," says Makri.

She takes a sip from a glass of klee and winces. Klee is a fiery spirit at the best of times, and Gurd's is not of the highest quality.

"Why do I drink this stuff?"

"It has reviving properties," I reply, and pour some for myself. I've always liked the spirit's dark gold colour. Warms a man before it even hits the throat.

"How did this happen?" I muse.

"What?"

"Everything. One day I was a Sorcerer's apprentice, the next day I was a mercenary, then I was an Investigator at the Palace and now I'm serving drinks to mercenaries. You couldn't say I've gone up in the world."

Makri shrugs.

"You're serving drinks because everyone else got sick. As for the rest, who knows? Anyway, do you want to go up in the world?"

"I'd like to get out of Twelve Seas."

"That might happen soon."

I sip some more klee, and wash it down with beer.

"True. If the Orcs swarm over the sea wall I'll probably have to move."

"I'm not moving an inch," declares Makri. "We ran away last time. I'm not doing that again."

Makri didn't really run away. She helped shepherd some important Sorcerers back into the city after our troops were defeated. If we hadn't saved Lisutaris we'd have even less hope of survival than we do now. Makri doesn't exactly see it that way.

"I'm making my death stand here."

I don't argue the point. She won't be the only one making their death stand, if only because there will be nowhere to run. I look over at her.

"Why did you want to find Tanrose's gold?"

"To pay for the university. In case there's a university left."

Makri looks depressed. She doesn't mind dying in battle but it's annoying that all her hard work at the Guild College will be wasted. It wasn't so long ago that she marched into the tavern with her arms aloft, celebrating her triumph in the exams, where she finished top of her year.

"If we could just find the Ocean Storm," I say, "the city would have a lot better chance of surviving. The Sorcerers Guild could still hold the Orcs off."

"Do you have any idea where it is?" asks Makri.

"No idea at all. Whoever finally ended up with it is powerful and smart. No one's picked up the slightest trace."

I haul myself to my feet.

"Time to get busy."

"What? Where are you going?"

"The harbour. Looking for whales, gold, and the Ocean Storm."

Makri leaps to her feet.

"I'm coming too."

I shrug.

"Okay."

"I get to share the gold if we find it."

"I'll consider it."

"I have plenty of ideas about what 'under the whale' might mean."

I raise my eyebrows.

"Really."

"No," admits Makri. "None at all really. But I might think of something. If we find it I can pay for the university. If we find the Ocean Storm too we can save the city."

"It's all starting to sound simple. We'll be heroes."

My bedroom is still full of Sorcerers. They've been cloistered in there for hours. I slip into my office, pick up both my magic warm cloaks, and hand one to Makri. We hurry down the outside steps then stride along Quintessence Street, which is cold and deserted. The oil lamps at the corners cast a feeble light, barely sufficient to navigate by. I speak a small word of power to light up my illuminated staff.

We pass a night-time Civil Guard patrol. They stare at us suspiciously before recognising us as familiar Twelve Seas characters. They walk off, swords at their hips, marching in an untidy fashion. Not for the first time it strikes me that our Civil Guards are not the most imposing bunch of men. Hardly enough to strike terror into the hearts of marauding Orcs. The King has some good troops, and there are some experienced mercenaries in the city. But for the most part, our defenders are poorly trained rabble. There was a time when every man in Turai, no matter what his profession, had undergone enough military training to take up arms at a moment's notice. Everyone could fight like a proper soldier. That's no longer the case. Back in those days there wasn't such inequality in the city. Now there are incredible riches at the Palace, and terrible poverty in the slums. In between the people and the King, our senate has become powerless and corrupt. Money, crime, corruption and drugs have ruined our fighting spirit.

"When's the card game?"

"Tonight."

"So really you're only out investigating in the middle of the night in a last desperate attempt to raise the money? As opposed to saving the city?"

"You're sharp as an Elf's ear, Makri."

Makri shrugs.

"It's a relief really. The notion of you becoming heroic was quite worrying."

We walk all the way down to the harbour. There's a watch tower at the end of the city wall, with a lookout post and a beacon on top. Great chains hang from the walls, covering the entrance to the harbour. I can sense the sorcery that's laid over the chains, strengthening them against assault. Since Cicerius sent more protection to the south of the city the whole area reeks of magic.

"Whales never come here," says Makri.

"I know."

"Except occasionally a dead one gets washed up. Can you remember when that last happened?"

"I can remember seeing the carcass of a whale when I was young, but it was long before the Battle of Dead Dragon Island. I don't think it was buried anywhere. Just rotted away on the beach."

"Maybe Tanrose's grandfather buried the gold on the beach?" suggests Makri.

"She said at the harbour. The beach is quite a way from the harbour."

"Perhaps he was confused?"

"Why would he bury his gold under the rotting carcass of a whale? Hardly the easiest place."

We stare out to sea.

"How about if we ask the dolphins?" suggests Makri.

"Are you feeling feverish?"

"No," says Makri, sharply. "Why did you say that?"

"Because you don't usually make insane suggestions. Okay, you do. But they're not usually dolphin-related."

"The dolphins might know something about a local whale incident."

"You're starting to sound like Dandelion."

Makri smiles.

"Maybe. But I want that money. I want to go to the university. Anyway, the dolphins once gave us a healing stone. Saved my life."

It's true. They did. And they gave me a handsome reward as well. Several valuable old coins, which I exchanged for a hefty purse of gurans. It was a good deal, though not one I ever talked about afterwards, not wishing the hardened inhabitants of Twelve Seas to know that I'd been accepting payment from dolphins. I'm still not convinced they can speak, though Dandelion claims she can communicate with them.

Makri takes out a thazis stick. She cups her hands carefully around a match as she lights it, preventing any sudden gust of wind from blowing it out. Matches are expensive items; it doesn't do to waste them. If I was any sort of Sorcerer I'd be able to light a thazis stick without a match. But I'm not and I can't. I take out a stick of my own and light it from Makri's.

"You might have let me try some of the thazis Lisutaris gave you," says Makri, accusingly.

"Doesn't she give you a supply of your own? For being her bodyguard?"

"No. Why would she? She doesn't want her bodyguard walking around intoxicated. And you might have let me try that special beer as well. What's the matter that you're so mean about everything?"

I'm stuck for an explanation.

"Habit, I suppose. You know what Twelve Seas is like. Full of leeches."

By this time we've reached one of the small gates in the wall. It leads through to the rocks outside the harbour. From there you can walk over to the beach. At a time of national crisis it's illegal for the gatekeeper to let anyone through, but the man on duty is a long-time resident of Twelve Seas, a man I've known all my life. I slip him a small coin and he lets us through the gate. He leers as we pass, probably imagining I'm off for some fun with a wench.

"It's not that reassuring that a small bribe gets us through the gate," says Makri, as we clamber over the rocks.

"I expect he'll charge the Orcs more. Are you sure Dandelion will be here?"

Makri nods.

"She always goes to the dolphins when she's upset."

Makri looks troubled.

"You think we have to apologise for making her cry?"

"I don't know."

"You do it," says Makri. "I can't make apologies. It never comes out right."

I can feel the tiredness and thazis affecting me as we clamber over the black rocks. Makri goes nimbly from rock to rock but I'm not as agile as I used to be, and I have to take care not to plunge into one of the icy pools. We finally make it to the edge of the beach.

"I can't believe I'm going to talk to the dolphins," I mutter. Again."

The dolphins in the bay are popular in Turai. They're regarded as lucky. I don't think they ever brought me any luck. I don't suppose they ever harmed me either. Maybe if I patted one on the head I might win at cards.

"There she is," says Makri.

I peer into the darkness. I can't see anything. Makri's Elvish eyes are far better at seeing in the dark than mine, and we walk quite a long way before I finally make out the outline of a young woman standing right at the edge of the water. She turns as she hears us approach. I hold up my staff, illuminating Dandelion's face. She still seems to be crying. I immediately feel uncomfortable. Makri treacherously takes a step backwards, leaving me to sort it out.

"Hello, Dandelion. Having a nice chat with the, ah . . . dolphins?"

Dandelion doesn't respond. Just stands there looking as miserable as a Niojan whore, or maybe worse.

"We wonder if you might be able help us."

Dandelion remains silent. I start to feel frustrated. There's no need to make such a meal of everything. It's not like Makri whacked her with her axe or anything, and God knows no one could have blamed her.

"Sorry to have made you cry, but you know . . . it was only a small argument. You have to expect that in a tavern. Especially in Twelve Seas. Happens all the time. If you think it's bad in the Avenging Axe, you should try visiting the Mermaid. It's weapons drawn all the time in there. People murdered every day. Hey, it's not like we meant it. Be reasonable, you can't expect Makri and me to watch every single thing we say just in case it upsets you. Goddammit, what do you expect from us? We can't all go around writing poetry about dolphins all the time. Some of us have to work, you know. I mean, you're hardly normal, Dandelion."

I pause.

"Good apology," says Makri. "One of your finest."

Dandelion brushes a tear from her eye.

"I wasn't crying about your argument. The dolphins just told me the Orcs are already here."

Makri and I draw our swords simultaneously, whirling round to fend them off. There's no one in sight.

"Where are they?"

"In the Avenging Axe."

Makri and I look at each other.

"We've just come from there. No Orcs around."

"Did they attack after we left?" says Makri.

Dandelion shakes her head.

"They've been there for days."

"For days?"

"Yes."

I sheathe my sword.

"Without anyone noticing?"

Dandelion nods.

"But the dolphins know all about it?"

"They can sense it," says Dandelion. "Because of the dragon line running up from their cave right through the Avenging Axe."

"But we've been living there," I protest. "We'd have noticed."

Dandelion shakes her head.

"The dolphins know."

I can't prevent myself from snorting in disgust. I can feel something of a headache coming on, not uncommon when talking to Dandelion.

"Maybe they just sensed Makri," I say.

"Hey!" says Makri. "I'm not an Orc."

"You're one quarter Orc. Probably enough to confuse a dolphin at long range."

"It's not Makri," says Dandelion, quite emphatically. "The dolphins like her."

I snort in disgust for a second time.

"They would."

"What's that supposed to mean?" demands Makri.

"It means it's strange the way these otherworldly creatures take to you. I still haven't forgotten the way the fairies in the Fairy Glade all flocked around you."

"Aha!" cries Makri. "I knew you were still annoyed at that. You couldn't stand it the way they ignored you."

"A man of my reputation does not depend for his status on a bunch of dolphins and fairies."

"The centaurs liked me as well," says Makri.

"Centaurs like anyone with breasts."

"The naiads were also friendly."

"Naiads have notoriously poor judgement. And will you stop bragging about how many non-Human creatures like you? It's nothing to be proud of."

"You've been jealous of me ever since I arrived in Turai," says Makri, hotly. "Always putting me down. Ever since I became Lisutaris's bodyguard you've been criticising me, just because I get to hear a few things and you don't. It's not my fault you got sacked from the Palace; you shouldn't have got so drunk all the time."

"What? Are you lecturing me? Am I actually standing on a beach being lectured by a woman with pointy ears?"

I notice Makri's hand straying towards her sword.

"Stop arguing!" yells Dandelion. "Why are you always arguing?"

I shake my head.

"The war. The Orcs outside the walls. It drives everyone mad. Apart from you, obviously."

Dandelion sighs.

"It's true. Turai is a sad place these days. And now the Orcs are in the Avenging Axe. Do you think that's why everyone's sick?"

"Who knows? We'll check it out when we get back. Meanwhile, could you ask the dolphins if they know anything about local whales?"

Dandelion looks puzzled. I explain to her the nature of our quest.

"Do you really need fourteen thousand gurans?" she asks. "Will it make you happy?"

"We plan to give it to the poor," I say.

"Oh. All right. In that case . . ."

Dandelion turns back towards the water and makes some odd noises. Very odd noises. I'd be more disturbed had I not heard her doing this before. Even so, it's a very strange experience. She makes a sort of whistling, clicking sound, then stares over the ocean, waiting for a reply. I notice for the first time that she has a piece of dried seaweed in her hair, a decoration so strange I can't bring myself to ask about it.

Dandelion converses with the dolphins for a while. She turns to Makri.

"They're pleased you got better."

She looks at me.

"They think you're drinking too much."

"Oh come on, you're just making this up. How the hell can dolphins know how much I drink?"

Dandelion faces back towards the ocean. I'm aggrieved. I refuse to believe the dolphins said I was drinking too much. Dandelion just slipped that one in herself.

After a lot more twittering and whistling, she lifts her arm, and waves goodbye.

"I told them we wouldn't let the city fall to the Orcs," she says.

"Anything on whales?"

Dandelion shakes her head. The seaweed seems to be fixed quite firmly, and remains in place.

"They didn't know what it could mean for treasure to be buried under a whale."

"Excellent," I say. "Tonight has been well worth the trouble. A long walk on a cold beach just to be insulted by a pack of dolphins."

I head back towards the rocks, followed by Makri.

"Maybe you shouldn't take it as an insult," she says. "Perhaps they were just worried about your health."

I'm not placated.

"Damned fish. They'd do better to worry about their own health. I'll be down on them like a bad spell if they keep spreading rumours about me. Drink too much indeed."

I bring out the small silver flask of klee I always carry, and take a sip. We re-enter the city through the small gate.

"Keep a lookout for anything that resembles a whale," I say, as we pass the harbour.

"I've already looked everywhere," says Makri. "There's nothing."

As we pass the large grain warehouses a voice calls out to us to halt. It's Captain Rallee.

"Captain. On duty tonight?"

He shakes his head.

"Then what are you doing here?"

I had the impression that Rallee spent every spare moment snuggling up to Moolifi, though I don't want to come right out and say it.

"Just looking round," says the Captain. He lowers his voice. "Would you say there's anything in this area that might be described as a whale?"

I look at him sternly.

"Have you been drinking, Captain? No whales around these parts."

"Well it might not be a real whale," says Rallee. "Maybe something else that could be described as one?"

The Captain looks at Makri.

"Any ideas? Any old Elvish words spring to mind?"

Makri shakes her head.

"They rarely talked about whales. Almost never, in fact. It's quite strange how few references there are to whales in Elvish poetry."

Captain Rallee looks at her suspiciously.

"Have you been studying the subject?"

"Certainly not. Thraxas, have I ever studied whales or whale-related topics?"

"Not to my knowledge."

"What are you doing out at this time of night?" asks the Captain.

"Just taking a walk," says Makri. "Nothing to do with whales. Whales didn't even feature in our conversation. Until you mentioned them. But even then, nothing about whales really springs to mind."

I bid the captain a hasty goodnight and drag Makri off.

"Damn it, Makri, do you practise being such a bad liar?"

"What do you mean, bad liar? I thought I was very convincing."

I shake my head in disgust. Damn Tanrose's mother's servant. She's obviously been blabbing to everybody. Soon the whole city will be down here looking for gold.

Chapter Sixteen

It's deep into the morning by the time we trudge back into the Avenging Axe. Makri goes straight up the stairs to check on Lisutaris but I take a walk through to the back of the tavern to check on Gurd. Though I try to remain silent, the slight noise of my entrance brings him round.

"Sorry. Didn't mean to disturb you."

Gurd manages a weak grin. That's more than any of the other malady sufferers have managed. Gurd was always strong, and I don't doubt he'll be up on his feet in a day or two.

"Just had to lie down for a while," he says. "Be better soon."

"You will be."

I marched all over the world with Gurd. I'd have been killed in battle long ago if he hadn't been by my side.

"The tavern . . . is everything all right?"

I reassure him.

"I've got it under control."

"What about Tanrose?"

"Also all right. She'll be better in a day or two. Don't worry, I can keep things going."

Gurd nods. I've never seen the old Barbarian looking so pale.

"Big card game tonight," whispers Gurd. "Sorry I can't play."

"It'll save you money. I'm on good form."

Gurd grins again, but his eyelids droop, and I leave him to sleep.

The scene in my office is not as riotous as I feared. Sorcerers are notoriously intemperate and I wouldn't have been surprised to find them all lying drunk on the carpet. They've remained sober. A sign of how serious things are, perhaps. Coranius the Grinder is sitting behind my desk. Tirini Snake Smiter is in my armchair. And Hanama, to my surprise, is sitting up. The malady is passing. She's still deathly pale but she no longer has the haggard look that comes with the illness.

"Feeling better?" I grunt.

She nods.

"I'll leave tomorrow."

I should be delighted. I realise I don't really care.

I shrug.

"Have you any information about the Ocean Storm?" asks Coranius.

"None at all. How about the Sorcerers Guild?"

Coranius shakes his head. The artefact has vanished from sight. No one has the slightest idea where it is.

"We've been discussing it with Lisutaris. It's a worrying situation."

It has to be worrying if he's talking to me about it.

"What about this woman Sarin?" asks Coranius. "Does she have information?"

"I don't know for sure. I don't think so. I think she killed a thief called Borinbax who had it, but it was gone by then."

"We must question her as soon as she recovers."

"She doesn't know where it is," says Hanama.

"How do you know?"

"I asked her."

"And you believe her?"

"Yes."

"Why?"

"I know Sarin much better than you realise," says Hanama. "She doesn't know where it is. She came here thinking you did."

I notice that the killer in question isn't in my office.

"Where is she?"

"She dragged herself downstairs," says Hanama. "She said she'd rather lie ill in a store room than stay here any longer."

Sarin has gone. It's good news, though once again I find that I don't much care. I ask Coranius a question.

"So many people have fallen sick here. And it's taking them a long time to get better. Especially Lisutaris. Is there something sorcerous about it?"

"Lisutaris thinks not," replies Coranius.

"What do you think?"

Coranius shrugs. He's a man of medium size. Sandy-haired, not imposing in any way. But he's one of our strongest Sorcerers, not far behind Lisutaris in terms of raw power.

"I can't find any trace of sorcery. But you're right, it is taking her a long time to recover . . ."

Coranius looks troubled.

"People fall sick in clusters all the time," says Tirini. "That's what the malady's like. I don't think there's any sorcery at work. We'd be able to detect it."

"We can't detect the Ocean Storm," says Coranius.

"We don't even know if the Ocean Storm really exists."

I sit down on the couch, keeping a fair distance between myself and Hanama. It's a little strange to hear matters of state security discussed in front of an Assassin. There again, she's number three in the Assassins Guild, and the Assassins Guild is an officially recognised body in Turai. In some ways she outranks me.

"I think it exists," says Coranius. And if we haven't found a trace of it, we've found plenty of traces of Orcish activity around the south of the city. Incursions by an Assassin, ships sighted off the coast, traces of spells of spying."

I remember what Dandelion said to me on the beach. The Orcs are already in the Avenging Axe. I tell Coranius. He frowns, very deeply.

"Who is this Dandelion?"

"A strange young woman with seaweed in her hair."

"Seaweed? Why seaweed?"

"I don't really know. Usually it's flowers. She has astrological signs on her skirt and she talks to the dolphins."

I'm expecting Coranius to laugh. He doesn't. He looks grave.

"The dolphins really said this?"

"According to Dandelion. But she's fairly crazy."

But Coranius isn't listening. He's already on his feet, heading for the bedroom. I follow along, and enter in time to find Lisutaris and Makri arguing fiercely.

"Damn it, give me my thazis," demands Lisutaris.

"No," says Makri. "The healer says you aren't to have any."

"The healer got sick!"

"So what? That doesn't alter anything."

Lisutaris, Mistress of the Sky, motions with her hand and her bag once more floats up off the floor towards her. Makri intercepts it, grabbing it from the air and placing her foot on it.

"Give me that bag!"

"No."

"Give me the bag or I'll blast you through the wall!" roars Lisutaris, then coughs mightily with the exertion.

"You can't blast me," says Makri. "I'm your bodyguard. Now calm down, it's almost time for your medicine."

Lisutaris sinks back on her pillow, meanwhile casting the most evil of glances at Makri, which Makri calmly ignores. Coranius and Tirini are looking rather embarrassed to see the head of their guild so discomfited. Lisutaris glares at them.

"Can't a sick woman have five minutes' peace? What do you want?"

"Thraxas reports that a woman of his acquaintance has talked to the dolphins. The dolphins say the Orcs are already in this tavern."

"Hey it's only Dandelion," I say. "I wouldn't worry about—"

"Be quiet," snaps Coranius.

"The dolphins said this?" says Lisutaris. "What were their exact words?"

I'm angry at Coranius ordering me to be quiet. I'm about to tell them they can go and talk to the dolphins themselves if they're so interested, but Makri spoils it by repeating Dandelion's words.

"You were there as well?"

Makri nods.

"Can this woman Dandelion really communicate with them?"

Makri shrugs her shoulders.

"Maybe. She did it before."

"Why were we not informed of this earlier?" demands Coranius. "The gift of talking to the dolphins is very rare, even among Sorcerers."

He looks at me accusingly.

"No one ever asked. And Dandelion is a strange woman. She thinks there's a dragon line running up from the dolphins' cave through the Avenging Axe."

Tirini laughs.

"Oh please. Not the dragon lines again."

"Do they exist?" asks Makri.

"No," says Tirini.

"Possibly," says Coranius.

"We don't know," says Lisutaris.

I'm feeling very dissatisfied with all this.

"Since when did the dolphins become so important? All they do is swim around eating fish."

Everyone ignores me.

"Makri," says Lisutaris. "Please fetch Samanatius. I need to consult with him about this."

Makri nods. She puts on her cloak then slings Lisutaris's bag round her shoulders.

"Leave my bag here!" says Lisutaris.

"No. You can't have any thazis." says Makri, then departs.

Lisutaris scowls after her.

"That woman is the nurse from hell."

Lisutaris takes a scrap of paper from the small table beside the bed, scribbles a message on it then mutters a brief spell, sealing the document.

"Thraxas, please send this to Cicerius immediately. We need him here."

"This is a lot of fuss about a few dolphins."

"Do as Lisutaris says," barks Coranius.

I walk right up to the Sorcerer and put my face close to his.

"No one orders me around in my own room, and if you take that tone with me again I'll pick you up and throw you down the stairs."

Coranius growls.

"Are you asking to die?"

"No. I'm asking you to mind your manners, and if you try using a spell I'll knock your ugly head off before you can get the words out."

It looks like I may have to do just that because Coranius isn't a man to back down, but before he can speak Lisutaris interrupts him.

"Coranius, desist. Thraxas is quite right. We're his guests and I've been taking up his bedroom for a week. He deserves our thanks. Thraxas, please send the message, it is rather urgent."

I nod at Lisutaris, then march from the room, still angry. Behind me Tirini Snake Smiter is complaining that her shoes are dirty because the place has never been properly cleaned. Sorcerers. I detest them. Apart from Lisutaris, possibly.

Before taking Lisutaris's message to the nearby Messengers Guild outpost, I answer the door to Moolifi. The Niojan singer is looking a little less glamorous than usual. Her hair is slightly dishevelled and she's not wearing any jewellery. She's holding a tray with a beaker of steaming liquid on it.

"I've just come from the kitchen. Dandelion asked me to bring this to Lisutaris."

I nod. Dandelion is caring for a lot of patients, and it's decent enough of Moolifi, who's a paying guest in the tavern, to lend a hand. I show her to the bedroom. I notice that underneath her gown—blue, well tailored, and more expensive than your standard Twelve Seas resident could afford—she's wearing a pair of high-heeled shoes, yellow with pink embroidery. Very like Tirini's, and quite similar to those worn by Anumaris Thunderbolt. The pink threads I found were a great clue. Narrowed it down to only every fashionable woman in the city.

As I walk along Quintessence Street I find myself humming "Love Me Through the Winter," Moolifi's most popular song. She's sung it once or twice more in the tavern, and it's still a great favourite. She's a good singer, no matter what Makri thinks. I shake my head at the thought of Captain Rallee pounding round the harbour, looking for buried gold. No wonder. He'll need a lot more money than he can earn if he's to keep hold of Moolifi.

After sending the message to Cicerius I wonder what to do. Tonight Glixius Dragon Killer, General Acarius and Praetor Capatius are meant to be arriving at the Avenging Axe to play cards. I hardly have enough money to sit at the table with them, and despite my best efforts it doesn't look like I'll be raising any more. With the money I've borrowed from Lisutaris and Dandelion, plus my own meagre savings, I can scrape together around 440 gurans. Not enough, faced with the wealth of my opponents.

I shake my head. Treasure and magical artefacts. I've been spending my days chasing phantoms. I should have stuck to some solid investigating. Small crimes, men cheating on their wives, petty thefts. That sort of thing. It suits me better, and I might have earned more.

I walk down to the public baths, pay the admission fee, and wallow in the pool for a long time. Given the poverty that exists in Twelve Seas, we're not so badly off for public baths. The King loosened his grip on the purse strings some years back and helped renovate several of the area's old bathing houses. Even the poorest citizen can get himself a warm bath every now and then, and that's not the case in every city by any means. Not everyone is as clean as the Turanians. We're well known for it.

I relax for the first time in a long time. By the time I leave the bathing house I'm feeling a little more like my old self. I call into Ginixa's bakery and buy four pastries and eat them as I walk along the road. A street urchin stands right in front of me and holds out his hand. Feeling moderately benevolent, I break one of the pastries in half and give a piece to him. He thanks me and runs off. And then I have a sudden flash of inspiration. Perhaps it's a reward from the gods for being charitable. Or perhaps the relaxation brought on by bathing. More likely it's the pastries; I generally think better on a full stomach.

Makri is in the back yard at the Avenging Axe, practising with her weapons.

"St. Quatinius once talked to a whale," I say.

"What?"

"St. Quatinius. Patron saint of this city. One of our most famous religious figures. He once talked to a whale."

"Why?" says Makri.

"The whale was full of religious knowledge. So the story goes, anyway."

Makri eyes me.

"And you've only just thought of this?"

"My thoughts rarely venture into the realms of religious mystery. Anyway there's a small fountain in the back streets off Quintessence Street. The statue in the middle is of St. Quatinius talking to the whale."

"And you've only just thought of that?"

"Do you want to come or are you just going to make sarcastic comments?"

Makri sheathes her swords.

"Number one chariot at investigating," she mutters. "He just remembers now there's a whale fountain in Twelve Seas."

We set off once more along Quintessence Street.

"I can't believe you didn't think of this earlier," says Makri. "Like maybe before we tramped all over the entire city searching for anything that looked like a whale."

"Don't exaggerate. Anyway, I told you. I have a mental blank on anything to do with religion."

"It's a fountain. With a statue of a whale. How much more obvious could it be?"

By now we're close to the street with the fountain. We turn the corner to find a riot going on. A mob is attempting to reach the fountain and the Civil Guards are trying to hold them back. The mob is mostly made up of beggars, but I can see a few shopkeepers in there, and one or two craftsmen. We stand on the corner and watch the struggle.

"It looks like other people were thinking the same thing," says Makri.

I nod. Apparently everyone wants to find out if there's gold under the statue. The mob advances. The Civil Guards put away their batons and draw their swords. The crowd hesitates, but doesn't retreat. Plenty of people in Twelve Seas are willing to risk a sword point for 14,000 gurans.

Before battle can be fully joined, a carriage thunders into the street, flanked by a troop of soldiers. The door opens and Prefect Drinius steps out, elegant in his snow-white toga. He holds up his hand and the crowd goes quiet. Turai might have become a disorderly place in the past few years, but the sight of the local prefect is still enough to quieten the mob. Drinius looks around him quite disdainfully, then starts to lecture the crowd. He isn't a bad speaker. Quite an effective orator in fact, given his total lack of talent at any other aspect of his job. Even the most useless of our senatorial aristocrats can often speak well in public. They learn the art at school, and later from private tutors. A man can't succeed in politics in Turai unless he has some skill as an orator.

The prefect castigates the crowd for their disorderly behaviour. He points out that at a time of crisis in the city, every man should be at his post, doing his duty, rather than scrabbling around for gold. He points out a few examples of heroic behaviour from Turai's glorious past. Then he reminds them all of the sacrilegious act they're about to commit, excavating under a statue of our city's patron saint.

"Nothing could ensure the downfall of the city more quickly than this profane act," he thunders.

By now the crowd have quietened. Drinius softens his tone, and assures everyone that if they all go home now, the riot will be forgotten about. Besides, he says, there isn't any gold under the statue.

"I too have heard these rumours. I don't believe a word of them. There is no gold in Twelve Seas. And if there were, it wouldn't be under this fountain. I was here when the Consul himself laid the first stone in its foundations. I witnessed its construction, as did many of you. It rests on good Turanian earth, not a mythical chest of gold."

Looking at the fountain, he has a point. It's a hefty piece of stonework. I don't really see how a lone sea captain could have buried anything under it. Makri thinks the same.

"At least you weren't the only one with such a ridiculous notion," she says.

Drinius brings his speech to an end. The crowd, by now thoroughly abashed, begin to drift off. It's a job well done by our prefect.

"It's strange how a man in a toga can still win over the masses," says Makri.

As we leave the street, soldiers are already starting to cordon it off. A gang of workers make their way in, with picks and shovels.

"What's going on?" asks Makri.

"Now Drinius has cleared the rabble out of the way, he's going to have a good look under the fountain himself, of course. You can't expect the local prefect to miss out on a treasure hunt. I doubt there's anything there, though. One man in a hurry couldn't bury anything under that fountain."

"Any more ideas?"

I admit I haven't.

"I thought the whale fountain was a breakthrough. I was wrong. I'm just going to have to go into the card game short of funds and hope for the best."

"You don't sound very confident," says Makri.

"I'm not feeling very confident."

"Why not?"

I shrug.

"Who knows? The war. The malady. My continual lack of success at everything."

Makri bats me quite a hard blow on the shoulder.

"Is this Thraxas I'm talking to? Fighter, gambler, drinker, and all-round notorious braggart? Get a hold of yourself. I'm expecting you to sit down at that card table and make them weep. So Glixius is rich? So Praetor Capatius owns his own bank? So what? Who's the best rak player? You or them?"

"Me."

"Exactly. So just get in there and give them hell. Did I ever tell you about the time I was faced with eight Orcs and two trolls in the arena and my sword broke?"

She has actually, but I don't interrupt.

"You didn't catch me complaining," continues Makri. "I didn't start wondering if I was any good. I just killed the nearest Orc with my bare hands, took his sword and got on with business as usual. I set a new record for multiple slaughter."

"They had records?"

"Of course," says Makri. "I was champion in every category. I'm expecting you to be down like a bad spell on your opponents tonight no matter what the odds."

We walk on towards the tavern. I am slightly cheered by Makri's encouragement. Not that she understand the intricacies of playing rak, of course, but even so, she has a point. It's not like me to become discouraged.

"You're damn right, Makri. I don't know what I was thinking. I'm going to give them hell. Nothing will get in my way."

We walk up the steps to my office. My outside door is open. I frown, and hurry inside. Standing there quite calmly is Horm the Dead, one of the most powerful Sorcerers in the world and a deadly enemy of Turai.

"I suppose this could be a problem," I say, and draw my sword.

Chapter Seventeen

In the past few years my office has hosted some interesting gatherings. Sorcerers, senators, thieves, murderers, Assassins, demagogues, Orcs, Elves and a few you couldn't really put a name to have all passed through my door. Even royalty. Princess Du-Akai was once a client of mine. However, I'd say that the present gathering matches anything in terms of the diversity of characters involved. We have, in the middle of the floor, Horm the Dead, Orcish Sorcerer and Lord of the Kingdom of Yal. Once seen flying over Turai on a dragon, trying to destroy the city with a malevolent spell, and almost succeeding. He's caused a lot of trouble for Turai, and the fact that last time he was here he sent Makri some flowers hasn't endeared him in any way.

On the couch is Hanama, Assassin, cold, ruthless, previously sick but now looking somewhat better. She brought Makri flowers too, an occurrence so strange I don't really want to think about it.

At the door to the bedroom stands Coranius the Grinder, as grim and short-tempered a Sorcerer as Turai can boast, which is saying something. Behind him is Tirini Snake Smiter, still glamorous, and behind her is Anumaris Thunderbolt, looking young, keen, but possibly glad that the others are between her and Horm.

Samanatius the philosopher is standing next to my desk, grey-haired, some way past middle-aged, but very upright. As if the assembly wasn't splendid enough, Deputy Consul Cicerius and his assistant Hansius thunder up the steps and in through the door, followed by two armed guards. When the guards see Horm they fling themselves in front of the Deputy Consul to protect him. Horm the Dead greets them all courteously.

"You received my message?"

Cicerius nods, but remains silent. He's slightly out of breath, due to thundering up the stairs, which he doesn't really have the constitution for. There's a long pause.

"I don't suppose it's any use telling you to get the hell out of my office?" I say.

"Ah, Thraxas. We do seem to meet often, don't we?"

"Your doing entirely. You just can't keep away."

"Really?" Horm looks thoughtful. "Perhaps you're right."

Horm wears a shiny black cloak. He has long dark hair tumbling down quite dramatically over his features, which are remarkably pale for a half-Orc. So pale that they lend credence to the common belief that he actually died and then came back to life in a ritual to increase his powers. Whether that's true or not, he certainly has a great deal of power. The city has fended him off so far but it says a lot for his strength that he's once more been able to walk undetected through Turai. He has a rather languid manner, as if bored by everything he encounters, but I know it's an affectation. Whatever brings him here, it's not boredom.

"I've been observing your investigations. If you don't mind me saying so, I'm rather disappointed."

"What?"

"I think you're losing your touch," says Horm. "I remember how you frustrated my best efforts in the matter of the Green Jewel. And once before, when you interfered with my transactions with Prince Frisen-Akan. How is the prince these days?"

There's an angry silence, tinged with embarrassment. No one likes to hear the heir to the throne of Turai mocked by an Orc. Unfortunately, it's hard to defend him. Although the matter was never made public, our prince did at one time have dealings with Horm, and everyone in this room is probably aware of the humiliating circumstances.

"And yet on this occasion you seem to have failed completely, Investigator. The Ocean Storm has eluded you. After it disappeared from the house of Borinbax you never came close to locating it. And as for the gold you seek, you're flailing around in the dark. It's interesting."

"Why is it interesting?" barks Cicerius. "And why are you here? Answer me before I instruct Coranius to eject you."

Horm looks slightly surprised.

"Eject me? Before listening to my offer? That would be rather foolish, would it not?"

He bows politely to Coranius. Coranius doesn't return the greeting. Horm transfers his attention back to me. Makri is standing at my side, waiting to pounce. She wears a spell protection charm, similar to mine. They're effective, but not necessarily against the sort of magic which Horm can produce.

"Why is Thraxas's lack of progress interesting? For no real reason, perhaps. The Investigator is not a man whose affairs will ever be of great concern to anyone. He possesses no great intelligence or perception. But I have noticed in the past that his dogged persistence does produce results. Though his adversaries are invariably superior to him in terms of intellect, he does tend to catch up with them eventually. I wonder if his failure on this occasion might point to a deeper malaise within your city? Nothing is going well for you now, either great or small. Your time has come. Prince Amrag will soon sweep you away."

There's some movement at the bedroom door. Lisutaris, Mistress of the Sky, has finally risen from her sick bed. I'd like to say she's looking her usual regal and impressive self but I'd be lying. She's pale, dishevelled and tired. Just like a woman who's not yet got over a serious illness.

"No one is sweeping us away," she says.

"Ah. The Mistress of the Sky." Horm bows quite extravagantly. "I am delighted to see you making a recovery. As I observed your illness, I felt for you. The malady can be very severe."

If Lisutaris is disturbed to learn that Horm has been observing her illness, all the while remaining undetected himself, she doesn't show it.

"It can indeed. But I'm well enough to see you off. Which I will, this moment, unless you can give me a good reason not to."

"Indeed," snaps Cicerius. "What brings you here?"

"This," says Horm, and, apparently from thin air, he produces a large conch shell.

"What's that?"

Horm looks disappointed.

"You don't recognise it? Why, it's the Ocean Storm, of course. With this in our possession, the Orcish Sorcerers can break down your sea wall and allow Prince Amrag's fleet to sail in."

"Amrag doesn't have a fleet within a hundred miles of Turai," says Lisutaris.

"So you would like to believe," says Horm.

He holds up his hand.

"Please, Coranius, desist. I perceive that you are about to attempt the sorcerous theft of the Ocean Storm. I assure you, it won't work. I have placed one of my own spells on it. If any sorcery comes near it, it will instantly disappear and be transmitted through the magic space into the hands of Prince Amrag's own Sorcerer, Azlax. Once that happens, you won't see it again until your walls are tumbling down."

Coranius glances at Lisutaris. Lisutaris frowns, and says nothing, probably a sign that she believes Horm to be telling the truth.

"How did you get hold of it?" asks Lisutaris.

"I tracked it from the moment it arrived in Turai. It went through various criminal hands, and eluded me for a while. I was up against some rather sharp minds. However, I eventually found it in the house of one Borinbax, and removed it just before a certain criminal you may have encountered before could do so. I understand she was moved to kill Borinbax for being careless enough to lose it."

"So why have you brought it here?" demands Cicerius.

"To make a bargain, of course."

"We don't bargain with Orcs," says Cicerius.

Horm raises his eyebrows.

"Really? I seem to remember you did exactly that when you allowed Lord Rezaz to enter a chariot in the Turai Memorial Race. It suited both your interests at the time."

He turns to Makri.

"You remember the occasion, of course. You benefited hugely at the races."

Makri narrows her eyes. It's true. She won a lot of money but it's not something she'd want bandied around by the likes of Horm, particularly as her success relied on some gross cheating by the Association of Gentlewomen, aided by Melus the Fair, resident Sorcerer at the Stadium Superbius.

"I didn't really win that much," says Makri, and manages to sound so guilty that all eyes turn towards her.

"Not enough to make a large donation to the Association of Gentlewomen anyway," continues Makri. "Even if I'd wanted to."

She pauses, and looks flustered.

"The Association of Gentlewomen did not cheat at the races. And Melus the Fair is not a secret supporter. It's an outrageous accusation."

"Have I offended you?" says Horm. "I apologise. I regarded your success at the racetrack as merely another example of your excellence in every field. Really, Makri, you are such a remarkable person. The finest sword-fighter in the land, the cleverest student in the city, and the most beautiful woman in the east or west."

He pauses. A slight smile plays across his face.

"Yet here you are, still employed as a barmaid in a cheap tavern, surrounded by imbeciles of the lowest order. Why not admit it? Turai will never recognise your talents."

"Did you bring me here to discuss Makri's talents?" says Cicerius, angrily.

"Yes," says Horm. "I did. And to propose a bargain. Or rather, a sporting venture. Tonight Thraxas will be engaged in a card game, playing some opponents who have the reputation of being the finest gamblers in the city. Thraxas has frustrated me in the past, and I would enjoy the opportunity to best him at one of his favourite pursuits."

It's my turn to sneer. I'm not about to sit down and play cards with an Orc who walks into my office uninvited and insults my intelligence in front of everyone.

"Why would we let you play? It's Humans only. Orcs not welcome."

"You see?" says Horm, once more turning to Makri. "You see how they hate the Orcish blood? You don't belong here."

"Yes she does," says Samanatius, speaking for the first time. "Makri will always be welcome in this city."

"Welcomed by you perhaps, philosopher," replies Horm, in a tone that's a good deal more respectful than the one he used towards me. "But you are a man of uncommon wisdom and civilisation. As for the others . . . Is the Deputy Consul really comfortable being in the same room as a woman with Orcish blood? Did he protest when she was banned from accompanying Lisutaris to the Palace? How about you, Lisutaris? Did you argue on her behalf?"

"We're at war," snaps Lisutaris. "There wasn't time to argue."

"Of course not. You're pleased to have the protection of her fighting skills. But it's a different matter when it comes to mixing in polite society. I imagine that Makri has encountered very little of polite society during her employment with you."

Lisutaris, Mistress of the Sky flushes slightly. Whether because of her illness, or because Horm has struck a nerve, I'm not sure.

"Well she's quite welcome here," I growl. "And you still haven't told us why I should let you join in our card game tonight."

Horm holds up the Ocean Storm.

"Because if you can beat me at the card table, Investigator, I'll hand this over to the city."

There's a pause while this sinks in.

"Which will give Turai some chance of survival," he adds.

"And what if he doesn't beat you at the card table?" says Cicerius. "What then?"

"Then Makri returns with me to the kingdom of Yal as my wife."

I doubt if Deputy Consul Cicerius has ever been lost for words before. He is now. He looks from Horm to Makri and back again. Coranius and Lisutaris do the same. I'm attempting to formulate a withering reply, but Samanatius beats me to it.

"Out of the question, Horm," he says. "Makri is not some chattel to be traded at your whim."

That's not quite as withering as I'd have liked, but it gets the conversation going.

"Abandon the notion, Horm," says Lisutaris. "You're not gambling for my bodyguard."

"He's completely insane," I yell. "Lisutaris, Coranius. Work some spell on him so I can throw him down the stairs."

Horm looks round at us.

"I don't believe any of you have the authority to make decisions on behalf of your city. Which is why I asked the Deputy Consul here. Well, Cicerius?"

Cicerius hesitates. To give him his due, he doesn't hesitate for that long.

"I refuse to consider it, Horm. A person cannot be traded as goods in this city. It's against the law."

"I understood that in time of national emergency, the laws could be superseded by the King? And if he was not in a fit state to rule, by the Consul? As your consul is unfortunately not in a fit state either, that power has devolved on to you."

Cicerius looks rather offended.

"I am not in the habit of making up laws to suit my own convenience," he says, sharply. "Not without a discussion and vote in the senate."

Coranius hasn't spoken up till now. He takes a step forward.

"It's not such a bad bargain for the city."

"Really Coranius," protests Lisutaris. She looks at him angrily, but Coranius is too senior a Sorcerer to be quelled by a look, even from the head of the Guild.

"Well it's not. We have here an item that may seriously harm Turai. We seem to have no other way of retrieving it other than Thraxas winning it at cards. So why not agree to the bargain?"

"Because it means gambling away a person's liberty, that's why not."

Coranius shrugs.

"One person is of little account compared to the welfare of the city."

"Coranius, this is outrageous. I refuse to discuss it."

"We have to discuss it."

Cicerius and Samanatius join in. Coranius stands his ground, and there's soon a heated argument raging around the room.

"Who knows?" says Tirini. "Makri might like being Queen of Yal. It has to be better than this tavern. Do you know, they have no servants to clean their rooms?"

"Can't you do something to circumvent this, Lisutaris?" demands Cicerius.

"Like what?"

"Use your sorcery, of course. There are four Turanian Sorcerers in this room. Simply remove the Ocean Storm from Horm's grasp."

Lisutaris shakes her head.

"No. He's telling the truth. It would immediately disappear into the magic space and end up with Prince Amrag."

"Then we have to agree to play cards for it," says Coranius.

Cicerius wavers slightly.

"I believe Thraxas does have a certain skill . . ."

"I refuse to countenance it," roars Lisutaris, then coughs mightily and looks unwell.

There's a pause in the discussion.

"Perhaps," says Horm the Dead, "we should ask Makri what she thinks?"

"Excellent idea," says Makri, quite briskly.

She turns to face the Deputy Consul.

"I'll do it if you let me into the Imperial University."

"What?"

"I'll put myself up for the stake if you allow me to enter the university. I'm qualifying as top student from the Guild College. It's enough to gain admission to the university. But they don't let women in. Or anyone with Orcish blood. If you promise to waive the rules, I'll do it."

"Don't be insane, Makri." says Lisutaris. "If Thraxas loses, you'll have to marry Horm."

"Thraxas is good at rak."

"Not that good, from what I hear."

"I'm number one chariot at rak," I protest. "Not that I agree to the bargain."

"But I do agree," insists Makri. "If I can go to the university."

All eyes turn to Deputy Consul Cicerius.

"It would require a change in the constitution of the Imperial University. Which would require a discussion in the senate."

He pauses, and looks troubled.

"I believe I could see it through the senate . . ."

"Then I accept," says Makri. "Thraxas, go and win the Ocean Storm."

"I don't want to do it," I say.

"Why not?"

"I don't want to play with you as the stake."

"Aren't you Turai's greatest rak player?" says Makri.

"As opposed to Turai's greatest braggart," mutters Coranius.

I draw myself up to my full height, which still leaves me a few inches short of Horm.

"I am both Turai's greatest rak player and Turai's greatest braggart. Unfortunately, I'm not Turai's richest man. It's going to be tough to compete against these rich senators. And what about Horm? How much money has he got?"

Horm draws a purse from the depths of his cloak. It's a very intricate little item, black leather with silver stitching. Though Horm is dressed entirely in black, I notice that a lot of the small details in his outfit are quite fancy. Silver stitching on his purse, a well-constructed necklace of shining black stones strung with silver, small earrings made from dragon scales, and some very elaborate inlaid silver on his scabbard. He's a half-Orc who cares about the details.

"I have one thousand gurans to hand," he says.

I turn to Cicerius.

"Well that's that," I say. "I've only got four hundred and forty. You can't send me in with a handicap like that. I need a thousand as well. You have to bring me up to his level."

Cicerius glowers at me.

"I can arrange for the money," he mutters.

"Then I accept the challenge. Horm, prepare to lose the Ocean Storm, your money, and anything else valuable you might have on you. I'm going to make you regret you ever came to this city."

"I always regret it," replies Horm. "But this time, perhaps not."

Chapter Eighteen

Gurd is still ill, and the news about the card game doesn't make him feel any better.

"Makri's the stake? That's a terrible risk."

"I wouldn't say that. I'll chase Horm from the table and everyone else as well. By tomorrow morning I'll probably be the richest man in Turai. *And* we'll have the Ocean Storm. I'll have saved the city. You think they might put up a statue of me?"

Gurd doesn't share my enthusiasm. Probably because he's too sick.

"What about the dolphins?"

This makes me frown. The winter malady can bring on some dementia, but even so, you don't like to hear a sensible man like Gurd talking about dolphins.

"What about them?"

"Dandelion. When she brought me medicine. She said the dolphins said the Orcs were already in my tavern."

"They were talking about Horm. Samanatius and Lisutaris have already discussed it."

"Samanatius? The philosopher?"

"The same. Apparently he's a repository of knowledge on the subject. No surprise really. Anyone foolish enough to teach philosophy in Twelve Seas might as well spend his time talking to dolphins. God knows why Lisutaris was wasting her time with him. Anyway, it's out in the open now. Horm's probably been popping in and out regularly while Lisutaris has been sick. He's good with his concealment spells, unfortunately."

There's a delicate knock on the door. Moolifi comes in, once more carrying a tray with medicine. Gurd struggles to raise himself in his bed. I help him up, and he puts the beaker to his lips. He thanks her, in his polite Barbarian way, and she departs.

"She's been a help," he whispers. "I wouldn't have expected her to."

"Me neither. Fancy singer that she is. Didn't expect to see her slinging herbal potions to the masses. Maybe she's taken a shine to us all since hooking up with old Rallee."

Gurd grins.

"Rallee. How often did we all fight together?"

"Plenty of times."

Gurd lies back down.

"We'll do it again. When I'm better."

"We will. The Orcs will be sorry they showed their faces. You don't take on Thraxas, Gurd and Rallee without regretting it quickly enough."

Gurd suddenly frowns.

"This game tonight. With Horm. Don't lose Makri. And don't let anything happen to the tavern."

"I won't."

I leave Gurd to sleep. Upstairs my office is still full of people. Sitting around my desk are Cicerius, Hansius, Lisutaris, Coranius, Tirini, Anumaris, Hanama, Makri, and Samanatius. Lisutaris still has a blanket draped round her shoulders, though Hanama appears to be well on the way to recovery. A hearty fire is burning in the hearth. There's a bottle on the table and each of them has a small silver cup in front of them.

"Thraxas. Join us for a drink."

I stare at the bottle suspiciously.

"The Abbot's Special Distillation? Makri, have you been stealing drink from my supply?"

"Certainly not," declares Makri. "Although as I'm about to be gambled away as bride of Horm, I wouldn't have thought you'd begrudge me it."

"I took it," says Lisutaris. "You should know it's no use trying to hide alcohol from a Turanian Sorcerer. We were just about to drink to your success tonight."

"Really?" I feel quite flattered. It's not every day the Deputy Consul drinks to my success.

The inside door opens, revealing Captain Rallee and Moolifi.

"Moolifi told me what's going on. You're gambling with Makri?"

"Yes," says Cicerius. "We're drinking to Thraxas's good fortune."

The Captain walks over and parks himself at the desk, squeezing himself and Moolifi in at the corner.

"He'll need it. There's a lot of good players coming here tonight."

It's true, there are. I'm expecting to vanquish them all, but in terms of my bargain with Horm, I don't need to. I just need to beat him. Whichever one of us lasts longest at the table wins our bet. It's quite possible that after I've taken all Horm's money, forcing him out of the game, I could then lose to Praetor Capatius, or General Acarius, but even if that happens, it won't affect the deal regarding Makri and the Ocean Storm.

Captain Rallee raises his glass.

"Good luck," he says, and we drink.

"I'm still working on some way to get the Ocean Storm out of Horm's hands," says Lisutaris. "He's got a lot of magic protecting it, but I'm sure we can come up with something."

"So try not to lose too quickly," says Coranius.

"I'm not going to lose at all."

I brandish my illuminated staff.

"You see this? I won it from an Elf lord, on a boat in the middle of the ocean while I was sharing a cabin with Makri. About as stressful a situation as a man could face, and I still came out on top."

At that moment Dandelion arrives, with potion. She's concerned to find Lisutaris and Hanama drinking klee.

"Stop fussing," says Lisutaris. "We're getting better. But thanks for looking after us."

"Indeed," says Hanama. "Thank you."

I'm quite startled to hear the Assassin saying thanks. Maybe the bout of the malady has brought her a little humility. No bad thing, though she'll probably be back to killing people in a day or two.

The door bursts open again. There was a time when my office was a private place. Now it's busier than the senate. It's Sarin the Merciless. She's not looking healthy, and she's not displaying any humility either, though at least she's not pointing a crossbow at anyone.

"What's this I hear about Thraxas playing cards with Horm for the Ocean Storm?" she demands.

"I'm about to win it for the city," I reply.

"It's not Horm's to gamble," says Sarin. "He took it from me."

I shake my head. The woman is still crazy from the malady. She's faced with the city's Deputy Consul, the head of the Sorcerers Guild, and a captain of the Guards, and she's trying to insist on her rights to a stolen item.

"The Ocean Storm is nothing to do with you," says Cicerius. "You should concern yourself with your defence in court. As soon as the malady passes I'm taking you into custody."

"I'll kill Horm," says Sarin. "And you. And anyone else who tries to rob me."

She shivers, and looks unsteady on her feet.

"It's time for your medicine," says Dandelion, brightly.

"Damn your medicine," says Sarin, and spins on her heel, marching out of the room.

I suggest to Cicerius that he might take Sarin into custody now.

"She can't leave the tavern," replies the Deputy Consul. "It's ringed with my men. We'll take her away tomorrow, if she's fully recovered."

"You really believe in this hospitality-to-sick-guests thing, don't you?"

"Of course," says Cicerius. "It's one of our oldest traditions. Our city is founded on its traditions."

"Even if those traditions are foolish?"

"None of them are foolish," counters the Deputy Consul.

Immediately a discussion starts up about the value of traditions in the life of the city. Lisutaris and Samanatius weigh in, as does Coranius. Everyone seems to have an opinion apart from Tirini Snake Smiter, who looks bored, and busies herself in front of a small mirror. Makri wades into the conversation, arguing quite spiritedly with Samanatius over some point of history. Samanatius listens, then counters her argument. Lisutaris puts forward a different point of view and Cicerius tells them they're all wrong. In no time at all facts and opinions are flying round the table covering everything from the traditions of hospitality in far-away Samsarina to the ancient ethics of the Orcish warrior class.

I'm not much of a man for these sort of discussions. I fill up my glass with the Abbot's excellent klee, drain the glass, then head downstairs, ready to play cards.

Chapter Nineteen

I'm sitting at the largest table in the tavern. Young Ravenius is on my left and General Acarius is on my right. Next to him is Praetor Capatius and then Casax, the Brotherhood boss. Directly across from me is Glixius Dragon Killer. Beside him is old Grax the wine merchant. There's an empty seat between Grax and Ravenius.

The front door of the tavern is closed. The public isn't being admitted. Cicerius has decided that with so much at stake, and Horm on the premises, it would be best to keep everyone away.

If the rich card players find it peculiar to be playing in humble Twelve Seas, they haven't said so. Rather, they seem grateful to have the opportunity to gamble. General

Acarius is quite effusive in his thanks. Since their friend Senator Kevarius had to close his house because of the malady, they've been searching for a good game, and if it means traipsing down to the poor part of town, they don't mind too much. Even Praetor Capatius isn't too objectionable. Like much of the senatorial class, he's very conscious of his status, but the prospect of an evening's gambling goes some way to making him forget about it. Indeed, with the people currently in the tavern, Capatius, Acarius and Glixius aren't as out of place as they might normally be. Some faces here are very well known to them. Deputy Consul Cicerius for one, who outranks everyone, and Lisutaris, one of our city's most famous residents. As for Grax the wine merchant, as a member of the Honourable Merchants Association, he's not unfamiliar with the city's aristocracy. He's a very wealthy man, and he's played with Acarius before. There's a good deal of surprised recognition and greetings when they all arrive. The Praetor wonders what the Deputy Consul is doing here, but Cicerius diverts the question.

Lisutaris, Coranius the Grinder, Tirini Snake Smiter and Anumaris Thunderbolt have all remained to watch the game. No surprise, given who's also due to attend. If it turns out that Horm the Dead is hatching some evil plot as yet unknown to us, the four Turanian Sorcerers should be able to take care of him. The Avenging Axe is now one of the best-protected buildings in the city. The whole area from here to the harbour is crammed full of soldiers and Sorcerers. If Prince Amrag is planning on sailing in tonight he's not going to find us unprepared.

Captain Rallee would normally play, but he's declared the stakes too rich for him, and is here merely to observe. The Captain puts a brave face on it but I know he'd rather be taking part in the game than sitting with Moolifi, no matter how much he likes her.

Karlox takes a seat close to his boss Casax, while Hanama and Samanatius both sit quietly at the edge of the room, observing the proceedings. As for Glixius, he greets Lisutaris politely, but he's his usual glowering self as he takes his place at the table.

"Who's the empty chair for?" he asks.

I slip away towards the bar for a beer. Makri frowns as I approach.

"You've already drunk a lot of klee," she says. "You need to keep your wits about you."

"I had one small glass of klee."

"You had four. I was counting."

"Makri, did we get married without me noticing? Since when are you keeping track of how much I drink?"

"Since I became the stake in your card game," says Makri.

I'm gripped by a moment of doubt.

"Do you want to back out? There's still time. I don't much like this."

"You seemed keen enough upstairs," says Makri.

"I got carried away when Cicerius offered me more money."

Makri laughs. I'm not feeling much like laughing myself. I've never sat down at a card table before without confidently expecting to win. But I was never gambling over a person's future before.

"What if Horm wins?"

"Then I'll be a fantastic Orc bride," says Makri. "And captain of the armies. You might see me outside the city walls one day, leading a phalanx."

"It's not funny. Tell Cicerius you've changed your mind. To hell with Horm. Let him keep the Ocean Storm. We'll beat the Orcs anyway."

Makri shakes her head.

"We won't. We'll all die. Anyway, this way I get to go to the university."

"We could think of another plan. You can get to the university some other way."

Makri raises her eyebrows.

"Haven't you spent the last three years telling me I have no chance whatsoever?"

"Yes. And now I've changed my mind. I don't want to play with you as the stake."

"Are you losing confidence again?" says Makri. "What's the matter with you? Just get in there and give them hell."

Makri pours me a beer and hands it over.

"Get confident."

Makri's dressed in her standard serving-wench attire, her chainmail bikini. It's still an impressive sight. Men look at her with lust and I'm sure I saw Tirini glaring at her physique jealously as she passed by. I drink the beer down in one gulp and hold out the tankard for another.

"I told you to get confident," says Makri. "Not hopelessly drunk."

"I'm a long way from hopelessly drunk."

"A glass of klee, please."

I recognise the voice. It's Horm, who's arrived as silently and mysteriously as ever. The collar of his cloak is raised, preventing anyone behind from recognising him.

Makri pauses briefly, then pours him a glass of klee. She holds out her hand for the money. Horm smiles, and drops a coin into her palm. The sight irritates me.

"Does Prince Amrag know you're gambling with the Ocean Storm?" I ask.

"Prince Amrag is no concern of yours," replies Horm.

"You're going to be in trouble when he finds out."

Horm raises an eyebrow.

"If you're trying to unsettle me before our game, you're wasting your time."

He smiles at Makri.

"My mountain kingdom is a wild and beautiful place. It will suit you perfectly."

Makri glares at him, and remains silent.

"She's never going to go there," I say. "I doubt you will either. Amrag will have you killed once he knows what you've been up to."

"Who is to tell him?"

Good point. I'm stuck for an answer.

"How about Deeziz the Unseen?"

"What? Deeziz? Deeziz is hundreds of miles away."

"Maybe not. I've an idea he might be close by."

For the briefest of moments, an expression of concern flickers over Horm's face.

"Absolute nonsense, Investigator. Deeziz the Unseen is not in Turai."

"Well you better hope you're right. Because if he tells Amrag what you've been up to, he'll be down on you like a bad spell and you can say goodbye to your mountain kingdom."

I'm pleased to have unsettled Horm. It's no bad thing to discomfort your opponent before you sit down at the card table. I'm working up a few more insults when we're interrupted by a lot of raised voices.

"Deputy Consul, surely you cannot be serious! Horm the Dead coming here? To play cards?"

It's Praetor Capatius. He's just heard the news and he's not pleased. General Acarius joins in, declaring that he's deeply shocked.

"What is the reason for this?" demands the General.

Cicerius won't say. He simply informs the gathering that it's for important reasons of state. It's part of our bargain with Horm that the other players mustn't know what's going on. Otherwise Horm might suspect that they were ganging up on him. It's reasonable. In his position, I'd have expected the same.

"This is intolerable," cries Capatius. "No decent man could put up with the company of that foul Orc."

"Why look," cries Glixius. "There he is now, standing beside Thraxas."

Every eye turns towards us. I take a hasty step to the side.

"Thraxas has bought him a glass of klee!" cries Praetor Capatius. "Cicerius, is the Investigator blackmailing you somehow? Tell us the truth and we'll throw him from the city walls."

"Silence," barks Cicerius. "Horm the Dead is not blackmailing me. I have allowed him to play for reasons which I cannot explain. Suffice to say it is important for the welfare of the city."

There are a lot of angry and suspicious looks as I walk towards the card table, followed all too closely by Horm.

"Are you telling us that Horm's presence has nothing to do with Thraxas?" demands Glixius.

Cicerius is slightly troubled. He hesitates, and naturally everyone notices. By the time I reach the card table it's firmly fixed in every mind that I've brought Horm the Dead to the Avenging Axe for reasons of my own, no doubt as the first part of a traitorous attempt to sell out the city.

I can sense the Sorcerers at the nearby table expending all their energies in checking around them for unexpected Orcish sorcery, probing the air for spells, and all the while wondering if there is some way of removing the Ocean Storm from Horm. Horm no doubt senses it too, but remains calm. He greets everyone at the table quite politely, and sits in the vacant chair.

"Are we ready to begin?" he asks.

There's a long pause, and a few uneasy expressions around the table. Finally General Acarius speaks.

"Who is dealing the cards?"

We don't have a designated dealer at our games at the Axe.

"We usually just deal ourselves," says Grax.

"I think a dealer might be better, in the circumstances," says the General.

"I assure you, I have no intention of cheating," says Horm, smoothly.

"I wasn't referring to you," growls the General, and looks straight in my direction.

"Yes," says Glixius, also looking in my direction. "A dealer might be better. There are some players whom one can never trust not to manipulate the cards in their favour."

"Are you calling me a cheat!" I roar, rising to my feet.

"I wouldn't dream of it," says Glixius. "Although it has struck me as odd before now how every time Horm the Dead troubles our city, you're involved in it somehow."

"Gentlemen, stop this," roars Cicerius. "The game must proceed. Try and act like civilised Turanians. Glixius, I assure you that Thraxas's continual involvement with Horm the Dead is nothing more than coincidence."

There seem to be a lot of eyes turned in my direction. I get the impression they're judging how many men it will take to throw me from the city walls. Quite a few, probably, though I have lost a pound or two since the yam shortage began.

"Who will deal?" says Cicerius, looking round.

Moolifi rises to her feet.

"I'll do it," she says. "I've dealt a lot of cards in my time."

I doubt if the music-hall singer would be Cicerius's first choice, but he's keen to get things underway. He nods, and asks if anyone has any objections. No one has, so Moolifi takes a seat at the table and picks up the cards. We're finally ready to play.

Chapter Twenty

There are several varieties of rak. Tonight we're playing palace rak, with the standard pack of forty-eight cards. Four suits, black, red, green and blue, cards numbered 1 to 8 followed by bishop, queen, king and dragon. Two cards are dealt to each player and if you like what you've got you make a bet. You get dealt another card and you can bet again. When your fourth and last card is dealt, if you still like what you've got, you can keep on betting. The highest hand you can have is four dragons. It doesn't happen that often.

The first two cards Moolifi deals me are a green three and a red eight. It's a poor start and I fold immediately. The next five hands are no better and I don't place a single bet. I'm not averse to bluffing when necessary, in fact I'm a master of the art, but I generally don't like to do it too soon.

There isn't a lot of action from anyone in the early hands. Everyone is treading cautiously. There's a long way to go and no one wants to find themselves financially crippled after only a few rounds. I sip my beer and study my opponents, looking, as always, for some telltale signs that might give me a clue as to their play.

Moolifi deals the cards quickly and skilfully. She seems to have dressed up a little for the occasion. She's wearing a long dress of dark red material, quite eyecatching in its way. It leaves her arms bare and I notice that though her limbs are slender, she's quite taut and muscled, rather like Makri. She's not soft, Moolifi. I'd guess she can take care of herself. As she deals out the next hand we're suddenly interrupted by a fit of coughing. Old Grax the wine merchant splutters violently then slumps in his chair, perspiration running down his forehead. Praetor Capatius, sitting next to him, draws himself back quite suddenly.

"He's got the malady!"

I'm already on my feet.

"No need to panic," I say. "There's a lot of it around."

I help Grax out of his chair. Makri comes to assist and we carry him back to the store room behind the bar, while Dandelion looks on with concern.

"You have more medicine?"

Dandelion nods. We're so used to this now that we take it in our stride. Grax is a tough old customer. A few days' rest and a good dose of the medicine and I've no doubt he'll be back on his feet.

Before I return to the table I draw Makri to one side and whisper in her ear.

"Moolifi is not quite what she says she is."

"What?"

"There's something not right about her. I don't believe a Niojan chorus girl would be so good with a pack of cards."

Makri looks puzzled.

"Why not?"

"Just a feeling. I wonder if she might be a Niojan spy."

"So what do you want to do?" says Makri.

"I don't know. Nothing, probably. I'm just mentioning it in case anything happens."

Makri nods, and I return to the table and retake my chair. There are a few polite enquiries over Grax's health.

"He'll be fine. There's a healer giving him some medicine right now."

No one is really that concerned. It would be unlucky to have a player actually die at the table, but apart from that, everyone is keen to get on with the game. Matters proceed quietly enough apart from a brief moment of excitement when Ravenius takes a large pot, beating Casax's three dragons with four sixes. Casax loses a lot on the hand but, like the cool gambler he is, he masks his disappointment.

So far Moolifi has dealt me nothing worth gambling on. It means I haven't made any serious losses but I haven't been able to get into the game either. I'm just starting to feel slightly twitchy when she sends me two queens in the first deal, giving me some hope that I might finally be on to something. When everyone has their first two cards, Glixius pushes thirty gurans into the centre of the table. The bet is covered by Ravenius. I slide thirty gurans across too. Acarius and Capatius do likewise. I sip my beer.

When the third card arrives it's another queen. I now have three queens and that's a good hand. I take a brief look at the archaically dressed ladies on the cards, put them back face down in front of me, and wait for Glixius to make his bet. He slides a hundred gurans across the table. I'm next to bet.

"I'll cover your hundred."

Ravenius considers for a few moments, then tosses his cards back to Moolifi, dropping out of the hand. General Acarius immediately folds as well. Praetor Capatius, however, confidently pushes forward his hundred gurans.

There's a lot of money riding on this hand and Horm isn't even involved. So far he hasn't made any sort of substantial wager. If I win this I'll go well ahead of him. If I lose, I'll be a long way behind.

When my next card arrives it's a nine. I'm disappointed, but three queens is still a good hand. It's Glixius to bet. He muses on his cards briefly, then counts out another hundred gurans and places it firmly in the middle of the table. A little too firmly, maybe. I get the impression he might be bluffing.

Ravenius shrugs. He hands his cards back to Moolifi, taking care not to let them turn over. Even when you're dropping out of a hand, you don't want your opponents to see what cards you were holding. It might give them some clues as to your strategy.

I can either call Glixius, or raise him further. I'm fairly confident I've got the hand won and I'd like to raise him but I'm aware that I don't have all that much room for error. Two hundred and thirty gurans is a hefty chunk out of my capital. I'd risk it for myself, but there's Makri to think of. I utter a silent curse. Now I'm having to think about Makri it's interfering with my normal aggressive style. I put in a hundred gurans and call Glixius, then lay down my three queens for all to see. Glixius turns over a run of 6, 7, 8, 9, all green. A straight flush which beats my three queens. And then he actually laughs, which is a very low-class thing to do at the card table.

"My game, I believe," he says, and scoops up his money like a man who's never seen a few hundred gurans before.

I'm seething inside though I don't let it show.

Cicerius approaches the table.

"Time for a break, gentlemen," he says. "There are refreshments at the bar."

General Acarius looks up sharply.

"Time for a break? We've hardly got started."

The Deputy Consul shoots him a serious look.

"It's time for a break."

Acarius shrugs, and the players rise from the table. I attempt to follow them to the bar but I'm immediately surrounded by a gaggle of concerned Turanian citizens, demanding to know what I'm doing throwing my money away in such a rash manner.

"You lost two hundred and thirty gurans in one hand!" hisses Cicerius. "It was far too adventurous. Have you forgotten what this game means to Turai?"

"I had three queens," I retort. "It was a reasonable gamble."

Cicerius snorts in derision, though I swear he doesn't know one end of a pack of cards from the other. Meanwhile Lisutaris has hobbled up, still with her blanket round her shoulders, and she doesn't waste any time expressing her concern.

"Thraxas! If you keep on like this you'll be out of the game in five minutes."

"I'm doing fine!" I insist. "Even the best card player gets the odd reverse. Look, Makri's got more at stake than anyone and she's not worried, is she?"

"She was burying her face in her hands the last time I looked," replies Lisutaris. "And I'm not surprised. Keep on the way you're going and we'll soon be buying her wedding presents."

"Could you try showing a little confidence in me?" I say trying to keep my voice somewhere below a bellow. "You can't expect me to play cards when you're on my back every five minutes."

Cicerius and Lisutaris both open their mouths. I'm guessing they're not about to express confidence in me, so I break free and head for the bar, where Makri is serving drinks.

"Nice going, Thraxas," she says. "So, will you visit me in Yal?"

"You're not going to Yal."

"I should probably start packing. How long do you think I've got? Half an hour maybe?"

"Just hand me a beer and save the sarcasm. Glixius got lucky. I'll get him next time."

"Horm's hardly bet a thing yet," says Makri. "If you keep losing he doesn't have to. He'll beat you by default."

"He won't beat me by anything. Give me the beer and stop worrying. I'm just warming up."

Hanama joins us at the bar, and I swear I've never seen the Assassin look so perturbed.

"I knew this was a foolish venture," she says. "I won't let Horm take you off to Yal, Makri. The instant Thraxas loses I'm breaking you out of here."

"I'm not going to lose."

"How long do you think we have?" asks Hanama. "I estimate half an hour."

I shake my head, and grab my beer.

"You shouldn't be drinking," says Hanama. "You need a clear head."

"Do I tell you how to assassinate people?"

"No. But I'm good at that."

Not wishing to bandy more words with irritating Assassins, I head back to the table, avoiding the eyes of those who are staring at me with a marked lack of confidence; which is to say, everyone in the tavern.

We're all about to take our seats again when there's a loud knocking at the front door. We'd ignore it, but someone shouts loudly for Casax. The Brotherhood boss sends Karlox to find out what's going on. Karlox draws back the bolt, disappears briefly outside, then comes back to whisper in Casax's ear.

"Damn," mutters Casax. "I'll have to leave you gentlemen for a short while. A little trouble back at the Mermaid. Karlox will sit in for me."

There are a few nods and grunts round the table. It's unusual for a player to leave the table mid-game, but not unheard of. Providing he has a friend who can take over his seat, it's common practice in Turai to let him rejoin the game when he returns. Casax hurries off and Karlox takes his seat. Casax is shrewd. Karlox is dumb. It's an excellent opportunity to remove some of the Brotherhood's ill-gotten money.

Unfortunately, it's not me who does the removing. Moolifi keeps dealing me dreadful cards and I can't get into the game. It's dispiriting, particularly as Horm the Dead suddenly makes a move, sucking the hapless Karlox into an unwise gamble on two eights and two dragons. Horm beats him with three bishops, and rakes in several hundred gurans. I curse. Horm has suddenly leapt ahead of me. I'm down to about 750 gurans, and I'd guess he's on around 1,500.

Casax returns fairly quickly, having sorted out whatever criminal problem he was faced with at his own tavern. If he's annoyed to see how much money Karlox has lost, he doesn't show it. He retakes his seat, picks up his cards, and carries on playing. By now we're deep into the night. The fire is crackling in the grate and the torches are burning brightly on the walls. The spectators keep their voices to low murmurs and the players huddle over their cards, deep in concentration. I lose another fifty gurans on a reckless bid which I don't follow through, and I start to curse Moolifi for the cards she's dealing me. Horm's pile of money seems to be growing steadily while mine is shrinking slowly. General Acarius is the other big winner, while young Ravenius is doing badly, as he often does.

Moolifi deals the next hand. She sends me a black dragon and a red dragon. Very promising. General Acarius puts in thirty gurans and I follow suit, along with several others. Before Moolifi can deal the third card, the General starts to cough, quite violently. Sweat pours down his face. Acarius has come down with the winter malady.

"Another one?" says Ravenius. "This is strange."

It is strange, and not conducive to concentrating on the game. I look over at Horm.

"Is this your doing? Are you making everyone sick so you can win?"

"Nothing to do with me," protests the Sorcerer.

We haul the General back into the store room, which is by now resembling a temporary hospital. Dandelion fusses around him with medicine, as brightly as she did her first patient. Personally I'm heartily sick of all invalids and wouldn't much care if they died, but Dandelion seems to have taken happily to the role of nurse, and will probably keep them all alive. Makri arrives to see if we need any help. Dandelion shakes her head.

"I can manage all the sick people."

Makri nods, and looks thoughtful.

"You're really good at this," she says.

"What?" says Dandelion.

"Looking after all these people. I'd have given up long ago. But you've got it all in hand. You're really efficient when you put your mind to it."

Dandelion looks surprised.

"Am I?"

I'm not arguing. Now Makri has pointed it out, it's obviously true. Dandelion might be strangely dressed and have a bizarre aversion to shoes, but there's no denying she's kept the place running during the winter malady crisis.

When the game is restarted my third card is a four, no help to my two dragons. Glixius raises the bet by a hundred gurans. It's something of a risk for me to go along with this but I do. I have a good feeling about my fourth card. I send up a brief prayer to St. Quatinius as Moolifi deals. My few moments of religious conviction have usually been at the card table.

My next card is an eight. I now have two dragons, an eight and a four. It's not a strong hand. Glixius raises another hundred gurans. I don't know if he's bluffing or not. I think about it for a while. I'd like to carry on betting, but if I do and I lose I'll be out of the game. My funds are already low. I could stand the humiliation of losing to Glixius but I've got more on my mind. I curse Horm and his ridiculous passion for Makri. It's ruining my game.

I shake my head, and hand in my cards, meanwhile sending up a strong protest to St. Quatinius for coming down on the side of the rich oppressors. Obviously all tales of the blessed saint helping the poor and needy are just lies.

Perhaps the saint is offended by my complaints. One hour and a series of bad cards later, I'm down to 300 gurans and things are not looking good.

Praetor Capatius wonders out loud if there's any food on offer. The praetor is a man with a healthy appetite and probably gets well fed when he's playing cards up at Senator Kevarius's house. Dandelion informs everyone that our temporary cook has just finishing preparing the famous **Avenging Axe** stew, and while Capatius isn't exactly enthralled at the prospect—being used to better things, no doubt—he's willing to try it. Cicerius takes the opportunity to suggest that all the players take another break to refresh themselves. Some head for the bar for food and drink and some wait at the table, probably annoyed at the interruption. As for me, the moment I leave the table I'm besieged by an angry mob.

"What the hell are you doing?" demands Lisutaris. "Do you want Makri to get carted off to Yal?"

"Have you forgotten how important this game is?" demands Cicerius. "I've never seen anyone throw their money away in such a wanton manner."

"How did you get a reputation as a good card player?" says Hanama. "It seems to be completely undeserved."

"A good card player?" sneers Coranius. "We might as well hand the Ocean Storm over to the Orcs and have done with it."

Lisutaris hasn't yet come up with any sort of spell for removing the Ocean Storm from Horm's grasp.

"You were meant to be buying me some time, not surrendering at the first opportunity," she says, quite angrily.

I hold my hands up.

"Will you all get out of my face? I'm doing my best."

"Your best?" says Lisutaris. "Is that why you're almost broke and Horm is piling up the money?"

"I've been unlucky with the cards. Are you sure that woman Moolifi is on the level? I think there's something odd about her."

"The only odd thing is that we have entrusted you with the welfare of Turai," says Cicerius. "I blame myself. I've failed the city."

Makri walks past with a tray of beer.

"Take two," she says to me. "You might as well enjoy yourself. Be sure to visit me in Yal."

"You're not going to Yal. I'm just getting into my stride."

I've rarely seen so many people looking unconvinced. At this moment, belief in Thraxas's gambling powers has hit an all-time low among the leading citizens of Turai.

Even the perennially cheerful Dandelion can't help frowning as she ladles out a bowl of stew.

"Please don't make Makri marry Horm the Dead," she says.

"Makri is not going to marry anyone," I declare, quite forcefully.

"Makri, you have to flee," says Hanama. "Get your swords and we'll fight our way out."

I notice some unfamiliar objects lurking on top of the food counter.

"Yams? Where did they come from?"

"Last consignment at the market," says Dandelion. "The new cook brought them down from Pashish."

I grab four large yams and retreat, clutching my stew. And as stew goes, it's not bad. I've tasted far worse. The temporary cook isn't such an incompetent as I feared. Managed to snare us some yams as well. I ignore all distractions, concentrating on getting the food inside me. It does me a power of good. It strikes me that it's little wonder my endeavours have been so ineffectual recently. I've not been eating well enough. It's quite understandable. You can't expect a man to go around solving crimes, finding treasure and beating everyone at cards if you're starving him at the same time. No one could stand it. With the stew, the yams and another beer inside me I start to feel a lot better. I feel so much better that I suddenly have a very good idea where Tanrose's mother's gold might be.

I take my empty plate back to the bar, ignoring all interruptions from discontented Turanians, and drag Makri to one side.

"Makri, I'm running out of money. I need more, and quickly. I just realised where the gold is and I'm going to get it. Take my place at the table for a little while."

Makri looks startled.

"I barely know how to play the game."

"It doesn't matter. Just put in your guran stake every time and don't get involved in any gambling. You can buy me enough time and I'll be back soon."

"Okay," says Makri. "I can do that."

She frowns.

"You're not about to flee the city in shame, are you?"

"Are you crazy? I've been in much more shameful situations than this and I never fled the city before."

"Yes you did."

"Well, not often."

"Doesn't this go against your agreement with Horm?" asks Makri. "You weren't meant to get any more money."

"No. No one was meant to give me any more money. Finding more money myself wasn't mentioned. If I happen across fourteen thousand gurans that's just his bad luck. Look after my place at the table and don't do anything crazy."

And with that, I depart, as swiftly as I can.

Chapter Twenty-One

The Church of St. Volinius is by far the most imposing building in Twelve Seas. It's solid rather than elegant, but it's richly decorated, the beneficiary of numerous bequests from the local merchants. If you want to get ahead in Turai, it's a good idea to keep in with the True Church.

I've had a few encounters with Derlex, the local pontifex, and his superior, Bishop Gzekius. They wouldn't regard me as a friend of the Church; in fact I've been denounced from the pulpit on more than one occasion.

The church is closed. Having no time to waste, I walk boldly up to the front entrance and mutter the opening spell, one of the few incantations I can use with any confidence. The door creaks open and I walk in, muttering another word to light up my illuminated staff. I glance at the walls. At the far end of the church, to the right of the altar where the pontifex gives his sermons, there is a picture of St. Quatinius and the whale. I've seen it before. I saw it briefly when I was talking to Nerinax the beggar and Pontifex Derlex came out of the church, but it didn't register properly then. Not till I was full of yams and stew did I remember that the painting was here.

On the floor underneath it there's a grating, and a small brass plaque: *Demetrius, first Prefect of Twelve Seas.*

In the vault beneath the grating lie the bones of one of the city's ancient notables. Untouched for centuries, apart, perhaps, from when Captain Maxius hid his gold here. I speak my opening spell again and the grating creaks open. So far so good. Underneath the grating is a large marble slab. I hesitate for a moment. I'm about to open a tomb. Some people might look on this unsympathetically.

"But it's for the good of the city," I mutter. "No one could hold it against me."

I use my opening spell again. The slab groans. It's a weightier item than I'm used to shifting. For a moment I think it's not going to work. I reach down and start hauling at it, adding my own strength to the strength of the spell. Finally the slab moves over a foot or so. I wipe the sweat from my forehead. That was an effort. Without the desperate circumstances I'd never have pulled it off. I reach down into the coffin below, and at that moment the front door flies open and Bishop Gzekius and Pontifex Derlex stride into the church. I have rarely seen two men look more surprised.

"What is going on!" roars the Bishop.

"It's Thraxas," cries Derlex. "He's robbing a grave!"

"Send for the Civil Guards," roars the Bishop. "He'll hang for this!"

Pontifex Derlex is aghast.

"Thraxas!" he cries. "Even from you, I never expected this."

He turns to go, to summon the Guards.

"It's for the good of the city . . ." I begin, but abandon the effort. There's no way of convincing them, and time is short. Though I'm not used to casting two spells in quick succession, I can still do it, just about. I mutter the words of my sleep spell and the Bishop and Derlex both tumble gracefully to the ground. Then I have to sit down. The effort has drained me completely. It'll be a week before I can use a spell again. I have to force myself to move, shaking my head and reaching down into the marble coffin. The first thing I touch is a wooden box, something of a relief as I wasn't looking forward to dragging up a lot of bones. I take it out of the grave. It's sealed and there's a small metal nameplate on it. *Captain Maxius.*

So there it is. The Captain's treasure. Buried under a whale, more or less. I tuck it under my arm, pick up my illuminated staff and hurry from the church. For a first attempt at grave robbing, it's gone rather well. With any luck the Deputy Consul can explain things to the Bishop, thereby preventing any rash attempt to hang me for my crimes.

Outside the church I'm about to climb back on my horse when a hand grabs me by the shoulder and yanks me backwards. I tumble to the ground and find myself looking at a fancy pair of black boots and the fringes of a rainbow cloak. It's Glixius.

"Stealing from the church?" he booms. "Just what I'd expect of you, Thraxas. Hand it over!"

I struggle to rise. It's an effort. I'm still weak from casting the spells. I once knocked out Glixius with one punch but there's no way I can do that just now.

"I need this money," I say.

"So do I."

"What for?" I ask, trying to delay him while my strength returns.

"Gambling debts," says Glixius. "To the Brotherhood. Casax, in fact. He just learned that one of my credit notes from last month is bad. It could be awkward."

He raises one hand.

"But killing you with a spell and taking the fourteen thousand gurans seems to be a solution to all my problems."

Glixius suddenly sags at the knees, and then pitches forward on to the ground. Makri has appeared silently round the corner and hit him with a small leather club. I look at her rather wildly.

"Who's looking after my cards?"

"Aren't you going to thank me for saving you?" says Makri.

"Thanks for saving me. Who's looking after my cards?"

"I saw Glixius following you out so I followed him myself."

"Yes, it was brilliantly done. So who's at the table?"

"Dandelion."

"Aaarrggghhhh!"

"Did you just scream?" says Makri.

"Dandelion is looking after my cards? Of course I screamed."

I struggle to get on my horse, frantic at the thought of the barefoot idiot sitting in for me at the card table.

"She'll be fine," says Makri. "I told her not to do anything rash."

"Are you insane, leaving her in charge? Do you want to marry Horm?"

"Well you weren't doing so well yourself," says Makri. "Shouldn't you be getting back to the Axe rather than standing here talking?"

I mount my horse and spur it forward. It's a risk riding at night in the city as it's illegal, but there are so many people exempted from this law in Twelve Seas at the moment, with soldiers, Sorcerers and Civil Guards scurrying round shoring up the defences, that no one pays me much attention. Makri, an inexperienced rider, follows me at a distance.

I stable the horse and rush back into the tavern. If Dandelion has blown my money then it's all over. Once a player is out of funds he has to leave the table, and can't return. I've a faint hope that Makri might have been joking about Dandelion. My heart sinks—even further— when I see that she wasn't. Dandelion is sitting in my seat, with a suspiciously small pile of money in front of her. I glance round wildly at the onlookers, focusing finally on Lisutaris.

"You allowed this to happen? Are you crazy?"

Lisutaris shrugs.

"Captain Rallee volunteered to take your hand. But Horm objected."

I turn to face Horm.

"Since when can an Orc come in here and start objecting to people?"

"There are limits to how many replacements a man can have," says Horm, smoothly. "There was general agreement on the matter."

I glare at them all.

"It's all right, Thraxas," says Dandelion, quite cheerfully. "I'm getting the hang of it now."

"How much of my money have you got left?"

"Er . . . almost fifty gurans."

I drag the idiotic barmaid out of the way and retake my seat, not in the best of tempers. I scowl at the assembled players.

"Most amusing. Dandelion filling in for me while you rob a man of his hard-earned money. Well I've got a surprise for you."

I slap the wooden chest down on the table.

"That wasn't the only money I have."

Now this isn't such a strange thing to do, in normal circumstances. A player is quite entitled to bring in more funds. But given that Horm and I are meant to be playing with a stake of 1,000 gurans each, I'm expecting some argument, at least from him. When I stare him in the eye, however, he merely lifts an eyebrow, professing not to care.

"I am already far ahead of you, Investigator. I have no objection to you squandering whatever else you have scraped together."

"Scraped together? Try this, you half-Orc excuse for a card player."

I open the chest and turn it upside down quite dramatically, expecting a shower of coins to cascade on to the table. Fourteen coins tumble out in front of me. Fourteen single gurans. I stare at them, and then shake the box, hoping for more. There is no more. Apparently the tale of the Captain's treasure grew in the telling. All around the table there are guffaws of laughter.

"Brought your life savings?" says Casax.

I'm still scrabbling around in the empty chest, looking for more money. I can't believe I've gone to so much trouble for fourteen gurans. Damn that Tanrose and her lying family. Behind me Cicerius snorts in derision. Lisutaris and Hanama might well be about to join him but we're interrupted by a very loud banging on the tavern door.

"Open up in the name of the True Church. We demand the immediate arrest of the grave-robber Thraxas!"

"What is this?" demands the Deputy Consul, startled by the clamour.

"Ignore them," I say. "The Church doesn't have the authority to go around demanding things."

"This is Bishop Gzekius and I demand the arrest of Thraxas under the authority of the Church!"

"It's a moot point," I say. "Anyway, you outrank the Bishop."

"What have you done?" demands the Deputy Consul.

"Nothing."

"They're saying you robbed a grave!"

"A small misunderstanding when I dropped in to pray. Well, gentlemen, I'd say it was time to get the game underway again."

Cicerius goes off to the front door, hopefully to pacify the Bishop. He has to. They can't drag me off for grave-robbing; the safety of the city rests in my hands. Me and my sixty-four gurans. It's not going to be easy. I need more beer. I twist round in my chair to yell at Makri, who's now returned to her post behind the bar.

"Beer!"

Makri looks at me strangely, clutches her brow, and falls to the floor.

"She's sick!" cries Dandelion. "She's got the malady!"

"But I want beer," I say, and start to feel that the world really is against me. Captain Rallee goes to help Dandelion carry Makri into the store room along with the other casualties. I ignore the commotion, and focus on the task in front of me. At a rough guess I'd say that Horm the Dead has around 2,000 gurans in front of him, and that's a lot of money to claw back. For most men, it would be an impossible task. Of course, most men haven't roamed the world with a sword in their hands and only their native wit to protect them. Most men haven't gambled their way around every card table in the west. You can't compare Thraxas the Investigator to most men; it's not a fair contest. I bang my fist on the table.

"Are we going to play cards or not? Moolifi, start dealing. And Dandelion, bring me a beer. Goddammit, do you expect me to sit here parched with thirst all night?"

The room goes quiet, Moolifi deals the cards, and I get on with the business of mounting one of the most heroic rearguard actions ever seen at the card table. With only sixty-four gurans to my name, I'm facing overwhelming odds, but I remain undismayed. Lisutaris needs more time to complete her spell. Fine. I'll get her some more time. I sip beer, study my cards, play with the utmost caution, refuse to be drawn, and even pick up a small win with three 4s. As the night wears on, I start to show the assembled mockers and doubters what a real genius at rak can do when he's backed into a corner. By the time Ravenius goes bust, unwisely believing that Casax is bluffing when he raises 500 gurans on one hand, I've built my stake up to ninety gurans and am exhibiting the sort of quiet determination that gets a man through a crisis when everyone around him is losing their heads.

Three hours later I'm still in the game. I call loudly for more beer, curse Moolifi for the bad cards she's been dealing me, and roar at Dandelion to bring me some more yams and make it quick.

Horm the Dead laughs. He's enjoying himself. He's still well ahead of me and he's no doubt expecting to be leaving the city with Makri in tow. I'll show him. By three in the morning there are only four people left at the table—Praetor Capatius, Horm the Dead, Casax, and me. Each of them has several thousand gurans in front of them. I have 180. Horm decides that it's time to force me off the table. When I raise a cautious ten gurans on a hand, he calmly looks over at the money in front of me, counts out 180 gurans, and pushes it into the centre of the table. If I cover his bet it will cost me everything I have, and I'll be out of the game if I lose.

I turn my head slightly, and notice Lisutaris shaking her head discreetly. A signal that she has not yet found a counter spell to attack Horm, and doesn't want me to risk losing yet. I turn back to my cards, and push all my money into the centre of the table.

"Let's see what you have."

Horm turns over two dragons and two kings. I turn over three 10s. My hand is superior. I scoop in the money and now I've got 360 gurans in front of me.

Cicerius appears at the table and says it's time we took another break. It brings complaints from the players. Praetor Capatius hasn't been doing so well for the past hour or so, and like any card player on a losing streak, he wants to carry on. Horm shrugs. He doesn't mind either way. I'd as soon carry on playing because I've got a strong suspicion that Cicerius is calling for a break so he can lecture me again, but we rise from the table anyway. I head for the bar but don't make it that far before I'm once more surrounded by the angry mob.

"That was very rash," says Lisutaris. "I told you not to risk everything before I'm ready."

"I knew what I was doing."

"I wish I knew what you've been doing," hisses Cicerius. "Did you really break into the church of St. Volinius and rob a tomb?"

"Yes. But only as part of an ongoing investigation."

"You know you could be hanged for this?"

"For what? For saving the city? I had to do it. Tell the Bishop it was vital war work. You ought to be getting behind me, not giving me a hard time. Who's the one that's doing all the work here? Who's the one that's making Horm look foolish at the card table?"

Lisutaris purses her lips.

"Good question. He has five thousand gurans and you have three hundred and sixty."

"I got off to a bad start. Now excuse me, I have a beer to pick up."

I break free and head for the bar, where Dandelion is handing a glass of klee to Horm.

"I want to see Makri," says Horm.

"You can't," replies Dandelion, firmly. "She's sick and she needs to rest."

Horm shrugs.

"This filthy city would make anyone sick. In my mountain kingdom, Makri will be healthy."

Hanama approaches silently.

"Makri isn't going anywhere near your mountain kingdom," she says.

"You trust Thraxas to save her?" asks Horm.

"Not for a moment. I'll save her."

Horm gives a languid smile, then departs without responding.

"Thanks for the vote of confidence," I say to Hanama.

"I have no confidence in you whatsoever," says Hanama. "And if you let Makri be taken by Horm I'll kill you myself."

Casax appears beside us. He's wondering what happened to Glixius Dragon Killer.

"Probably still trying to find the money he owes you," I tell him. From the look on Casax's face I can tell that he'll be wanting words with Glixius at the first opportunity. I'm pleased. Even if you're a powerful Sorcerer, it doesn't do to offend the Brotherhood.

Captain Rallee is looking rather weary. No doubt he'd rather be in bed, but with Moolifi dealing, he has to stick around. Moolifi is sitting beside him but her attention is taken by Tirini Snake Smiter who's at her side, talking about clothes.

"I adore your dress. The new Samsarina line is definitely you. And those shoes; I swear mine can't compete."

They both stretch out a foot, rather genteelly, to compare shoes.

"Such a beautiful pink," says Tirini.

"Thanks," says Moolifi. "But they're not quite perfect any more. I seem to have lost a few threads from the embroidery."

I glance at the shoes. It's hardly noticeable, but there are a few pink threads missing. Pink threads like the ones in my pocket. The ones I took from the place where Makri fought the Orcish Assassin. I don't quite know what that means, but I have a bad feeling as we sit down again to play.

Chapter Twenty-Two

Capatius, Horm, Casax and I resume the struggle. The air is thick with thazis smoke and the fire burns brightly in the huge hearth, kept alight by the occasional word from one of the Sorcerers. No one looking at Lisutaris, Coranius, Anumaris and Tirini would guess that at this moment they were busy working on a spell to defeat Horm, but I know they are. Three of them are anyway. Tirini is probably planning her outfit for the next reception at the Palace.

Deputy Consul Cicerius sits with Samanatius. I'm a little surprised to see that Cicerius apparently regards the philosopher as worthy of respect, as does Lisutaris. I wouldn't have guessed the practical Cicerius had much time for that sort of thing.

With 360 gurans I still can't afford to do anything rash. So far tonight I've rarely tried bluffing, though it's something I'm good at. But Praetor Capatius, being obscenely rich, likes trying to throw his weight around, and it goes wrong for him in spectacular fashion when he tries to bluff Horm out of a hand and Horm coolly stands up to him, and triumphs. The Praetor is left almost moneyless, and scowls mightily as he throws in his cards.

"I'm out," he grunts, and stands up, stretches his limbs, and heads for the bar to see if there's any stew still on offer. The praetor is a large man, and a healthy eater, and if he's used to more exotic fare that the Avenging Axe stew, it's not a bad meal for a man who's just been beaten at cards in the early hours of the morning.

As Casax, Horm and I battle on I can feel the eyes of the audience on us. I've worked my way up to 400 gurans, and when Moolifi deals me three kings I raise a hundred. Horm drops out but Casax follows me. Once more I'm forced to put in everything I possess. My nerves are straining as Casax turns over his cards, but I win the hand. I've now got 800 gurans and I'm back in the game. Casax is rattled and the very next hand he stays in far longer than he should and I end up taking another 300 gurans from him. Now I'm the one with the momentum. Horm plays quietly and cautiously while I systematically win hand after hand from Casax in an exhibition of card playing that will undoubtedly go down in history. When I finally chase the Brotherhood boss from the table, grinding him to dust with a lethal combination of masterly betting skills and a few lucky cards, he rises to his feet wearily, throws his cloak around his shoulders and walks away without even offering a parting insult. His henchman, Karlox, glowers at me evilly but I ignore him. Thraxas, number one chariot at rak, and no one can deny it.

"Just you and me, Horm," I grunt, and call for beer.

Horm sips his glass of klee, and stares at me for a few moments. I can't read his expression. He has turned out to be a better card player than I expected.

"Indeed, Investigator. Just you and me. For the Ocean Storm, or Makri."

"Myself, I'm more worried about the money."

"Are you serious?" says Horm.

"Women and magical trinkets are never in short supply. Personally I prefer a solid pile of cash."

Horm hesitates. For the first time ever, I seem to have disconcerted him.

By now it's quite likely that everyone in the tavern knows the nature of our bet. It's been obvious from the start that this is no ordinary game, and as the whispers and rumours have spread the intensity of the interest has grown. There's hardly a sound save for the crackling of the fire. I'm suddenly gripped with a thirst that can't be satisfied by normal beer alone. I tell Horm and Moolifi that I need to collect something from my room, then hurry upstairs, returning with a bottle of the Grand Abbot's Ale. I open the bottle and pour some into my tankard.

"Are you quite ready?" says Horm, now a little more irritated.

Moolifi deals the cards. She gives me a black 8 and a black bishop. Horm checks his cards idly, lays them face down in front of him and pushes 100 gurans into the middle of the table. I cover the bet. Moolifi deals again. This time she gives me a black 7. Bishop, 8 and 7, all black. It's a hand that's worth pursuing. Horm raises 200 gurans and I again cover his bet, quite calmly, giving nothing away.

Moolifi deals me the fourth and final card. It is a black queen. I have a straight run in the same colour. It will beat anything except four of a kind. Horm studies his money for a while. It's laid out in neat piles in front of him, unlike mine, which is strewn around messily.

"I have seven thousand gurans," he says. "Around the same as you, I'd judge."

He pushes it all into the centre of the table, and looks me in the eye.

"It's your bet," he says.

I count my money. I have enough to cover the bet, just. If I go along with it one of us will be forced from the table. With this one bet I can save Makri and rescue the Ocean Storm for Turai. Or I could lose everything. My straight run is a good hand. Horm's might be better. I could back out, escape with the loss of just a few hundred gurans. I wonder if Horm is bluffing. I can't tell. I take a sip of my excellent beer and think for a few moments.

I remember once when I was fighting as a mercenary away in the south, the captain of our company tried to force me out of a game by betting 100 gurans on a pair of 2s. One hundred gurans was all the money I had in the world and I'd had to fight hard and long to earn it. I covered his bet. I lost. I ended up fighting for six months as a mercenary and I was worse off than when I started. Gurd had to buy me food on the way home, and it was lucky he was with me or I'd have starved to death in some far-off land.

I start sliding my money across, pushing each ragged bundle of coins in one after the other. It takes me a few moments to count out the seven thousand. I stare at Horm.

"So, what do you have?"

"The Ocean Storm isn't yours to gamble," comes a voice, familiar but not entirely normal. It's Sarin, looking quite crazy. She's pointing a crossbow, illegal inside the city walls, but still her favourite weapon. From the wild look in her eyes I'd say she was deep in the grip of the fever. As a powerful Sorcerer in an alien land, Horm is undoubtedly protected by some powerful spells. But I don't know how safe he is. A full-size crossbow at such a short distance is a very deadly weapon. At this range the bolt would go right through a normal man and through the man behind him as well. I've seen it happen, and I wouldn't want to be the third man standing behind them either. I wouldn't lay much money on Horm's spells saving him from harm.

Before anyone can move, Sarin fires the crossbow. As soon as she releases the string, I jerk my head towards Horm, expecting to see him driven back from the table, but instead I find that Moolifi has raised her hand and caught the bolt, which is quite impossible. No one can catch a crossbow bolt in mid-flight; you can't even see it in the air. There are a few gasps from around the room. I turn towards Moolifi.

"Are you by any chance another Sorcerer in disguise?"

"I am," says Moolifi.

"I'm guessing Deeziz the Unseen?"

"Then you have guessed correctly," says Moolifi.

"Ridiculous," cries Horm. "Deeziz isn't a woman."

"I assure you I am. Though it's suited me till now to hide myself with veils and sorcery."

All around the tavern chairs are tumbling over as Lisutaris and her fellow Sorcerers leap to their feet. They're not the only ones. Captain Rallee is already upright, a baffled expression on his face as the shocking news that he's been dating the most famous Sorcerer in the Orcish lands sets in.

I turn towards Lisutaris.

"You see? I told you Deeziz was in the city."

But Lisutaris isn't listening to me. She's already speaking a spell. I get myself out of the way quickly but

Deeziz remains in her chair. She appears quite untroubled. She raises one hand and moves it a few inches. There's a sort of ripple in the air, and nothing more.

"You can't harm me," says Deeziz. "I've negated your sorcery."

"We'll see about that," growls Coranius the Grinder, and lets loose a powerful bolt. Or tries to. The shaft of purple lightning that flies from his hand travels no further than a few inches before dissipating into the air.

"You are wasting your time," says Deeziz. "I am more powerful than any of you."

"I doubt it," says Lisutaris.

"Whether you doubt it or not, it's true."

Deeziz the Unseen rises gracefully to her feet.

"I spent ten years on a mountaintop while you attended parties and balls, Mistress of the Sky. I took my skills to new heights while Sorcerers in Turai cast horoscopes for princes. You doubt my power? Me? The Sorcerer who made you fall sick and sapped your strength?"

"The Sorcerer who fooled me into thinking she was a singer from Nioj!" roars Captain Rallee.

I can see why he's upset. It was hardly civilised of Deeziz to trick him. If we get out of this alive, it's not going to do his reputation in Twelve Seas any good at all.

"Disguising yourself as a beautiful woman when all the time you're a foul Orc!" continues the Captain.

Deeziz looks slightly pained.

"That's uncalled for, Captain. I wouldn't say I was foul."

She waves her hand again, and the Human disguise drops from her features. Her skin darkens, her hair turns black, her features become a little stronger. She looks at me.

"Do you think I'm unattractive?"

"Er . . ." I hesitate, and look round for support.

"I think you're still very pretty," says Dandelion.

"Good features," adds Tirini.

"I think you're very beautiful," says young Ravenius, then looks abashed as everyone stares at him. "For an enemy Sorcerer, I mean."

"Even so," I say, "you can see why the Captain's angry."

"The Captain was a most pleasant companion," says the Orc Sorcerer. "And made my stay in your city much more bearable than it might otherwise have been. But enough of this. Lisutaris, I'm disappointed in you. Your sorcery is less powerful than I've been led to believe. Deputy Consul Cicerius, you are a fool. And as for you . . ."

She turns towards Horm the Dead.

"Your life will not be worth living once Prince Amrag learns that you were willing to gamble the Ocean Storm away for the sake of a woman."

Horm moves very swiftly, trying to fire a spell at Deeziz, but she waves her hand once more, sending him crashing backwards against the wall. Nothing could demonstrate her power more than the ease with which she defeats Horm. I'm hoping Lisutaris has some brilliant plan for beating her, because I certainly haven't.

Deeziz snaps her fingers and the Ocean Storm rises out of Horm's cloak and flies into her hand. She looks at it thoughtfully for a few seconds, then towards Cicerius.

"Perhaps it was harsh of me to call you a fool. After all, you did what you thought was best. You sent troops and Sorcerers to the south of the city to guard the sea wall. But as you will see, that was a mistake."

"What do you mean?" asks Cicerius.

"I mean it's what we wanted you to do. I have created panic and suspicion in Turai. I have planted rumours of Orcish incursion. I've caused phantom Orcs to be seen around the harbour. I've spread rumours of Orcish fleets around your shores. I have introduced Orcish Assassins inside your city to bring panic. I've made you send so much of your defences to the southern walls that your other walls are now insecure. Your Sorcerers Guild has insufficient power left to guard the rest of the city."

Deeziz looks again at the Ocean Storm, and then, bizarrely, she starts to sing. She sings a verse of "Love Me Through the Winter," Moolifi's most famous song. Not emotionally, like the times she performed it for an audience, but quietly. Everyone looks on, quite mystified. If the most powerful Orcish Sorcerer arrives in your midst, the last thing you expect them to do is to start singing.

Moolifi halts, and looks towards Lisutaris. "I've sung that song every day since I arrived here. It's based on a powerful old Elvish invocation. I wove spells into it to baffle my enemies, and bring you to ruin. And now it's done."

"What's done?"

Deeziz tucks the Ocean Storm into her elegant little bag.

"Are you aware that this tavern stands on a dragon line?" she says.

"Yes," says Lisutaris.

"It runs right through the city to the northern gate, where the river enters Turai. I've sent the power of the Ocean Storm along the dragon line. In around thirty seconds a wave of incredible power will flow down the river, breaking all your defences and smashing the gate. As soon as that happens, Lord Rezaz will march into Turai."

"Rezaz is nowhere near Turai," cries Coranius.

"On the contrary, he and his army are about to march through your shattered northern wall."

At this moment Lisutaris once more attempts to fire a spell at Deeziz. Deeziz brushes it off quite nonchalantly.

"Your sorcery is useless against me. But not against Lord Rezaz's army, perhaps. So it would be better for Prince Amrag if you were not around to use it."

With that, Deeziz the Unseen raises both arms in front of her, chants a short sentence, and there's an almighty explosion. I'm thrown backwards and crash into the wall, and pass out immediately.

Chapter Twenty-Three

When I wake up, it's dark and I'm very confused. Not the sort of confusion that comes from indulging too freely in Gurd's fine ale, and coming round on the floor wondering what day it is. More the sort of confusion that makes me wonder who I am and what my name is.

I stand up, looking around me dumbly. I'm in a large room. There are tables, chairs, half-finished drinks and a lot of cards scattered around. I'm the only person in the room. There's a fire in the hearth, burning low. It's still confusing. I can't make any sense of it at all. I notice my throat is very dry. There are drinks all over the place but I'm drawn to a bottle on the table where the cards are. I pick it up and glance at the label. *The Grand Abbot's Ale.*

Odd name for a beer. I raise it to my lips and drink it all down.

And then it comes back in a flash. The Grand Abbot's Ale restores my memory. I'm Thraxas, private Investigator, currently engaged in a game of cards with Horm the Dead and various others. Except Horm and all the others don't seem to be here any more. The last thing I remember is Deeziz the Unseen casting a spell. I'd guess it was some powerful spell of confusion. Powerful enough to knock me out, despite my spell protection charm. I wonder if it worked on everyone else. From the way they've all wandered off, I think it has. Particularly as the card table is still loaded with money. People in Turai would have to be very confused indeed to leave money lying around in public.

My cards are still on the table. I flip them over: 7, 8, bishop, queen, all black. I turn over Horm the Dead's cards: four kings. It's a better hand than mine. He would have won. Of course, technically, the game hasn't finished yet. We never got round to declaring our hands. But he's no longer at the table, while I'm still here, which makes me the winner. Thraxas, number one chariot at the card table. I toss the cards in a heap then scoop all the money into my bag.

I walk past the bar and into the rooms beyond. Gurd's room is empty. No sign of him or Tanrose. I check the store rooms. Also empty. I hurry upstairs. I have a feeling there's something badly wrong but I can't quite put my finger on it. My office is empty and so is my bedroom. There seems to be a lot of noise outside. I hurry along to Makri's room. Makri is lying on the floor, drenched in sweat, barely conscious. Lisutaris is beside her, unconscious. I kneel down beside them. Makri opens her eyes.

"Are you confused?" I ask.

"Compared to you, no," says Makri. "What happened?"

"Deeziz. Enemy Sorcerer. Cast a powerful spell downstairs."

"I heard a bang," whispers Makri. "I found Lisutaris wandering in the corridor. I dragged her in here."

"You see anyone else?"

Makri shakes her head.

The noises outside get louder.

"What's happening?"

"I think the city has just fallen to the Orcs."

"What?"

Makri attempts to sit up, but fails. She's very weak, and the effort of dragging Lisutaris into her room has taken the last of her energy. I tell her to wait while I check on events outside. I walk along the corridor and go into the small cupboard which contains a ladder leading to the roof. It's an awkward climb, not one that I've made for a while. By the time I struggle on to the roof the noises outside are deafening. People are screaming in panic and confusion. I look north. Dragons are swooping over the city and smoke and flames curl over the Palace. Lord Rezaz the Butcher has taken the city and the population is fleeing as best they can. I struggle back down the ladder, and head for my office. I put on my magic warm cloak, take my sword, my illuminated staff and my grimoire of spells. I put a bottle of the Abbot's klee in my bag, along with thazis and the large joint of venison Lisutaris sent me. It's a heavy load, though not much to be taking away from the city I've lived in all my life.

I now have to get myself, Makri and Lisutaris to safety. I'm concerned about Gurd, but he's not around and I've no way of locating him. It's possible Tanrose has taken him off somewhere. Or it's possible he's just wandered off and has been killed by the Orcs.

Back in Makri's room I ask Makri if she can stand. She shakes her head.

"The Orcs have taken the city. We have to get away."

Makri scowls.

"Orcs? In the city? We have to fight."

She attempts to rise, but fails.

I pick her up.

"My swords," says Makri.

I pick up her swords and her favourite axe and head downstairs to the back of the building. Luckily the cart is still in the stables. Everyone in the tavern must have been too confused to take it. I dump Makri in the cart and run back upstairs. I don't know how much time I have. The Orcs will be sweeping through the city. If resistance has completely crumbled it won't take them long to reach Twelve Seas. I pick up Lisutaris and carry her downstairs. I throw her in the cart then set about getting the horse affixed to the reins.

When I make it out into Quintessence Street I'm greeted by a scene of terrible panic. People are running everywhere, screaming that the Orcs are here and we're all going to be slaughtered. It's quite likely. But I've encountered Orcs many times, and I haven't been slaughtered yet, so I'm not about to give up now. I drive the horse forward through the crowd, all heading south towards the harbour in a desperate effort to escape from the invaders.

I have no thoughts of staying and fighting. With dragons swooping over the Palace, and Lord Rezaz's army inside the walls, we're already beaten. I don't intend to lose my life in a dark street in Twelve Seas for no reason. I spur the horse on.

Makri emerges from her stupor.

"What's happening?"

"We're leaving Turai."

"Why?"

"It seems like a good time for a fresh start."

Makri opens her mouth to protest, but lacks the strength, and she sinks back into unconsciousness. Our progress is interrupted when the wagon becomes hemmed in by people and we come to a halt. I look around impatiently for some means of escape but there's nowhere to go. If the Orcs arrive now we're finished. Neither Makri nor Lisutaris are in a fit state to be of any help.

At this moment a dragon flies overhead and a troop of heavily armed Orcs advances into Quintessence Street, sending the crowds fleeing in terror. There is a terrible panic as people dive through windows into houses, climb walls, anything to escape. For a moment I consider just picking up my sword and confronting the Orcs. I can kill three with my sword and another four or five with a spell before I die. That's not too bad. I notice the alleyway on the right looks familiar. I once climbed out of the sewers into that alleyway. There's a manhole cover there. I take Lisutaris in one hand, Makri in the other and drag them over the side of the wagon. It's fortunate that neither of them are heavy women or I'd never make it. When I reach the manhole cover the Orcs are no more than fifty yards away. I open the cover, drop Makri and Lisutaris through it, clamber inside, and pull the cover over my head. Then I descend the ladder as quickly as I can, because if the water level in the sewer is high, Makri and Lisutaris will be drowning by now.

The water is several feet deep. Makri is struggling to stand but Lisutaris is floating face down. Praying that I haven't actually killed Turai's leading Sorcerer, I drag her out of the water.

"What are you doing?" croaks Makri, slightly more animated after being dumped in the sewer.

"Escaping. The Orcs are right overhead. Can you walk?"

Makri nods, and then falls over.

"No, seriously," I say, dragging her to her feet. "Can you walk?"

"I'm strong," says Makri, and falls over again. For a moment I wish I'd just stayed and fought the Orcs, but I grit my teeth and start dragging Makri and Lisutaris through the sewer. It's a tough job but at least I know where I'm going. I've been here before. I was once chased through this sewer by Glixius Dragon Killer, curse his name. I wonder if he had something to do with the appearance of Deeziz in the Avenging Axe. I wouldn't put it past him.

My illuminated staff lights the way but progress is painfully slow. The last time I was here it wasn't only Glixius I had to worry about. I encountered an alligator as well. Damn these sewers. And damn Makri and Lisutaris for being too ill to walk. If an alligator arrives I'll feed them to it and make an escape myself.

After what seems like hours Lisutaris grunts, and starts to come round.

"What's happening?"

"You got hit by a spell of confusion and the Orcs have taken the city. We're escaping through the sewers."

"We have to fight!" cries Lisutaris.

"It's too late to fight."

"We can't run away!"

"Can you remember any spells?"

Lisutaris looks blank.

"Spells?"

"The things you do sorcery with."

The Sorcerer looks puzzled.

"Oh yes. Spells. No, I can't seem to remember any."

"Then we'd better keep moving. We're not far from the outlet on the shore. If we're lucky we'll be far enough away from the Orcs. I don't expect they'll scour the coastline tonight."

Now that Lisutaris is conscious again, the going is a little easier. I sling Makri over my shoulder. Even though she seems to be unconscious she keeps hold of her bag containing her two swords and her axe. At least she's not leaving the city empty-handed.

When we arrive at the outlet on the shore the beach is lit up with explosions. Some Sorcerers at the harbour are putting up resistance and the last ships are leaving the dock, crammed with refugees. People who couldn't make it on to a ship are streaming along the rocks towards the beach, fleeing through the winter night in all directions. Fire and smoke hang over the city although there doesn't seem to be a general conflagration. I'd guess that the Orcs won't burn Turai; they want it as a base to gather strength during the winter.

We're too far from the harbour to reach any of the ships. I don't see anything to do except start walking.

"No good," gasps Lisutaris. "I'm too weak."

The lingering effects of the malady, followed by Deeziz's spell, have taken all of the Sorcerer's strength.

Makri comes awake and slides off my shoulder.

"There's an empty boat out there," she says.

I can't see any boat. Nor can Lisutaris.

"I can see it," says Makri. "I have Elvish eyes."

Makri looks at me.

"I've got the malady," she says, and sounds quite unhappy.

"You'll recover. Lisutaris, can you bring the boat in?"

Lisutaris shakes her head.

"I can't remember any spells."

I drag my old, out-of-date grimoire from my bag. Most of the spells in it I could never use and the few that I could are no good in the circumstances. Maybe the head of the Sorcerers Guild can make something of it. I thrust the book at her. Lisutaris looks at it hopelessly.

"I can't read it."

I explode with exasperation.

"Could you make an effort? I've just dragged you from the Avenging Axe to the beach via a sewer. The least you could do is remember a simple spell. Here."

I take out some thazis from my bag. It's still fresh and green. Lisutaris's eyes light up and she rolls a thazis stick with nimble dexterity. Without even thinking about it she mutters a word, causing the stick to light, and inhales deeply.

"Of course," she says. "I'm a Sorcerer. I do spells. Let me see that book."

The Mistress of the Sky flips over the pages while I light the book with my illuminated staff, trying not to make it to bright for fear of attracting attention. There's no saying that a dragon won't suddenly decide to practise its fire-breathing technique on the hopeless survivors who throng the beach.

Lisutaris snaps the book shut, and utters a few words, a spell of bringing.

"The boat is coming."

"Good. So is a dragon."

The dragon, flapping its wings languidly, appears over the city walls, heading our way. A small boat heaves into view. A tiny fisherman's craft, with one sail. I sling Makri over my shoulder again and splash through the water towards it, flinging her over the side then climbing in myself. Lisutaris can't make it over the edge and I have to haul her in. The dragon is getting ominously close.

"Use a spell," I scream. "Get us out of here."

Lisutaris snaps her fingers and we begin to drift out to sea. The dragon turns its head towards us but doesn't follow. Dragons are not keen on flying over water.

Lisutaris lies down on the deck.

"More thazis," she mutters. "I want more thazis."

I hand the sorceress my thazis pouch. She rolls herself another stick.

"When I get my strength back," she says grimly, "I'll come back and chase those Orcs all the way to the mountains."

I gaze towards the shore. Maybe I'll come back with her, and help chase the Orcs. Or maybe I'll just keep going till I reach the furthest west, and see if anyone there needs an Investigator. The way I've been feeling about Turai recently, just keeping going doesn't seem like such a bad option.

What with the malady, Deeziz's spell and the thazis, the greatest Sorcerer in the west is once more out of commission. She falls asleep as we drift away from the shore. I haul both Lisutaris and Makri into the small cabin, cover them with their cloaks, and go back on deck, looking towards Turai. Flames and smoke tower over the Palace and dragons still swoop down from the sky. I let the boat drift with the current, and I wonder if I'll ever see the city again.